THE
UNADOPTABLES

Hana Tooke

Viking

VIKING
An imprint of Penguin Random House LLC, New York

First published in the United States of America by Viking,
an imprint of Penguin Random House LLC, 2020

Published simultaneously in the UK by Puffin Books, Ltd.

Visit us online at penguinrandomhouse.com

Library of Congress Cataloging-in-Publication Data is available.
ISBN 9780593116937

1 3 5 7 9 10 8 6 4 2

Design by Lucia Baez   •   Text set in Fournier MT

For my wonderfully weird family.

THE
UNADOPTABLES

❧ ZERO ❧

Little Tulip Orphanage, Amsterdam, 1880

LITTLE TULIP ORPHANAGE
❧ *Rules for Baby Abandonment* ❧
Rule One: The baby should be wrapped in a *cotton* blanket.

Rule Two: The baby should be placed in a *wicker* basket.

Rule Three: The baby should be deposited on the topmost step.

IN ALL THE YEARS that Elinora Gassbeek had been matron of the Little Tulip Orphanage, not once had the Rules for Baby Abandonment been broken. Until the summer of 1880. Five babies were abandoned in the months that followed and, despite the Rules being clearly displayed on the orphanage's front door, not one of these babies was abandoned *sensibly*.

The first baby arrived on a bright morning at the end of August, as dew glistened on the city's cobblestone streets.

Swaddled in a pink cotton blanket and placed on the appropriate step was a baby with cocoa-bean eyes and blond fuzz on its head. However, the way in which Rule Two had been disregarded left no room for forgiveness. The child was snuggled inside a tin toolbox, which had been wrapped with emerald-green ribbon, as if it were a present.

"Ugh!" Elinora Gassbeek squawked, looking down at the toolbox baby in disgust. She signaled a nearby orphan to retrieve it. "Put it upstairs."

The orphan nodded. "What name shall I put on the cot, Matron?"

The matron curled her lip. Naming children was tedious, but necessary.

"She's got a lotta fingers, Matron!"

The baby was sucking its thumb, making loud slurping noises that sent ants crawling up the matron's spine. She counted the child's fingers. Sure enough, it had an extra digit on each hand.

"Name it . . . Lotta."

The second baby arrived on a blustery evening in September, as a mischievous wind rattled the orphanage's many wooden shutters.

An orphan walked into the dining hall, cradling a coal bucket as if it were a bouquet of flowers. Something was *whimpering* inside the bucket. Peering in, the matron was displeased to find a raven-haired infant, wrapped in a soot-stained shawl, blinking up at her.

"Poor thing was abandoned beside the coal bunker," the orphan said.

"Disgraceful!" Gassbeek screeched, referring to the breaking of Rule Two *and* Rule Three. "Take it away."

"A name for him, Matron?" the orphan asked nervously.

Elinora Gassbeek took another reluctant look at the coal-bucket baby, its charcoal-blackened nose, and the shabby shawl wrapped snugly around it. The cotton shawl looked like it had, possibly, been brightly colored once. Now, however, it was a mottled shade of gray, with a barely discernible pattern of darker-gray ovals. Like rotten eggs, the matron thought.

"Name it . . . Egbert."

The third baby arrived on an unusually warm afternoon in October, as ladies with parasols paraded on the sun-warmed street.

Sitting on a bench outside, in her finest puffed-sleeve dress, Elinora Gassbeek opened her picnic hamper and found a wriggling baby, wedged in amongst the cheese sandwiches and almond cake. It had a shock of curly red hair on its head and was babbling incessantly.

No blanket. No basket. Not on the front step.

The matron screeched, shrill and loud like a boiling kettle. The picnic-hamper baby immediately fell quiet, its eyebrows squeezing together in a frightened frown. Up and down the street, curious faces appeared in the windows of the tall, narrow brick houses, and the strolling ladies came to a halt. Elinora Gassbeek gathered her wits and forced a smile for her neighbors. An orphan wove through the throng toward her.

"She wasn't in there a minute ago," the girl insisted, picking the baby up delicately.

"Take it away," Elinora Gassbeek said through gritted teeth.

"Yes, Matron. But . . . a name?"

The orphan rocked the now-silent baby, gently brushing fennel seeds from its hair. The matron shuddered.

"Name it . . . Fenna."

The fourth baby arrived on a gloomy morning in November, as a blanket of fog curled over the canal behind the house.

The delivery bell on the second floor jangled, rung from a boat on the canal below. Using the pulley system attached outside the window, an orphan hoisted the bucket winch up. As it emerged from the fog, Elinora Gassbeek's eye began to twitch. Inside the bucket was a baby, wearing a wheat sack and a sad frown. Two holes had been cut in the bottom of the sack, to allow its unusually long legs to poke through.

The matron hauled the wheat-sack child inside, cursing the madness that had befallen her orphanage.

"Put some clothes on it," she cawed at the orphan hovering beside her.

She looked at the baby's wonky ears, its gangly limbs, and the wheat-colored hair that stuck out from its head at the unruliest of angles. Printed on the wheat sack were the words SEMOLINA FLOUR. The matron groaned.

"Name it . . . Sem."

The fifth and final baby arrived under a full moon in December, as the constellations shone brightly above Amsterdam's skyline.

Elinora Gassbeek had sent an orphan out onto the orphanage's roof to investigate a strange noise. Wedged behind the chimney stack, inside a coffin-shaped basket, was a baby, cooing contentedly up at the starry night sky. It had hair as dark as midnight and eyes that were almost black.

Gingerly, the orphan brought the coffin-basket baby inside, where it immediately began to wail. Careful not to touch the infant, the matron reached down and pulled a toy from its clutches: a cat puppet, made from the softest Amsterdam cotton and dressed in fine Antwerp silk. A faint ticking noise emanated from the toy, but the matron was tutting too loudly to hear it.

"Ridiculous!"

She tossed the puppet back in the basket, on top of the black velvet blanket in which the baby was swaddled. On the corner of the blanket, embroidered in white thread, was a name:

Milou.

❋ ONE ❋

Little Tulip Orphanage, Amsterdam, January 1892

THE LITTLE TULIP ORPHANAGE was an unusually tall house, wedged in the middle of a long row of unusually tall houses. In the small window of the very top floor, a girl with unusually dark eyes gazed down at the frozen canal below her. Milou tracked the falling snow as it settled over the ornate rooftops like a layer of cake frosting. Crowds were gathering on the ice below, their pink-nosed faces beaming. Bicycles had been swapped for toboggans, clogs for skates, and cries of delight mingled with the neighing of cart horses.

The view became steadily more blurred as Milou's breath misted the cold window, and with a final heavy sigh, she turned away. As she did so, a frozen piece of peeling paint on the wall beside her fell to the floor with a *clink*. Even the dormitory's floorboards had developed a thin layer of frost, and Milou's eyeballs were so cold that it hurt to blink. The small fireplace on the adjacent wall was empty and dark, as always.

"Frozen orphan," Milou said to the red-haired girl sitting on the bed opposite her. "Sounds like some sort of fancy dessert, don't you think, Fen? I wonder if that's Matron's new plan; if she can't market us as potential sons and daughters, perhaps she hopes to sell us as ice cream."

Fenna grimaced and rolled her eyes, then went back to hand-feeding stale crumbs to a small gray rat nestled on her lap.

Milou scrunched her nose and pushed her mouth into a pinched pout. "Iced orphan!" she cawed, in a perfect copy of Matron Gassbeek's squawkish tone. "Come and get your iced orphan! Best iced orphan in all of Holland! Only five cents a scoop!"

Fenna's eyebrows unfurrowed and the corners of her mouth twitched. Milou felt a twinge of satisfaction that warmed her from the inside, ever so slightly.

"We'd better hurry," Milou said, turning serious. She rubbed a circle on the window and squinted at the clock tower at the other end of the road. "There's only four more minutes until laundry inspection; Gassbeek will pull out our arm hairs if we're late again—"

A prickling shiver started at the tips of Milou's ears and ran down the back of her neck. It was not a shiver of cold but a shiver of *warning*.

Footsteps sounded in the hallway. The girls shared a panicked look. Milou jumped down from the windowsill. Fenna rolled backward over the bed, the rat clutched to her chest. As Milou grabbed an armful of laundry from the end of a bed, Fenna hid the rat in her picnic basket, a mere moment before the dormitory door burst open.

A boy's head appeared in the doorway, possessing two oddly proportioned ears and a straggly tuft of blond hair. A gangly body followed immediately after, with spidery limbs that appeared to belong to four entirely different species of spider.

"There you are!" he said, breathlessly, his long fingers fiddling with the hem of his grease-stained shirt.

"Oh, Sem, it's only you," said Milou with relief. "What is it?"

Sem grinned lopsidedly. "We have *visitors*."

He spoke with such breathless hope that a ghost-like fluttering started in Milou's belly. There was only ever one kind of visitor that could make Sem so eager.

Adopters.

Fenna gave a tiny gasp.

"Visitors," Milou repeated.

It had been months since anyone had come to the Little Tulip to look for orphans. What if today was the day? What if her parents had finally returned for her? She couldn't remember them, of course, but she had theories. An entire Book of Theories, in fact, which at that moment was tucked into the left sleeve of her smock. In all her theories, her parents were clever and brave. In all but one, they were desperately making their way back to her. Perhaps, after twelve long years, they'd finally succeeded.

"Milou," Sem urged. "We need to hurry."

"Just a moment."

She clambered over three beds to get to the one she shared with Fenna and Lotta. Fingers trembling, Milou reached under the bed and pulled out her coffin basket, which was always packed and ready, just in case. Inside, on top of everything, was her cat puppet. Milou ran a finger over its foot, where the words "Bram Poppenmaker, Puppeteer" were written in swirling red letters. The puppet was cradling a lock of red, curly hair, which had been tied with an emerald-green bow. Milou placed it aside and reached into the basket to move two pieces of paper: a charcoal portrait of herself, and a poster advertising the famous Parisian circus troupe Cirque de Lumière. Tucked beneath these treasures was a neatly folded bundle of fine Amsterdam velvet.

Sem sat on the bed beside her, his legs tucked up under his chin. "Milou—"

"Just one minute."

He gave her that look again—the one she knew said he thought she was silly for holding on to the hope that her parents would come back for her. He'd never held that kind of hope; he'd only ever shown disdain for his birth parents. Milou reckoned that if *she'd* been abandoned in nothing but a wheat sack, she might have felt the same way. He didn't understand that she just *knew* she'd find her family one day.

It was a question of *when*, not if.

Milou slipped the black velvet dress over the stained cotton one she was already wearing and ran her fingers over the plush smoothness of it. If it *was* her real parents arriving, they should recognize her old baby blanket. It was a snug fit; Sem had taken it out as much as he could over the years, and soon the dress would not fit at all.

Sem looked at her outfit with a frown, then carefully adjusted her collar. Milou repacked her basket and grabbed her cat puppet, holding it over her thumping heart. When she'd been much younger, she'd been certain the puppet had a heartbeat of its own. It had soothed her through many cold, sleepless nights until, several years ago, it seemed to have stopped, and Milou realized that she had likely imagined it all along.

Perhaps the cold, sleepless nights would finally end now.

Perhaps today would be the day she finally left this place.

"Perhaps we should hurry?" Sem said impatiently, walking toward the door with Fenna.

Milou stood and followed them out of the room. Their dormitory was on the fourth floor of the old, narrow canal house—a building mostly constructed of deep shadows and loose floorboards and barely held together by peeling paint. Milou stomped down the treacherously steep stairs, past the mending rooms on the third floor, the laundry rooms on the second, and the schoolrooms on the first. Sem practically flew ahead of her, hopping down three steps at a time. Fenna seemed to glide, her feet as silent as they were nimble.

The ground floor was the only part of the orphanage that didn't look like a mere sneeze would demolish it. In the main foyer, the marble floor was polished to a shine, the walls were painted a charming shade of violet, and a tall grandfather clock ticked and tocked in the corner. A motley collection of children were arranging themselves in a line against one wall; younger ones at one end, older ones at the other. They were all frantically trying to make themselves presentable: rubbing at grease stains, tucking in shirts, adjusting petticoats, pulling up socks. But there was no disguising what they really were: scruffy, hungry, *desperate* orphans.

Sem and Fenna slipped into the line just as three small brown rats darted across the marble floor in different directions. A girl with a waistcoat over her blue cotton dress was scrubbing at a raven-haired boy's fingers. She shot Milou a worried look.

"What took you so long?" Lotta asked, then noticed Milou's dress and the cat puppet in her arms. "Never mind. Quick, help me get this charcoal off Egg's hands."

Milou took Egg's other hand and began rubbing at it with the inside of her sleeve. The charcoal smeared, leaving his hands an interesting shade of gray.

"Gassbeek wanted another portrait," Egg said, his voice full of worry as he peeled his hands from theirs and carefully adjusted the soot-stained shawl that hung around his neck. "I didn't have time to wash."

"Don't worry," Milou said. "It's just—"

The prickling shiver started at the tips of her ears again. The sensation intensified, until it felt as if a thousand needles were pricking at her earlobes. Milou pulled Lotta by the arm and shoved her in line beside Sem. She had just positioned herself next to Lotta when a familiar sound echoed out from the hallway leading to the Forbidden Quarters.

Click. Clack. Click. Clack.

All twenty-eight children straightened as if pulled by invisible strings.

Click. Clack. Click. Clack.

Twenty-eight staccato breaths sucked in, in quick succession.

Click. Clack. Click. Clack.

Twenty-seven sets of wide eyes fixed firmly on the wall

ahead. Milou peered through lowered lashes at the darkened hallway to her left.

Click. Clack. Click. Clack.

Matron Gassbeek's boots emerged a moment before the rest of her; twin points of polished bloodred leather, with low, pointed heels that were just as sharp as the expression on the matron's face when the rest of her appeared.

Every monster that Milou had made up for her bedtime stories was based in some way on Gassbeek: the brutal sneer of a gargoyle, the soulless eyes of a werewolf, the skin-itching screech of a banshee. If the matron hadn't been so filled with hatred and menace, she would probably have looked like any other middle-aged woman, but her vileness had transformed her features into something monstrous.

Gassbeek walked agonizingly slowly up and down the line, sneering with every *click* and scowling with every *clack*. Milou kept her eyes lowered and her spine straight, her shoulders not too low but neither scrunched up to her still-tingling ears. Finally, the matron clucked her tongue in disapproval and stamped one boot.

CLACK!

All twenty-eight children flinched.

The doorbell *dinged* and then *donged*.

"Our guests are here, so do *not* disappoint me," the matron cawed, already looking thoroughly disappointed in every single one of them.

Gassbeek *click-clacked* to the front door, paused to pat her tightly coiled hair, and stretched her mouth into a hideous smile.

The door swung open and snow swirled in. Milou couldn't help herself; she leaned forward from her spot at the far end of the line as the adopters stepped over the threshold, two dark silhouettes in the midst of the snow cloud. Milou squeezed the cat puppet to her chest, right against her jittery heart. Her ears tingled again; her breathing grew shallow.

The door slammed shut and the snow dropped to the floor, revealing two tall figures in black cloaks with hoods drawn over their heads. Even from the other side of the hall, Milou could see their cloaks were made of Amsterdam velvet; the subtle shimmer was unmistakable.

Her fingers sought the little label on the cat puppet's foot. Could this be Bram Poppenmaker? Had he brought her mother too? She knew without doubt she would recognize them. They would look like her. *Different.*

As the adopters reached up to their hoods, Milou felt as if she had an entire graveyard of ghosts fluttering around in her stomach. But it was not midnight-dark hair and almost-black eyes that emerged from those hoods. The ghosts in Milou's belly turned into solid, heavy tombstones.

Two heads of honey-blond hair.

Two pairs of ice-blue eyes.

Two *disgustingly* cheerful smiles.

❧ TWO ❧

THE GOLDEN-HAIRED ADOPTERS SHOOK themselves free of snow and turned to face the lineup. Milou tried to ignore her deep disappointment and squeezed her cat puppet to her chest, staring down at her boots.

They weren't her parents.

"*Welkom!*" Gassbeek chirped, smiling like a wide-eyed marionette. "*Kindjes*, this is Meneer and Mevrouw Fortuyn. Everybody say *Goedemorgen!*"

"*Goedemorgen*," chimed twenty-seven small voices.

Milou's tongue felt as if it were coated in cobwebs. She tugged on the collar of her baby-blanket dress, the tightness of which was now becoming suffocating. A hand reached into hers and squeezed, and Milou gave Lotta a tight smile.

"Come into the warm!" Gassbeek was cooing, as she flounced around the adopters and ushered them across the marble floor. "The *kindjes* are ever so excited to meet you."

"*We* are ever so excited to meet *them*," Meneer Fortuyn said.

He was a tall man, and his wife was even taller. They stood in the middle of the foyer and ran their gaze up and down the line as if they were perusing a shop-window display.

"How delightful," Meneer Fortuyn said.

"Delightful indeed!" Gassbeek snorted, her joviality slipping for an instant. "As I'm sure you'll remember from the advertisement, there is no doubt *whatsoever* that I provide the finest orphans in all of Amsterdam. Obedient, hardworking, and well-mannered. And the older ones can all read and write."

"Oh, this is even better than buying a new handbag!" Mevrouw Fortuyn said brightly. "Look, Bart, there are so many of them to choose from!"

Gassbeek's smile took a steep climb up her powdered cheeks. Milou dug her fingers deeper into the soft cotton of her cat puppet.

"Then by all means start your inspection," Gassbeek crooned. "We'll start with the smallest."

The first orphan, a small girl with blonde ringlets and an entire constellation of freckles on her face, took a hasty step forward. The matron lowered her reading spectacles onto the tip of her nose and squinted at her clipboard.

"This is Janneke," Gassbeek squawked. "Aged three-ish. She can count to ten and is beginning to wield a sewing needle without drawing blood. Janneke comes with a wicker basket and a yellow cotton blanket."

The Fortuyns beamed down at the toddler. "*Hallo, liefje.*"

Milou felt a tug on her sleeve. She looked at Lotta, who was studying the adopters with a thoughtful expression.

"I bet you a hole-less sock they choose Janneke," Lotta whispered. "Seven times out of eight, adopters choose the youngest one. A child with freckles increases the odds. Mathematically speaking, we've lost this one already."

"It's probably for the best," Milou whispered back, eyeing the Fortuyns as they moved steadily down the line toward her. "They look like grave robbers to me."

Lotta raised her eyebrows in question.

Milou leaned in a bit closer to her. "Black boots, dark cloaks. All the better for sneaking around at night, stealing corpses to sell for medical research. Perhaps they'll choose Sem, on account of those excellent shovel-wielding arms of his."

Sem coughed and gave them a pointed look. Milou turned her gaze back to her boots.

Her Book of Theories suddenly felt uncomfortable in her sleeve. Perhaps her parents would arrive after the worst of winter had passed. It made sense. Traveling was difficult at this time of year, she reminded herself. She just had to be more patient.

"And what is your name, *liefje?*" Meneer Fortuyn said, now only a few children away.

Milou's stomach twisted once more as she noticed Fenna fiddling with the hem of her apron and looking down at her feet.

"This is Fenna," Gassbeek crowed, reading from her clipboard. "Aged twelve-ish. Fully literate with adequate handwriting. Her cooking skills are second to none. Fenna comes with a picnic hamper, but, alas, *no* blanket."

"What lovely red hair," said Mevrouw Fortuyn, gripping Fenna's chin. "It reminds me of my favorite shade of lipstick. Tell me, Fenna, do you sing?"

The foyer fell suddenly silent, except for the clunking gears of the grandfather clock. Mevrouw Fortuyn cleared her throat. Fenna's shoulders scrunched together, and she squeezed her eyes closed.

"Oh, it's no good asking her questions," Gassbeek said with a sigh. "She's a mute, that one. *However*"—the matron's voice pitched upward—"she would make a gloriously *quiet* daughter."

"A mute?" Meneer Fortuyn said, his voice curious. "I suppose it might be good to have a silent child—"

"Oh, absolutely not, Bart!" his wife cried. "What would our friends think? I couldn't bear the gossip. Next!"

Fenna shuffled backward as Egg stepped eagerly forward. He wiped a charcoal-stained hand on his trouser leg, then held it out to them. The Fortuyns stared at his filthy hand and made no move to take it.

"This is Egbert," the matron said. "Aged twelve-ish, of unknown East Asian heritage. He can name every capital city in the world and shows plentiful promise at both calligraphy *and* cartography. Egbert comes with a coal bucket and"—she scowled down at Egg—"that shawl."

"An artist?" Meneer Fortuyn asked, and grimaced as he pointed to the stick of charcoal that was wedged behind Egg's left ear.

"Egbert is, well, yes, he is *artistically inclined*," Gassbeek said, as if she were admitting that Egg liked to eat dead frogs. "*However*, he'd be very useful for drawing portraits, or—"

Meneer Fortuyn held up a hand. "We have just redecorated our home. White silk curtains from Beijing and cream upholstery from Rome."

"Charcoal *stains*," Mevrouw Fortuyn added, nodding toward Egg's shawl in disdain. "As you can quite clearly see."

The adopters moved down the line.

Sem tumbled forward, as if the floor had suddenly tilted. The Fortuyns took a hasty step back. Sem managed to lock his legs rigidly and slap his arms to his sides. His nose turned bright red.

"This is Sem," Gassbeek said. "Aged thirteen-ish. An expert in dressmaking. Handwriting is . . . well, let's say his handwriting has *character*. Sem comes with a wheat sack, but no basket and no blanket."

"I thought *girls* learned sewing?" Mr. Fortuyn said.

Mevrouw Fortuyn turned to Gassbeek. "Why is he not apprenticed, if he's thirteen?"

"Clumsier than a three-legged donkey." Gassbeek sighed. "He keeps getting sent back from every job I've found him. *That said*, his height makes him my number-one cobweb duster. Very useful indeed. I could give you a discount on this one."

Sem reddened in embarrassment, and his smile faltered.

Mevrouw Fortuyn shook her head. "I don't think so. Look at him, Bart, how would I ever find suitable outfits for such a beanpole of a boy? And don't even get me started on that disastrous hair. No. Just no."

Sem slunk back into line, his shoulders slumped lopsidedly. Milou let out a small growl, ignoring the sudden needle pricks on her ear tips telling her to watch herself. She shook her hair over her face. Peeking through a thin slit of ebony, she saw the adopters turn enthusiastically to Lotta. Mevrouw Fortuyn's eye twitched slightly at the sight of Lotta's waistcoat, but her friend's beautiful golden pigtails, tied with emerald ribbons, seemed to reignite the woman's interest.

"Lotta, aged twelve-ish," Gassbeek sighed, reading from her clipboard in a monologue. "Mastered the twelve times table by the age of four. She is familiar with concepts such as Pythagoras's theorem and pi. Lotta comes with an empty toolbox, a yellow cotton blanket, and three reams of emerald-green ribbon."

Meneer Fortuyn scoffed. "What use does a *girl* have for knowing about Pythagoras?"

Lotta's fists clenched at her sides.

"Oh, don't worry," Gassbeek said quickly. "I assure you, she's house trained and docile, as a girl should be."

Milou felt Lotta bristle beside her, and the two girls shared a side-eyed look of contempt.

"That ghastly waistcoat will have to go, and the dress will need more frills." Mevrouw Fortuyn bent down so that her nose was level with Lotta's. "But oh my, aren't you a pretty little doll?"

Lotta narrowed her eyes.

"Say *hallo*, Lotta," Gassbeek warned.

"*Hallo*," Lotta said in a voice as sweet as syrup. She raised one hand and gave them a six-fingered wave. Then she uncurled her other hand and made it a slow, twelve-finger wave.

There was a long pause, in which Milou could hear some mumbled counting. Then the Fortuyns sidestepped, and, despite the wall of ebony hair covering her face, Milou felt their gaze land on her.

It was time for her performance.

"This is Milou," Gassbeek said. The matron cleared her throat, but Milou kept her hair over her face. "Aged twelve-ish.

She can recite the Grimm Brothers' fairy tales and has a pleasant enough singing voice. Milou comes with a small coffin, that strange little dress she's wearing, and a puppet."

"But does she come with a face?" Mr. Fortuyn asked.

"Milou?" The matron *clacked* her boot in warning. "Move your hair immediately."

"Mill-oo," Mrs. Fortuyn mused. "What kind of a name is *Mill-oo?*"

"Not one I would have chosen," Gassbeek said with a sigh. "You're more than welcome to choose a proper name for her." *CLACK.* "Move your hair, girl."

Milou felt another prickle on her left ear, like a needle of cold air, but she ignored it. She didn't need her Sense to tell her that she was risking the matron's wrath.

"Is she deaf?" Mrs. Fortuyn asked.

"No," Gassbeek snarled. "She isn't."

"Milou?" Lotta's whispered voice was tinged with fear. "What are you doing?"

The ear prickling returned a mere moment before the matron seized a fistful of Milou's hair and pulled her head up. It was all the time she needed to arrange her expression. She scrunched her nose and bared her teeth, and with her head tilted away from the light, she knew her almost-black eyes would look like dark, empty pits.

The Fortuyns gasped.

Milou smiled. It was not a sweet smile. There were no

dimples. It was a smile the matron herself had taught her: all teeth and no soul.

"*Goedemorgen*," Milou growled, using her best werewolf voice.

The adopters' wide eyes roamed across her face, traveled down her ill-fitting black dress, then back up again. Milou stared up at them through spider-leg lashes. The Fortuyns shared a look: crinkled noses and a not-so-subtle shake of their heads.

"We'll take that one," Mrs. Fortuyn announced, pointing to a dark-haired boy in the middle of the line. "He seems ever so sweet."

Milou's heart did a little dance of triumph.

Gassbeek twisted her fist one more time, then let go of Milou and grinned.

"An excellent choice!" she cried in delight, *click-clacking* toward a side table, upon which lay a huge leather-bound tome. "Let me prepare the adoption certificate for you." Her smile vanished as she faced the orphans. "The rest of you, back to work."

The grandfather clock ticked and tocked, rats scratched in the darkest corners of the room, and the orphans moved on silent feet to attend to their chores.

As they made their way up the stairs, Milou smiled to herself for a performance well done. Then she cast a sideways glance at her friends. Lotta was scowling, Sem looked bewildered, Egg was still trying to wipe charcoal off his hands, and Fenna looked like she wanted to climb into one of the many shadows and hide. Milou's smile slid to the floor.

"She won't forget what you did," Sem said quietly. "It'll be worse than head-shaving and caned fingers this time."

Milou swallowed. "I had no other choice. I can't get adopted; you know that. Whatever the matron does to me, I can take it."

Sem didn't look convinced, but he gave her a small smile. "I hope it's worth it."

Milou clutched her puppet and ran her fingers once more over the label on its foot, ignoring the tiny stab of doubt trying to worm its way into her heart.

She hoped it was all worth it too.

Hope was all she had left.

MILOU'S BOOK OF THEORIES

Lotta says all theories must be based on evidence and that the power of deduction can solve any mystery. Gassbeek insists that my parents abandoned me because I was an "unwanted little freak," but I believe the evidence tells an entirely different story. I was abandoned with more clues than any other orphan I've ever known. My parents would never leave me without good reason.

Evidence

- Cat puppet made by Bram Poppenmaker. Had a heartbeat.
- Coffin basket with claw marks down the left side of it.
- A length of white silk thread stuck inside the wicker weaving.
- Blanket made of expensive Amsterdam velvet.
- Name stitched in white silk thread.
- Two drops of blood on blanket stitching.
- Left on rooftop of orphanage, under a full moon.
- My Sense, which warns me of danger.

The Werewolf Hunter Theory

My parents are werewolf hunters (Sense, claw marks, and full moon). They were being chased by werewolves, so they climbed to safety (rooftop). Worried that I might get hurt (babies do not make very good werewolf hunters), they decided to leave me somewhere until it was safe to return for me (orphanage). To let me know that they cared for me, they left clues to both my identity and theirs: They quickly stitched my name onto the blanket, pricking a finger in the process (thread and blood drops); and my father left me a clue to show he is Bram Poppenmaker (cat puppet). They'll return for me, no doubt, when I am old enough to train as a werewolf hunter.

❧ THREE ❧

AFTER A MEAGER LUNCH of Fenna's signature cabbage broth, Milou spent an hour helping Lotta winch down bucketload after bucketload of clean laundry to a sledge waiting on the frozen canal. She then spent the following hour helping Lotta winch bucketload after bucketload of *dirty* laundry up from a different sledge. By the time the grandfather clock began to chime seven o'clock, Milou's arms felt like noodles, and her hands were covered in friction burns.

"Holy Gouda, I can barely feel them anymore," Lotta said, wiggling all twelve fingers. "At least if Gassbeek does cane you, you probably won't notice much."

Gassbeek had gone out into the city shortly after the

Fortuyns had left and had yet to return. Even when the matron was gone, her presence was felt, like a malevolent spirit that filled every shadow-strewn nook and draft-battered cranny of the Little Tulip. It wouldn't have surprised any of the children if the matron had eyes in the walls or spies at the windows. If they slacked on their chores even slightly, Gassbeek would know. And so, the orphans worked as diligently as if the matron were hovering over them, barking her endless orders.

Milou was growing increasingly anxious about what punishment Gassbeek had in store for her. The matron would be planning something terrible, Milou was certain of it. Her Sense was certain of it too, it seemed. Even a mention of the matron sent a wave of shivers across the tips of her ears.

"Maybe she's fallen into the North Sea Canal," Milou said hopefully, gazing out the laundry-room window toward the smog-blurred docks to the north. "She could be floating off to some faraway ocean as we speak."

"Doubtful," Lotta said, as she retied a blonde pigtail that had come loose. "Her buoyancy would be compromised by those heavy dresses she wears. It wouldn't take her long to sink."

The grandfather clock continued to *dong* in thunderous tones, and Milou heard the hurried footsteps of orphans spilling out of rooms and hurrying upstairs. She closed the laundry-room window and then rubbed at her tingling ears.

"Come on," Lotta said, a hint of exasperation in her voice. "Let's get you to bed before your ears convince you that the matron is plotting your murder."

Milou followed her out of the room, worry twisting her insides. When they reached the dormitory, there were ten children elbowing each other for room around the single bucket of water, into which they dipped their toothbrushes and hastily scrubbed their teeth. When the children moved on, Milou peered into the bucket. Its contents were now slightly yellow, with bubbles of spit floating on the surface.

She went to the open window and plunged her toothbrush into the snow on the window ledge. Egg was sitting on the roof, his charcoal pencil scratching away on a corner of an old pillowcase. He lifted a makeshift telescope, made of metal piping and recycled spectacle lenses, and pointed it toward the horizon, seemingly unaware Milou was there. She put her toothbrush in her mouth, shuddered as the cold touched her gums, scrubbed, then spat into the bucket.

"You're letting even more cold in, Egg."

"Yes, but I've nearly finished adding the eastern dockland. Look."

Milou peered over his shoulder at his pillowcase map. "The tiny ships on the river look wonderful. With your leg shaking like that, it looks like they're bobbing up and down on the water."

Egg beamed at her, then shivered again. "I suppose it is rather cold. I'll finish it tomorrow."

He carefully handed her his mapmaking supplies, climbed back in through the window, and closed it behind him. She tucked them into his coal bucket, then wriggled through the narrow gaps between the beds to the rear of the room. Bedsprings creaked as their inhabitants clambered in. Milou tucked herself in between Lotta and Fenna, then pulled her Book of Theories out from her sleeve.

"Could we have a cheerful story tonight?" Lotta asked. "I don't think I'm in the mood for ghouls or werewolves."

Pale faces emerged from beneath bedsheets all around the crowded room to nod in agreement. Beside Milou, Fenna shivered, then snuggled in closer, and Milou felt the tickle of rat fur against her arm as her friend cuddled the creature to her chest.

"I have been working on a new theory." Milou smiled, all thoughts of the matron vanishing the instant she opened her homemade notebook, flicking through its worn, scribble-filled pages. "In it, my father, Bram Poppenmaker, is a puppet maker by day, air-balloon aviator by night."

As murmurs of interest rippled across the dormitory, Milou licked her dry lips and began her story.

"On a moonlit night, twelve years ago, a family of three sailed the skies above Amsterdam. They flew higher than the hawks, smoother than the starlings, and faster than the falcons."

Lotta coughed pointedly. "I'm not sure that's how balloons work—"

"It's how *this* one worked." Milou turned the page and resumed her storytelling voice: half raspy whisper, half singsong. "The balloon was midnight black, speckled with silver stars. Below hung the grandest gondola there ever was. At its bow, a snarling wolf, carved from ebony, with giant emeralds for eyes. At its stern, dangling from a horizontal pole, was my basket, placed there so I could watch the stars twinkle above me.

"The Poppenmakers had just flown past Centraal Station and over the royal palace, when, suddenly and unexpectedly, a storm began." Milou's voice deepened. "Lightning forked and thunder boomed. From the east came a swirling vortex of furious winds. My mother lowered the balloon, hoping to escape the worst of it, but the wind knocked the gondola into the rooftops. My basket caught on a chimney stack, wedging so firmly that as the air balloon carried onward, the ropes holding me snapped, and I was left behind."

Milou paused for dramatic effect, then grinned behind her notebook at the sounds of breaths being sucked in and then held. The rat in Fenna's embrace gave a little squeak as if it had just been squeezed. She let them wait another few heartbeats, then continued.

"There was nothing my parents could do. As the wind blew them further and further away from me, my mother did her best to turn the air balloon around, while my father considered jumping out to get to me as soon as the balloon got low enough. But the storm had other ideas.

"The air balloon was blown higher and higher, across oceans, spinning and turning until, a few days later, they crash-landed at the North Pole, surrounded by a family of very confused polar bears. The balloon had a huge tear in it and lay, deflated and limp, alongside the upturned gondola. My parents, with their quick wits and excellent survival skills, built a house out of ice. My father used old puppet strings as fishing lines, and my mother befriended the bears by singing them lullabies.

"But it is hard to find balloon-fixing supplies in the Arctic. To this very day, they are still patching the balloon up and desperately trying to make their way back home."

"That doesn't explain why you were in a *coffin*," Sem said in a slightly muffled, disembodied voice from beneath the covers of the bed opposite hers.

"Well, yes, I'm still working on that bit, but—"

"Nor does it explain the claw marks," Egg added.

"I'll admit, it's not my most convincing theory, but—"

Milou's words died away as her left ear began to tingle wildly. She looked at the closed dormitory door. A heartbeat later, a familiar sound echoed in the hall beyond it.

Click-clack-click-clack.

There was a collective rustle of bedsheets as the orphans

tucked their heads under the covers again. Tiny rodent feet scampered up her arm and over her head as Fenna's rat darted away. Milou heard a puff of air blown from small lips, and the single candle that lit the room hissed and died.

Click-clack-click-clack.

The beds creaked and squeaked beneath shivering bodies.

Click-clack-click-clack.

The matron entered the room, and made her way past each bed, pausing every now and then.

Click-clack-click—

Through a hole in her blanket, Milou saw the pointed toes of the matron's boots stop, adjacent to her bed. Her ears tingled as the boots turned, one at a time, to face her.

"Get up," Gassbeek hissed, tearing the blanket from Milou's grip. "Lotta and Fenna, you too." The matron whacked the two lumps shivering in the bed opposite. "Sem and Egg as well."

"Why them?" Milou asked, her heart thudding in double time as she staggered out of bed.

The matron merely smiled her signature smile, all teeth and no soul, then *click-clacked* out of the room.

In the pale light of the moon that streamed in through the threadbare curtains, her friends climbed out of bed with matching expressions of dread.

What was the matron up to?

Gassbeek was waiting in the foyer. There were dirty footprints leading across the marble floor, toward the dining hall. The same floor Sem and Egg had scrubbed clean earlier. Surely, they wouldn't have missed such obvious marks. Was this what the matron had called them down for?

The five of them assembled in a line, shivering in their nightclothes under the matron's glare. A strange oily smell hung in the air, tickling Milou's nostrils in an unpleasant way.

"Your behavior earlier today was unforgivable," Gassbeek said, her gaze boring down on each one of them.

Milou frowned. "But I'm the only one who misbehaved, Matron."

The matron's eyes hardened. "The five of you have been here *twelve* years. I have never had an orphan stay beyond ten before. No matter how hard I have tried to convince potential parents that you might make suitable adoptees, you have persisted in presenting yourselves as the unadoptable little brats that you are. And you, Milou, are the most irredeemably monstrous child I have ever had the misfortune of knowing. It's little wonder your real parents didn't want you."

"That's not true—" Milou began, feeling for the reassuring lump of her Book of Theories—and all the evidence that showed her parents *had* loved her—before realizing it was still under her pillow.

She took a shaky breath. Arguing with Gassbeek now would only make things worse. Her friends looked terrified, and this was all her fault. The matron was going to punish them all, just to spite her.

Milou held out her hands. "Please, just cane me. I am the one who behaved badly, they've done nothing wrong."

Gassbeek sneered. "Oh, there won't be any caning today. I've realized that won't solve my problem at all. No, I have another plan. I've decided that the five of you have outstayed your welcome."

Milou's heart thudded. "What do you mean?"

"The law states an orphan can remain until adulthood," Lotta said. "You can't just throw us out. The Kinderbureau would not allow it."

"They care only about paperwork," Gassbeek snorted. "To them, you are nothing but names and numbers in a book. As long as the paperwork adds up, they will not look too closely. I can do whatever I please."

"But that's illegal!" Lotta cried.

"I will offer you one final chance at redemption," the matron said, ignoring Lotta. "I will allow you to attend *one* more lineup. Whoever is not chosen during the next inspection will find themselves nameless and homeless."

"You can't do this," Egg pleaded. "We'll starve, if we don't freeze first."

"Perhaps you should have thought about that sooner."

"It could be weeks before the next lineup," Lotta said, turning to the others. "Egg could paint some freckles on our faces, perhaps? We'll just have to try harder."

Milou kept her eyes on the matron. She knew there was something else coming before the matron spoke. She could see it in the way Gassbeek's mouth twitched in the corner. Milou looked at the footprints again. She realized then they were far too large to be a child's and not pointy enough to be the matron's. She also noticed there were *two* sets of prints.

"Actually, Lotta *liefje*," Gassbeek said. "The lineup will begin right now."

❧ FOUR ❧

THE STRANGE SCENT OF oil mingled with the ashy smell of smoke as Gassbeek led them down the dark corridor toward the dining hall. Adopted or banished, they would all be leaving tonight. Milou's parents would arrive one day and find her *gone*.

Milou clasped her cat puppet over her heart like battle armor, pretending that the pulse she felt through it was its heartbeat returning, not just her own, pounding hard enough for the two of them. Would it be better to go with this new family, to live who-knew-where? Or should she allow herself to be banished and try to find her parents herself?

She followed Gassbeek and the others meekly into the dining hall, where long, narrow tables lined the walls.

"Here they are," Gassbeek announced to the visitors that Milou still could not see beyond the matron's tall form. "*Kindjes*, form a line."

A fire crackled at the far end of the room, and Milou wondered who these adopters might be, to warrant such a welcome from Gassbeek. The unexpected fire did not, however, explain the oily smell of smoke that hung in the air, tickling Milou's nostrils unpleasantly.

"Quickly now." Gassbeek grabbed Milou's arm and shoved her into place before spinning with a rustle of her silk dress toward the visitors. "The oldest orphans I have, as you requested."

With the matron now out of the way, Milou saw that two men stood beside the fireplace. The taller one was wearing a finely tailored gray suit, with a fur-trimmed overcoat and a tall top hat. His face was half-covered by a huge mustachio, which erupted from under his nose in two long curls and spread out toward his thick muttonchop sideburns. There were rings on almost every finger and a long tobacco pipe hanging from his mouth. A younger man, barely into adulthood by the looks of it, was dressed in simple black trousers and woolen coat. A bowler hat rested on his head, tipped down so that the top of his face was in shadow, leaving only a pointed chin on display.

"At least she's bettered our odds by keeping the little ones upstairs," Lotta whispered. "We each have a twenty percent chance now."

"*Kindjes*," the matron crooned. "This is Meneer Rotman."

She rolled the r in Rotman far longer than was necessary. Milou's ears tingled, and she squeezed her cat puppet more tightly.

"*Goedenavond*," the man with the mustachio said, his voice a deep baritone. "It is a pleasure to make your acquaintances. My name is Bas Rotman, and this here is my apprentice, Pieter."

Pieter nodded his head once, his face still hidden, and his arms crossed behind his back. He did not speak, nor did he look up from the floor.

"Say *hallo*," Gassbeek cooed.

Four croaked *hallos* sounded. Milou had never seen her friends look so worried before. Their expressions stabbed at her. If only she hadn't angered the matron, they'd perhaps have had enough time to find families that loved them for who they were. They'd at least have a *chance*.

The five of them stood, straight-backed and trembling, waiting for the matron to take out her clipboard and begin listing their sellable qualities, but Gassbeek merely crossed her arms. They would be getting no help from her, Milou realized. If Milou wanted to be adopted, she'd have to make it happen herself.

"Meneer Rotman is a very wealthy sugar merchant," Gassbeek said. "And he is looking for an heir to join him on his many travels aboard his ship."

In the flickering firelight, Milou saw her friends' faces waver between hope and despair. Their hands reached out toward each other, forming a line of solidarity.

A realization settled over her. It wouldn't be right to take this one last opportunity for herself. They all deserved a fair chance at being adopted, of being *happy*. This was her chance to make things right by one of them.

She had to do something.

Something bold.

"Good evening, Meneer Rotman," Milou said, giving him a small curtsy.

The others looked at her in surprise. The matron's eyes narrowed, but Milou knew it didn't matter if she angered Gassbeek further. The damage was already done.

"We are honored to meet you," Milou continued. "Might I introduce us all?"

The merchant's mustachio twitched. "That would be . . . *delightful*."

He took a long drag on his pipe, then blew a cloud of pipe smoke. As the smoke curled around them, Milou's ears began to tingle again. She looked down as she rubbed them and noticed that her shadow seemed to be . . . quivering. She frowned, wafted the smoke away, and cleared her throat.

"This is Lotta," Milou said, pushing Lotta forward a step. "The cleverest girl in all of Amsterdam. She's a mathematician *and* an engineer. She once made a telescope for Egg out of some old reading glasses and a metal pipe."

"It's amazing what you can find in a canal," Lotta said, beaming. "I found a working compass in there once too."

"Her parents were undoubtedly well-regarded scientists from Bavaria," Milou continued. "It's the only explanation for her cleverness. And with her extra fingers, there is no knot that she cannot tie or untie. She would make a fine merchant's daughter, sir."

Rotman's only response was more mustachio twitching and a short nod. Behind him, Pieter shifted slightly on his feet, his gaze remaining downcast.

Milou pushed Sem forward. "This is Sem. The kindest boy in all of Amsterdam. He always puts others before himself, and those ears of his are a testament to how good he is at listening. What he lacks in grace, he more than makes up for with his sewing skills. I'm convinced his parents are dressmakers from Paris who make magnificent haute couture designs out of the most mundane materials. He fixes all our clothing and once even gave me stitches when I split my chin open. He would make a fine son, sir, if you ask me."

"She's being a little too complimentary," Sem said quietly, his cheeks flushed. "I can fix clothes fairly well, though. And sails too, probably."

The matron clucked her tongue. Rotman's eyes narrowed. He nodded again, and Milou stepped quickly over to Egg and nudged him forward.

"Egbert is the most talented boy in all of Amsterdam," she said. "He has drawn an entire map of the city on an old pillow-case, just from sitting on the roof. It is remarkable, and covers the north of the city, all the way from Centraal Station, the city docks, the Amstel river, and down to the watery flatlands of the polders to the south. No doubt he gets this talent from his parents, who were most likely traveling painters from the Far East. Surely a merchant like yourself would delight in having a son with such promising skills in cartography. He could help you explore the world."

Egg made a small noise, half giggle, half gasp, and Milou saw he was holding the corner of his shawl with a white-knuckled grip. He shot Milou a quick, grateful smile.

Rotman took another deep puff on his pipe and blew out a large cloud of smoke that hit Milou right in the eyes. As she fanned the smoke away, she noticed her shadow elongating. It stretched across the floor until it hit the merchant's sealskin boots.

Milou frowned. Was it *pointing* at him?

She looked behind her, but there was nothing there to cast such a shadow. Then she looked back down. The shadow was still there, wavering in the last strands of smoke, like a long shadowy finger pointing straight at Rotman's toes. Her ears tingled so suddenly and sharply she let out a little gasp.

A draft howled in through a wall, and then the smoke was gone and so was the shadow. Egg's elbow bashed her arm, and Milou tore her gaze from the floor. Fenna was looking at her expectantly.

"And this is Fenna," Milou croaked.

"I'm assuming Fenna is also an ideal child with impressive parentage?" Rotman asked.

There was cold amusement in his voice, Milou realized. As if he were laughing at her. As if he found her . . . *ridiculous*.

Milou stared at Rotman hard for a moment, trying to work him out. He certainly dressed like a rich merchant: extravagantly. His features were neither handsome nor repellent, but there were deep lines on his forehead, as if he spent a lot of time frowning. And his hands were clean and looked soft, which, Milou thought, was odd for a seafaring merchant.

Rotman stared right back, unsmiling.

Milou's ears tingled uncomfortably.

"Fenna is the *sweetest* girl in all of Amsterdam," Milou said finally, clearing her throat and making sure she held the merchant's gaze. "She doesn't talk, but this is only because her parents were probably mime artists from London. She doesn't smile often either, but when she does it's like an entire galaxy is twinkling in her eyes. She makes the best breakfast cake you could ever hope to taste. I imagine a cook would be very useful on a ship, sir."

"That sounds wonderful," Rotman said blandly, his mustachio twitching yet again.

To Milou's surprise, Fenna lifted her gaze to the merchant's and gave him a timid smile.

He puffed out another mouthful of smoke. "What delightful little *creatures* you have raised, Matron."

Milou looked from him to the matron, to the once-again-quivering shadow that was now wrapping itself around the merchant's ankles. The matron looked thoroughly pleased with herself, and Rotman's smile remained unmoving.

It was a parody of a smile, Milou realized, much like the matron's: all teeth and no soul.

Something was wrong, but she couldn't work out what.

"And what about you then?" Rotman asked. "What delightful skills do you have, young lady?"

"Me?" Milou said, her voice ragged. She lowered her chin and tilting her head just so, blinking up through spider lashes. "I'm the most irredeemably monstrous child you could ever have the misfortune of meeting, sir. You wouldn't want a child like me. Also, I think you smell funny, so I don't think I'd like you much as a father."

Her friends gasped.

The matron's eyes widened in fury.

Rotman tipped his head back and laughed.

It was a strange laugh: like a seagull. And it seemed to

go on forever. In which time, an unshakable worry had settled over Milou like an itchy blanket.

Rotman did not behave like any adopter she had ever met before. He did not coo over them. His smile, and his laugh, seemed . . . wrong. He was looking at them in the same manner that Gassbeek did: as though they were *things*. *Creatures*, he had called them. Why would a man who so obviously did not like children want to adopt a child?

"Pieter!" Rotman said, holding his hand out toward the younger man. "Pass me a handkerchief, would you?"

Pieter reached into the inside pocket of his coat and pulled out a white handkerchief, then held it out for Rotman to take. Milou saw that there were scratches all up the younger man's arms. Some were scabbed over, some seemed fresher. As if sensing Milou's gaze, Pieter quickly put his arms back behind himself and went back to staring at his feet.

As Rotman's chuckling subsided, Milou noticed her shadow was still twitching and stretching outward, pooling thickly at the merchant's boots. Her ears tingled. It couldn't be a coincidence. Her Sense had never failed to warn her of danger before, but now it seemed to be trying to warn her more *urgently*.

"Well, Matron," Rotman said, wiping a tear of mirth away with his handkerchief. "I am most impressed. It is just as you said, the most remarkable orphans I have ever come across."

Gassbeek preened at his words, and Milou felt queasy.

"Now." He clapped his hands together. "I suppose I must choose which of you I shall take home. My ship, *De Zeehond*, is spectacular. It is the fastest vessel in all of Europe and has sailed every ocean in the world. It might be an unusual home, but I guarantee it will be an adventurous one."

"Would I really get to travel?" Egg asked.

"Oh yes," Rotman said, smirking. "We will travel to places you've never even heard of."

"What about a mother?" Sem asked. The hope in his voice made Milou's heart ache.

Rotman's mustachio twitched again. "You will have a female . . . guardian. Her name is Dolly."

Pieter's shoulders immediately stiffened, Milou noticed. The others were looking at Rotman with awe-filled gazes and hopeful smiles. They didn't seem to notice anything strange about him.

"It is such an impossible choice you give me, Matron," Rotman said, taking another long drag on his pipe, blowing it out in a thick and disgusting plume right in their faces.

As the oily cloud of smoke dissipated, Milou realized the merchant was staring at her. He smiled that odd smile of his. Then he gave her a wink.

"I suppose I shall just have to adopt all five of them."

✳ FIVE ✳

MILOU STARED AT THE others. In the flickering light, their smiles were wide enough to swallow the moon. She clung to her cat puppet.

He wanted all five of them?

He wanted to adopt . . . *her?*

Milou blinked up at him. She wanted to say something, anything, to make him change his mind and leave, but her tongue felt too heavy to move.

"Are you . . . sure?" Gassbeek squawked, her expression one of utter shock. "You want . . . *all* of them?"

"Oh yes, I'm quite serious, Matron," Rotman said, his smile gone. "This little girl has convinced me, well and truly, that these children are perfect. In fact, I find them all *adorable*."

He said "adorable" in the same way that someone might describe a bad smell. He was, Milou decided, a terrible performer, uncommitted and sloppy.

A six-fingered hand grabbed Milou's and gave it a little shake. Lotta gave her a delighted smile. She wrapped her arms around Milou's middle. "Oh, Milou," she whispered. "Thank you."

Milou opened her mouth to respond, but all that escaped her lips was a strangled croak.

"Well," Gassbeek spluttered, her mouth flapping open, then closed, "that's marvelous!"

Rotman took another long drag on his pipe. In the cloud that erupted around them, Milou watched her shadow tremble. Her ears didn't tingle, they *burned* icily. Milou felt a wave of panic wash over her. This was wrong, all wrong.

What had she done?

"Pieter!" Rotman barked, snapping his bejeweled fingers at his apprentice. "Go and ready the carriage while I discuss the *transaction* with the matron."

Milou sidestepped to get out of Pieter's way as he strode swiftly and silently from the room, the scratches up his arms hidden once more.

"*Kindjes*," Gassbeek said. "Go and pack your belongings. Wait in the schoolroom until I call you down. Meneer Rotman, we have *much* to discuss. Please follow me to my office."

Without a backward glance, Gassbeek and Rotman strode out of the dining hall, toward the Forbidden Quarters, leaving a trail of oily smoke and five stunned, silent orphans in their wake. Down the hallway, the grandfather clock *donged* once to mark the half hour.

"I don't believe it!" Sem said happily.

"Neither do I." Egg grinned. "We're going to travel!"

Lotta beamed up at Milou. "We're free, all thanks to you!"

Fenna let out a tiny giggle, no louder than a hiccup.

But Milou shook her head. "No. We can't leave with him. He doesn't like children."

Lotta frowned. "What are you talking about? He's just offered to adopt all five of us. That suggests he likes children very much. *Five times* as much as your average adopter, in fact."

"He's not what he seems," Milou insisted. "There's something wrong about him. I'm not quite sure what, but he was definitely not telling the truth. Perhaps he's a pirate, or a smuggler. He might even be worse than the matron."

"Enough with your theories." Egg let out a sigh. "Milou, I know you thought your parents would come for you if you stayed long enough, but you don't have a choice anymore. This is our only way safely out of here. That doesn't mean you have to give up. Perhaps Meneer Rotman can help you find them, like he'll help me find my real home. He seems *nice*."

"No, he doesn't," Milou said. "I think his apprentice is scared of him. Pieter barely looked up from the floor. And did you see the scratches on his arms? They were the kind you might get in a sword fight. Or from a whipping."

"Milou," Lotta said. "You're being dramatic. And why are you rubbing your ears like that?"

"You know why. My Sense has been warning me. I thought at first it was telling me not to anger the matron by speaking up, but then I realized it was Rotman it wanted me to be wary of. That man is the very definition of creepy. Dangerous, even."

"Holy Gouda." Lotta rolled her eyes. "Not that again. Your ears do not have magical danger sensors, Milou. It's scientifically *implausible*."

"Why would he come so late at night, if he wasn't up to no good?" Milou said. "And why wouldn't Gassbeek have the other orphans come down, too? She looked so smug, as if there was some secret that we weren't in on. This whole lineup is what's *implausible*. Adopting all five of *us*? The most unadoptable children in all of Amsterdam."

"He requested the oldest ones," Egg said.

"No adopter has *ever* requested the older ones," Milou said. "Not once."

Milou saw it. The tiniest flicker of doubt in Lotta's eyes.

"And no adopter has ever called us a *transaction*," Milou added. "That's a business word, not a parenting word."

Sem's eyebrows furrowed.

"This is silly," Egg said. "Let's just get our things and wait in the schoolroom like the matron told us."

He turned back toward the foyer, tugging Fenna and Sem along with him.

"No adopter has ever said we are *adorable*," Milou called after them.

It was Fenna who faltered this time.

"Something's not right about him," Milou pleaded. "You have to believe me."

"Milou, you have no proof that he's lying," Egg said, turning to glare at her. "All you have is a wild imagination that *always* gets us into trouble. We aren't in one of your spooky stories now. This is real life. And this is the first time we've been offered a chance at a real home. I'm not giving it up because your ears told you we should."

And just like that, the others turned away too. Reluctantly, Milou followed them into the gloomy darkness of the foyer. She looked back to the hallway that led to the Forbidden Quarters. Soon, Rotman would have the paperwork he needed to take the five of them away, to whatever fate he had in mind for them. She had to do something. But what?

Milou could still see the wispy trail of oily smoke leading beyond that red line, past the iron plaque on the wall that read: NO ORPHANS BEYOND THIS POINT. Beneath the last curls of smoke, she thought she saw a thin, finger-shaped shadow, pointing shakily *over* the red line.

"If it's proof you need," Milou called, as her friends began climbing the stairs, "then I'll get you proof."

Sem turned, his eyes widening as he realized what she was about to do. In three long strides he was down the stairs and reaching for her, but Milou had already crossed the hallway and stepped over the red line. Sem hovered on the threshold, reaching out to her, and the others appeared behind him.

"Milou," Lotta whispered. "You can't. If Gassbeek catches you—"

"Any punishment would be worth it to prove to you that his promises are emptier than our hungry bellies," Milou said. "He may have convinced you with his pretty words, but I don't trust him."

Sem reached for her again. "Please, Milou—"

She took three backward steps down the corridor before he could grab her. The others stood on the other side of the line, too scared to step over it. Fenna shook her head at Milou, pleading with worried eyes.

"I promise I'm not overreacting," Milou said. "And I would never lie to you. But if you don't believe me, then I'll have to convince you."

MILOU'S BOOK OF THEORIES

The "Secret Spy" Theory

My parents are spies. They were posing as undertakers that night (coffin basket), when they were attacked by an assailant with a metal hand (claw marks). One of them was injured (blood drops), and narrowly missed having their arm ripped off (snagged white thread). They climbed to safety (rooftop). Worried that I might get hurt (babies do not make very good spies), they decided to leave me somewhere until it was safe to return for me (orphanage).

For them to have been gone this long, they would have an extremely dangerous mission, like keeping the young Princess Wilhelmina safe from an evil villain, perhaps. I haven't heard any of our neighbors gossiping about this, but that's the thing about spying, it's all top secret. Spies are stealthy and brave. They do the jobs no one else dares do, to protect others.

❋ SIX ❋

THE ORPHANS OF THE Little Tulip had often discussed
what might lie beyond the shadowed hallway of the Forbidden
Quarters. The only thing they knew for certain was that the
matron's chambers were situated in the only place no orphan
had been before: deep down in the Little Tulip's underbelly.
Milou's theories ranged from a dark dungeon filled with rodent
skeletons floating in glass tanks to a factory that turned rat
hides into pointed leather boots, polished crimson with mouse
blood. No one had ever been stupid enough, or brave enough,
to step over the red line to find out.

Until now.

The only thing keeping Milou's heart from bursting out

of her rib cage was the fact that she had her Sense to help her. In the pipe smoke that still curled down the entire length of the long, dark corridor, that thin shadowy finger seemed to keep beckoning her forward. Milou tiptoed, one hand running against the wall to steady herself, the other clutching her puppet, toward a thin strip of flickering light at the far end.

She *had* to do this.

Onward she crept, until finally she reached the small flickering oil lamp, beneath which lay a wooden staircase that spiraled down into a gloomy abyss. Milou flinched as the first step creaked beneath her. Her breath stuttered as the second one groaned, but she knew turning back was not an option. The spiral stairs wove down and down, drawing Milou toward who-knew-what, until she finally emerged in another hallway. She stopped on the threshold. Dumbstruck.

It was as long as all the orphanage's many hallways, but twice as wide. The walls were covered in a blue-and-white floral wallpaper; no peeling paint in sight. Along one wall there were two large bookcases filled with ornaments, and a chest of drawers with an elegant oil lamp placed on top. On the opposite wall were three doorways, the furthest of which was outlined by a ring of light. Next to the stairwell was a coat stand, laden with fur coats. The air was warm and toasty, filled with the scent of burning coal.

No skeletons. No glass tanks. No cold.

As the heat seeped into Milou's frozen limbs, fury began

to burn inside her. How could the matron let them freeze and suffer above, while living a life of *luxury* right beneath them?

In the walls beside her and under the floorboards, Milou could hear the telltale pitter-patter of small, rodenty feet, the sort that sent Gassbeek into fits of terror. It seemed she wasn't the only thing making its way toward the cozy warmth of the matron's office. Milou felt a tiny twinge of satisfaction that Gassbeek was, through her own sheer greediness, provoking her own phobia by luring the very creatures she feared so greatly toward her private quarters.

It wasn't enough to dull Milou's rage, however, and she swallowed down an angry lump in her throat. The warmth of the hallway wrapped around her shoulders and ankles, drawing her toward the furthest door. She crept up to the very edge of the doorway and pressed her ear against it.

"You drive a hard bargain, Matron," Rotman was saying. Milou heard him blow out a puff of smoke. "You want money *and* my help in exterminating your rodent infestation? That was not in the advertisement."

"The rats are all over the house now," Gassbeek said, her voice tinged with barely contained panic. "I cannot . . . bear the foul creatures. I hear ships are often riddled too; you must have a better solution than traps that don't work. Furthermore, I should think it a bargain considering you're getting five able-bodied workers out of this. Had I known you would take them all, I would have asked sooner. It is merely a favor I ask of you, in honor of our new partnership."

Partnership? Milou's fingers gripped her cat puppet tightly.

"Not to mention that taking on multiple new apprentices every year will rouse immense suspicion against you," Gassbeek continued. "Especially if the Kinderbureau were to investigate and find those children had all . . . vanished. I am the only matron in Amsterdam who is not only capable of, but willing to eliminate that suspicion for you, Meneer Rotman."

"Oh? And how will you do that?"

"How I do it is none of your concern. You need only worry about paying me *adequately* to do it."

"Very well, I will return to the city docks this evening and send my rat exterminator to you. Though it is probably best that your other orphans don't meet Dolly. No point frightening them."

Milou frowned. The woman he'd claimed would be their mother was a rat exterminator?

"Excellent," Gassbeek squawked. "We have a deal then?"

"They were all quite pale and skinny. Working a ship like mine isn't for the weak, Matron. It would not do if I had to throw them overboard before the journey is even over. I need them to last long enough to pay off the investment before I come back for more."

Milou's grip on her cat puppet tightened. She had been right about him, then. He wanted cheap, disposable *workers*, not heirs. A rat skittered past her toes and darted under a bookcase.

"When will you return?" Gassbeek asked. "I can ensure the next batch are fattened up a little."

"I have a tight schedule this spring," Rotman said. "I'll return in August. But I must ask: the dark-haired girl, the one who looks like she should live in a graveyard. Is it likely she'll give me much trouble? Her little performance just now makes me think she's not one to listen to rules."

"Milou?" the matron scoffed. "Don't worry about her. As long as you have the others under your thumb, she'll follow. Sentimental little brat, that one."

"Then we have a deal, Matron. In return for a steady supply of orphans each year, I will provide you with coin and rid this place of vermin—both the rodent variety and the urchins you can't shift."

"I will need an hour to sort out the paperwork." Gassbeek sounded supremely satisfied, Milou thought furiously. "Will that be long enough for you to retrieve Dolly?"

Milou had heard enough. She had an hour to tell the others what she'd learned and try to formulate a plan. She pushed away from the wall and turned back toward the stairs, coming to a sudden halt after just a few steps when she realized her friends had tiptoed down the hallway after her.

"Milou?" Sem said.

"Sem!" Milou hissed. "What are you doing here!"

"We came to get you—"

The sounds of scraping chairs and creaking floorboards

were heard. The office door creaked open, and light and smoke spilled out into the hallway, a shadowy outline of Rotman stretching up the wall.

"It's been a pleasure doing business with you," Rotman said, his booming voice filling the hall.

Milou realized they would never make it up the stairs without being seen or heard. The others seemed to come to the same conclusion. They stood, staring at each other in wide-eyed horror.

MILOU'S BOOK OF THEORIES
The Illness Theory

Perhaps my parents have an unfortunate medical condition that means they are temporarily unable to look after me? This could even be a phobia of some kind. Like a fear of babies and young children. Gassbeek's fear of rodents turns her from an evil witch to a quivering wreck anytime she even hears a rat. And Egg has a phobia of earwax. Even saying the word "earwax" makes him tremble. Babies are a bit like earwax: sticky and weird-smelling.

My parents will just be waiting until they are well enough to look after me again. Or until I'm old enough not to give them nightmares.

❧ SEVEN ❧

ROTMAN STEPPED OUT OF Gassbeek's office, preceded by a huge fog of pipe smoke. Milou shoved at her friends. The children moved quickly and silently. Fenna curled under the fancy chest of drawers, Egg tucked himself between the two bookcases, Sem and Lotta slid into the first doorway, and Milou buried herself in the thick fur jackets on the coat stand. Something small and hairy shuffled past her ankles.

Milou heard the matron's *click-clacks* accompanied by the heavy *thud-thud-thud* of sealskin boots going past. She had never been as thankful for the deep and hungry shadows in the canal house as she was then. Still, her heart thumped painfully against her chest.

"I'll have them ready and waiting," Gassbeek crowed, her voice echoing down the stairwell.

"I can see myself out from here, Matron. You get started on that paperwork. I need it looking believable when it comes to sneaking them past the customs officials."

"Don't worry, my paperwork is always flawless."

Click-creeeeak-clack-creeeeak.

Milou carefully made a peephole between the coats as Gassbeek's footsteps retreated. She noticed a thin arm sticking out from underneath the dresser, reaching toward a little gray rat.

Fenna.

Click-creeeeak-clack-creeeeak.

Fenna grabbed the rat around its middle, but the beast twisted and sank its teeth into her hand. Fenna's arm disappeared back under the dresser as the rat scurried up and over it, knocking into the vase and making it wobble.

The matron emerged from the stairwell and stopped, suspicious.

Milou adjusted her peephole. Gassbeek stood there, her face lost in shadow, out of reach of the flickering oil-lamp light.

Click.

Clack.

Click.

Clack.

Gassbeek approached the dresser and stilled the vase.

Then she bent down, as if to look underneath. Milou quickly drummed her fingernails against the wall behind her. Gassbeek bolted upright. Milou added a small rat-like squeak.

With trembling fingers, the matron lifted the vase and held it over her head, weapon-like. Milou stopped drumming. She had hoped Gassbeek would simply run back to her office in fear. Closing her peephole, Milou pushed herself against the wall and held her breath. She tried to push herself further back, clutching her cat puppet to her chest as if it might quiet her pounding heart. Her head hit the wall with a small *donk*.

Click.

Clack.

Click.

The fur coats were wrenched away. Milou blinked up at the matron.

Gassbeek's face contorted from fear to fury. "You!"

The matron reached out and grabbed the cat puppet. Milou tried to clutch it to her chest. They struggled, Gassbeek growing increasingly red-faced with fury as Milou refused to let the puppet go. Then, with a sickening ripping noise, the matron tore the cat's head right off.

"No!" Milou watched in horror as Gassbeek threw the puppet's head aside and raised the vase above her head, ready to strike.

Milou's eyes squeezed closed.

Gassbeek let out a bloodcurdling scream.

Not a scream of fury, Milou realized, but a scream of utter terror.

Milou's eyes snapped open again.

Gassbeek was staring at the wall next to her, eyes like full moons. Her shrill scream continued. A movement by the dresser caught Milou's eyes. Fenna's little gray rat was standing atop it, directly in front of the oil lamp. Milou turned to look at the wall beside her, to where the rat's shadow stretched across the wall: a huge twitching nose with whiskers as long as swords. It opened its mouth, teeth like daggers. And raised its paws, claws like scythes.

Gassbeek's scream suddenly cut short. The vase dropped from her hands and rolled across the floor. The matron fell forward, crashing into the wall. She clutched her throat, gasping, croaking, dragging her nails down her throat, and then clutching at her chest.

Milou took a step toward her, heart hammering.

Gassbeek slid down the wall and landed with a *thud* on the floor. The hallway fell silent, except for her gurgling, the same sound water makes as it disappears down a clogged drain. *A death rattle*, Milou thought. The gurgling stopped abruptly, Gassbeek's hand fell slackly to her side, and she stared blankly up at the ceiling.

She didn't move again.

MILOU'S BOOK OF THEORIES

The Unthinkable Theory

What if I truly am an *orphan*? A proper orphan, I mean. Perhaps the only way my parents would have ever given me up was if they were dead.

Until the other theories are disproven, however, this theory is not worth even thinking about.

Dead parents don't climb roofs.

Dead parents don't leave clues.

Dead parents don't come back.

⚹ EIGHT ⚹

THE MATRON LAY, LIMBS splayed awkwardly like a discarded marionette, on the polished wood floor of the Forbidden Quarters. Her eyes stared unblinkingly at the ceiling, her neck twisted to the side and her mouth was open in a silent scream.

Milou clutched the headless body of her cat puppet over her sputtering heart. A door creaked open beside her, then stopped with a *thunk* as it hit the matron's supine body. Lotta peeked out, looked down, and gave a yelp. Sem's head emerged from the doorway above her. Egg appeared from between the bookcases, and, one bony limb at a time, Fenna crawled out from under the dresser, clutching her rat-bitten hand. The five of them stared down at Gassbeek.

"Is she dead?" Sem asked finally, looking to Lotta. "Check her to see if she's alive."

"No." Lotta hiccupped loudly. "I don't want to touch her. You touch her."

Sem paled. "I'm not touching her!"

Fenna shook her head as she stared at Gassbeek.

"Neither am I," Egg added. "She looks dead. Milou, you touch her. You like dead things."

"I don't like *real* dead things. I . . . oh, fine."

Milou knelt beside the matron, extended a hand, then hesitated. She *really* didn't want to touch the matron either. Instead, she waved a hand in front of the matron's face, but Gassbeek didn't blink. Milou stood and quickly backed away, the others following suit.

"Can someone really be frightened to *death*?" Egg asked.

They all looked to Lotta, who merely shrugged. "I'm a scientist, not a doctor."

The little gray rat emerged, darting over the matron's dress and off toward the office's open door. Milou thought she saw the matron's foot twitch, but when she looked again, Gassbeek was lifeless. Fenna made as if to chase the rat, took one step closer to the matron, then shook her head and hurried back to huddle between Lotta and Sem, who both wrapped an arm around her.

Lotta hiccuped once more, then turned to Milou. "What

did Rotman mean about *believable* paperwork and *sneaking* us past the dockyard's customs officials?"

"He and Gassbeek struck a deal," Milou said, quietly and flatly. "He pays her to make all records of us disappear, then he'll work us until we're broken or dead. And in August he'll come back for a fresh group of orphans."

They all stared at her.

Lotta shook her head in disbelief. "But that's against the law."

"Since when has Gassbeek cared about any laws but her own?" Sem said quietly, staring around at the opulent hallway, then down to the lifeless form at their feet.

"I should have known. A *girl* would never be allowed to engineer a ship," Lotta huffed. "He'd no doubt have me doing his laundry. We should have listened to you, Milou."

Wordlessly, Milou reached out and squeezed her friend's hand.

"Well, we can't stay here," Egg said. "The authorities might think we killed her."

"We can't just run," Lotta said. "The Kinderbureau will send a new matron. Perhaps we could explain . . ."

Sem shook his head. "You really think they'll believe us? We can't take that chance. Egg's right, we need to leave."

"But we've got nowhere to go."

No one spoke, and the silence hung heavy in the still-oily air.

Milou held her puppet's body tight, then went to pick up its head. As she leaned forward, something small but heavy fell from the puppet's open neck, landing between her feet with a soft *thud*. The tips of her ears turned icy cold, and she sucked in a short, sharp breath.

A round piece of silver glinted in the lamplight, and Milou sank to her knees in front of it.

"Milou?" Egg dropped down on one side beside her, Fenna on the other. Milou's throat felt too tight to get words out. With trembling hands, she put her puppet aside and picked up the glimmering item.

"What is it?" Sem asked, and he and Lotta crouched in front of her.

Milou swallowed. They all leaned in.

It was roughly the same diameter as a guilder coin, and the thickness of Milou's pinky finger. The surface was tarnished silver, inlaid with a neat line of tiny crystals, shimmering like stars, around which curled a golden crescent moon. There was a loop at the top, with a thin chain running through it, and at the bottom, the smallest clasp she had ever seen. Milou lifted the lid and found an intricate clock face, each roman numeral sitting below a tiny golden star. In the middle was a painted-blue disk, only partially visible from behind a cutout in the clock face, displaying the sun and moon cycle.

The pocket watch's gears had long since fallen silent, and the hands were completely still.

"Well, that explains the puppet's supposed heartbeat," Lotta said. "I told you there is *always* a logical explanation."

Milou turned the watch over in her hand, revealing a delicate inscription, so small she had to lean right in to read it:

> Beneath the stars I found you.
> 52:284040, 4:784040
> Under the moon I lost you.

The icy chill spread from her ears down her neck to her shoulders as she read the inscription again.

I found you.

The chill grew seemingly heavier, colder, pricklier.

I lost you.

The first two lines had been engraved in neat type, but the final line had been scratched on.

"Geographical coordinates," Egg said, almost reverently, pointing at the numbers between the writing.

Coordinates.

Milou's breath hitched inward once more.

I lost you.

Milou ran her fingers shakily over the coordinates. Things that were lost could be found again—if you knew where to look.

"I'm leaving," she said, the words finally bursting from her lips. Four shocked expressions settled on her. "This is a message from my parents—and before you say anything, this isn't one of my wild theories. This is *proof.* I'm going to find them. And I want you to come with me. Let's leave this place together and never look back."

"Milou," Lotta said softly, despairingly, "we need papers. The only plausible way out is adoption, and no one except that horrid merchant wants to take us."

Milou uncurled the watch's chain and slipped it over her head, a plan already blossoming in her mind. Her Sense prickled her ears in encouragement.

"Then we'll just have to adopt ourselves."

❧ NINE ❧

AS THE OIL LAMP flickered, the rats scratched, and Gassbeek lay lifelessly still, Milou, bright eyed and tingly eared, faced her friends and began to explain.

"It's simple, really," she said, her head swirling as if she'd just spun in a thousand circles. "And so obvious. We know Bram Poppenmaker, my father, made this puppet. Which means, most likely, he or my mother made this watch. They must have hidden it because they knew an orphanage matron might steal it, and they were definitely right about that. My point is, it's a proper clue. On its own, the puppet was useless at telling me how I could find them, but together—"

"Milou!" Lotta said, exasperated.

"Yes?"

"You still haven't explained how you plan to get us out."

Milou shook herself, trying to stop the maelstrom in her mind. "It's easy. We write ourselves an adoption certificate, using my father's name, and then we just *leave*."

Egg frowned. "And go where, exactly?"

Milou held up the pocket watch and pointed toward the numbers etched on the back of it. "Here, of course!"

"But where do those coordinates lead?" Sem asked.

"Gouda knows," Lotta said. "It could be anywhere in the world. Milou, we need a *proper* plan. Rotman will be back soon. I suggest we go back up to the dormitory and pretend to be asleep. In the morning, we can act as if—"

"Actually," Egg said, eyes agleam, "those coordinates are within a hundred-kilometer radius of the city." He held Milou's pocket watch up for them to see. "Amsterdam sits just over fifty-two longitude, and just under five latitude. It took me seven attempts and twice as many canings to get that information out of Gassbeek when I started making my map. I didn't think she'd ever tell me, but I guess she wanted to shut me up—anyway, it was worth it. But we'd need a much more detailed map than mine to find the exact location of these coordinates." Egg's smile widened. "Just as well I know where we can find one."

Milou hugged him.

"Wait," Lotta said. "Even if we do find this location, there's no guarantee that it'll lead us anywhere useful."

Milou was about to argue—to point out that her parents wouldn't have left her coordinates that led nowhere—but stopped herself just in time.

Lotta needed logic in order to be convinced, not optimism.

"If we stay, we'll be in trouble no matter what we do," Milou said softly. "If we leave, there's a chance—maybe just a small one, but a chance—that we can be rid of this place, rid of the chores, rid of the *lineups*—forever."

They all looked at Gassbeek.

The grandfather clock chimed the quarter hour.

Sem got to his feet. "We need to decide now. Milou's right. We'll never have a chance like this again." Milou beamed at him, but her smile faltered slightly as he shook his head gently. "I'm not coming just to help you find your birth family, Milou. You know how I feel about the people who *discarded* us here. I'm agreeing because it's the only chance we'll ever get to leave this place on our own terms."

Milou swallowed hard. "I understand."

Egg stood too. "I've never belonged here," he said, glaring at the matron. "None of us have. There's nothing but pain here."

He and Sem looked expectantly at the girls.

"We do this together, or not at all," Sem said. "I'm not leaving any of us behind."

Fenna stood too and nodded in agreement.

Lotta sighed, holding up a hand for Milou to pull her up. Then she nodded. "All right, I'm in."

Lotta, Sem, and Fenna left to gather their belongings and some supplies. Milou took Egg's hand and dragged him toward the office, carefully stepping over the matron's body. The door to Gassbeek's office opened with a creak that sent goose bumps up Milou's arms.

"Quiet!" Egg hissed behind her. "You'll wake every dead dog in the neighborhood."

Milou pushed the door fully open. Egg edged around her, into the warm glow, where mere minutes ago, Gassbeek and Rotman had been plotting their nefarious deeds.

She stepped in behind Egg. It was like walking into a wall of warmth. A large fire burned brightly in a huge fireplace made of marble and iron, above which hung a charcoal portrait of the matron in a gold-painted frame. A huge oak desk took up the entire center of the room, two elegant oil lamps on either end. And in the middle of the desk lay a thick, leather-bound book, with the words "LITTLE TULIP ORPHAN RECORDS" stamped across it in bold letters.

"There it is!" Milou said, hurrying around the desk.

"This stuff looks like it belongs in a mansion," Egg said, loosening his shawl slightly. "Those lamps alone could have paid for new clothes for every one of us."

"Gassbeek was as crooked as a corkscrew," Milou said, her lip curling in disgust. She looked at the well-stacked fire. "It's so warm in here. And yet she left us to freeze."

"Let's be quick," Egg said, sitting down in the desk chair, his feet dangling high above the luxurious gray carpet.

Milou opened the record book to the most recently written-on page, which showed the name of a girl who'd been adopted six months earlier. At the bottom of the adoption certificate, Gassbeek had signed her name in a scratchy scrawl.

"Why isn't the Fortuyn adoption from this morning listed in here?" Egg asked.

"She was clearly too busy trying to find someone to sell us off to, to record it. Can you copy her signature?"

Egg pulled out a blank sheet of paper from the desk, took a quill from the ink pot, and made a few practice squiggles.

Milou looked between Egg's paper and the record book. "Outstanding! I can't tell the difference at all."

Egg gave her a bright smile and turned the page over to a blank form. His quill hovered over it. "Are you sure your parents will agree to this?"

"Of course," Milou said without hesitation. She placed her cat puppet on the desk in front of him and pointed at the label sewn into its foot. "Here. This is how you spell Bram Poppenmaker."

Egg gave her a small smile and began filling out the adoption certificate. He finished the final signature, blew on the ink, then tore off the top sheet, leaving the certificate's imprint on the pink sheet below.

"We are officially no longer orphans," Milou said, her mouth stretched into a grin that nearly met her ears.

"Well then, Milou *Poppenmaker*," Egg said, returning her grin. "Shall we get out of here?"

"Just a moment." Milou snapped the record book closed, heaved it up, and stepped out into the hallway.

She nudged the next door open. The matron's bedroom was as luxurious as the rest of the Forbidden Quarters, but Milou didn't pause to examine it. She skirted around the large four-poster bed, toward a more-familiar-looking woven laundry basket. Pulling dirty dresses and underskirts aside, she buried the record book at the bottom of the basket.

"Just in case." She grinned at Egg. "I reckon that'll take the next matron a while to find!"

The grandfather clock began to strike the ninth hour, the first *dong* rattling the ceiling. Milou and Egg were running up the spiral staircase as the second *dong* rang out. As the third strike ricocheted off the walls, they were over the red line and back in the cold gloom of the foyer, shivering as they ran. The others were already waiting.

Sem had his wheat sack slung over his shoulder, Milou's coffin wedged in his left armpit, and Egg's coal bucket dangling from his long fingers. Lotta was clutching her tin toolbox and an armful of the matron's fur coats. Fenna held her picnic basket.

"It doesn't feel right," Lotta whispered, as the fourth *dong* rang. "Leaving the other orphans behind."

Egg took his coal bucket from Sem. Milou gathered her own coffin basket into her arms.

"We don't have a choice," Sem said.

The fifth *dong* echoed across the marble floor.

Fenna lifted the lid of her picnic basket, revealing a bundle of mostly moldy vegetables.

Lotta handed out three of the matron's coats. Fenna and Egg huddled into one, and Sem had one to himself, leaving Lotta and Milou to share the last one.

"That's it then," Milou said. "We're ready. Let's go." The certificate of adoption was tucked into her breast pocket, and she held a hand over it. She took one last look around the foyer, as the sixth *dong* chimed. "Ready?"

The others nodded eagerly, and they hurried to the front door as the seventh *dong* rattled the room.

This was it; they were finally escaping. Milou was going to find her parents.

Sem's hand clasped around the door handle as the eighth *dong* struck.

Milou heard a loud whinny from outside, and her ear tips were assaulted by a pinch so sharp she cried out. "Sem, don't—"

But Sem had already yanked the door wide open, letting in a cloud of oily smoke.

A large, ring-bedecked hand wafted the smoke away, and a mustachioed face grinned down at them.

"Ah, *kindjes*," Rotman said. "I see you're all packed and ready."

❈ TEN ❈

THE CHILDREN STOOD THERE, staring up at the merchant in silent horror, as the ninth and final *dong* echoed around them. Milou clasped the pocket watch as her Sense prickled frantically at her scalp and neck.

The merchant's gold-toothed smile tightened. "Aren't you going to let me in?"

A wave of icy shivers, colder even than the winter air blowing in from outside, ran down Milou's spine and urged her forward. She nudged Sem aside and glared up at Rotman.

"No," she whispered.

Rotman's mustachio twitched.

"No," Milou growled. Then, more bitingly: "*No!*"

She grabbed the edge of the door and began heaving it closed, but it crunched on something before she could close it fully. On the other side of it, Rotman roared in pain. Milou looked down to see the merchant's sealskin boot half-inside, wedged at the ankle. He pushed at the door, knocking Milou backward into Sem.

"You little—"

Hands appeared from behind her, reaching out to push the door back. The five of them pressed forward. Milou kicked at Rotman's foot until, finally, the sealskin boot was pulled away. The heavy front door closed with a thunderous *thunk*, rattling the windows and shutters to the side of it.

Sem slid the bolt across, and they all took a step back.

Rotman pummeled the door. "Open up!"

Milou peered out the side window at him. He looked nothing short of murderous as he battered his fists against the door. Window shutters opened on the house across the road. Then more followed. Realizing he was being watched, Rotman stopped banging the door and straightened his tailcoat. He shot Milou a furious glare. Adjusting her coffin basket on her hip, Milou closed the shutter, looking helplessly to the others.

"There's no other way out," Sem said. "We're trapped."

The doorbell *dinged-donged*.

"The bucket winch!" Lotta said, spinning on her heels and dragging Milou toward the staircase with her.

Ding-dong-ding-dong.

They hurried up the steep stairs, baskets, bucket, wheat sack, and toolbox bumping and clunking as they ran. Milou grabbed the staircase railing as she and Lotta skidded around the corner and thundered up the next set of stairs. The laundry room was lit by a thin column of moonlight streaming in through a broken plank in the window shutters. It was a narrow squeeze past the tubs and tables to the small window.

"It'll probably take two at a time," Lotta said, opening the window with an earsplitting screech. The laundry bucket was suspended on the other side, swaying in the icy wind that blasted in at them. "Egg and Fenna, you first."

Egg peered eagerly over the window ledge. He held a hand out to Fenna. "Ready?"

The doorbell *ding-dong-ding-dong-ding-donged.*

Rotman was going to wake the other orphans at this rate. Not that they would be brave enough to go investigate. They didn't know the matron was dead and wouldn't answer the door.

Fenna climbed up next to Egg. The suspended basket swayed, and the rope groaned. They climbed into the bucket together. It was a tight squeeze, especially with a picnic hamper and coal bucket in there too.

"Ready?" Lotta said, then she began turning the crank handle.

Milou watched as the bucket descended with a *creeak-*

clunk-creeak-clunk. She let out a long breath when they touched the ice and began to climb out.

Lotta's arms spun quickly, the winch crank squealing as she wound it back up again. Milou slipped out of the coat they shared, her skin erupting into a million goose bumps.

Sem peered nervously over the edge. "But the canal—"

"It's frozen, Sem," Lotta said impatiently. "If it can hold a hundred ice-skating families, it can hold five children. Now shush your face and get in the bucket."

Sem climbed into the laundry bucket, and Milou followed quickly behind, careful to keep her eyes only on the round bucket as she climbed in, ignoring the height and the biting wind that stabbed like icy daggers at her exposed skin. The bucket swayed from side to side, and Sem wrapped half of his stolen fur coat around Milou's shoulders. Lotta passed them the coffin basket and wheat sack, then piled her toolbox into Milou's arms.

"See you in a minute," Lotta said.

"What about you?" Milou asked, suddenly fearful. "You can't operate the crank and lower yourself down."

Lotta gave her a wry smile. "I'll need you to unlatch the bucket and then attach the hook, nice and taut, to the railing on the other side of the canal. Okay?"

"But how—"

With a sudden, grinding squeal, the bucket began to lower

them down onto the canal. Sem's arms tightened around Milou so much she could barely breathe, but before she could wriggle enough to get room to tell him off, the bucket hit the ice with a scratchy thud.

They scrambled out, Sem's limbs tangling with hers, and unhooked the bucket.

"I hope she has a plan," Milou rasped, the cold night air catching in her throat.

The four of them slipped and slid across the width of the frozen canal. Fenna climbed up the stone bank first, pulling Egg over the iron railing. Milou gave her the hook, and she clicked it onto the topmost rail.

"I'll help you up," Sem said.

But Milou shook her head. "Lotta—"

Lotta was a dark silhouette in the laundry-room window. Milou watched in awe-filled horror as Lotta reached up toward the taut line of rope, her hands wrapped in something Milou couldn't quite make out. Then she leapt into the air.

A scream lodged in the back of Milou's throat, but she swallowed it down again.

Lotta knew what she was doing. Lotta *always* knew what she was doing.

Lotta's cloak billowed out around her as she slid down the rope and glided over the canal like some sort of nightmarish wraith. Milou's swallowed scream came back up as a delighted giggle. Lotta was *spectacular*. She hurtled down toward them at a dizzying speed, and just as her maniacally grinning face came into view, she let go and dropped to the ice. She landed, tangled in a mass of skirts and fur coat, with an *oof*.

"Stupid dresses," she huffed as she straightened herself out. "So impractical."

Milou and Sem slid over to her and pulled her up.

"Are you all right?" Milou asked.

Lotta stood on shaky legs, her pigtails in disarray and a wet rag in her left hand. She nodded and threw the rag aside. A few streets away, a whistle blew, then another.

"Rotman stopped ringing the doorbell," she said, her face turning serious. "We need to run."

❄ ELEVEN ❄

SEM BOOSTED MILOU ONTO the pavement, then pulled himself up after her. Together they hoisted Lotta up and over the railing. Frost glistened on the cobblestones, and the street was deserted and quiet, except for a wind that whistled over the canal and through the tiny gaps between the towering houses. The air was sharp, stinging Milou's lungs as she took deep, ragged breaths. The cold enveloped every inch of her, clinging to her cheeks like tiny claws of ice. It made her jaw ache and her shoulders squeeze up toward her ears.

She wriggled deep into Lotta's fur coat.

The five of them stood at the canal edge, staring up at the towering form of the orphanage just across from them.

"We're free," Sem said, his voice a disbelieving whisper.

Milou hoisted her coffin basket onto her hip and used her other hand to tuck the pocket watch under her collar. "Not quite yet. Which way next, Egg?"

Egg had his pillowcase map held out in front of him and Fenna, his brown eyes glinting as surveyed it. Then he folded it, tucked it back into his coal bucket, and nodded toward a bridge at the other end of the street. "That way."

They had made it only a few steps when Milou's ears prickled urgently. A chill blew over her forehead. A mere moment later, they heard wheels scraping on nearby cobbles and a whip cracking.

She tugged Lotta toward a narrow gap between two houses, nudging the others ahead of her. Rotman's carriage rattled around the corner just as Milou pushed herself into the darkened alleyway. The horse snorted, its hoofbeats slowing. Peering carefully around the wall, Milou watched as Pieter pulled the carriage to a stop next to the railing, where the bucket winch's rope was still hooked.

The door opened, emitting a puff of smoke, and Rotman stepped out. He limped up to the railing, reaching out to touch the rope, which led right to the still-open laundry-room window. He looked up and down the street, the moonlight casting a silvery glow over his furious expression.

Milou ducked her head back into the shadows, her heart galloping.

"He knows we've left," she whispered. "And he's blocking our route."

"We'll just have to go the long way around then," Egg whispered back. He tucked his pillowcase map back under his arm. "Follow me."

They hurried through the narrow alley, huddled closely together in their fur coats. Egg paused at the end of the alleyway, and they all strained their ears. A cart passed by, its wheels squeaking with each rotation.

"That wasn't him," Egg whispered softly. He leaned forward. "I think it's clear now."

Milou felt a little tingle at the base of her spine. "Go. Quick."

They darted across the street, their boots tapping a hurried rhythm, and into the next alley. They walked quickly and in single file, like ducklings following a mother duck, with Egg at the front, over bridge after bridge, each canal a frozen sheet of glimmering ice. The canal houses had always reminded Milou of Sem: tall, gangly, peculiarly proportioned, yet full of character and charm. But she realized that looking down at Amsterdam from the dormitory window was one thing. To be walking its streets for the first time in her life was something else entirely. From down on the ground, the pointed, jagged roofs loomed like gaping jaws. Milou felt as if they were being swallowed up by the city. The canals all looked identical, as did the bridges. It was as if they were running around in circles, trapped in a maze, but Egg led them with confidence, turning his pillowcase map this way and that.

After a short but heart-galloping while, Egg came to a sudden halt. His face was lost in the shadows, but Milou heard his sharp intake of breath.

"We're here," he said, pointing to a canal house across the street. "Kerkstraat 189."

Much like the Little Tulip, Kerkstraat 189 was built of black bricks, its windows painted white in contrast. An octagonal sign dangled from a wrought-iron bar sticking out above the door. Milou squinted up at it.

BRAAKENSIEK EN ZOON
LITHOGRAPHER AND DEALER OF MAPS

"I heard one of our neighbors talk about this place a few months ago," Egg said. "It took me weeks to find. I had to climb across four other rooftops to spot it and add it to my map. Look."

There, in the ground-floor window, were several large maps.

Tingles danced across Milou's ear tips, and a giggle escaped her lips. She and Egg shared a delighted smile. They checked that the street was empty, then emerged from the alley and huddled in front of the window. Egg's expression was nothing short of reverential.

"Is that really what Nederland looks like?" Milou asked, pointing to one of the maps. "It looks a bit like a rabbit's head."

"That's just the northern province," Egg said, setting his coal bucket by his feet. "Here, we want this one."

He pointed to a map of Amsterdam, running his fingers over the glass as he surveyed it. Finally, he jammed his finger on a point southwest of the city. "That's it right there. We can follow the Amstel River down here for a few kilometers, then head west. If I copy this section of the map, I can probably get us fairly near Milou's coordinates."

"Fairly near?" Milou asked, clasping the pocket watch tightly. "How are we going to find the exact spot?"

Lotta stepped up beside Egg. She tapped her forefinger against the bottom corner of the map. "Using this scale." Then she tapped a point near the coordinates, at a tiny junction. "Egg just needs to get us to the start of this road here. I can get us to the exact spot."

"How?"

Lotta smiled. "Math, of course." She took a tape measure out of her toolbox and handed it to Sem. "Here. Measure my stride, from rear heel to front toe."

Lotta stepped one foot forward and held her pose as Sem measured the distance between her feet. Milou rubbed her arms for warmth as Lotta and Sem repeated their measurements a few more times. After just a few minutes, Egg had finished his map, and Sem was handing the tape measure back.

"Don't you need to make your . . . calculations?" Milou asked Lotta.

"It's fine. I'll do the math while we walk. Come on, we should hurry."

They were already limping by the time they reached the Amstel River, just as a distant church clocktower chimed ten o'clock. Milou felt as if her coffin basket had a heavy body inside it; her arms ached as much as her empty stomach. The river meandered past factories and warehouses. Every now and again, they would hide behind whatever they could find as a boat went past, but for the most part, the snow-drenched streets were empty, as the people of Amsterdam sought shelter from the cold.

Milou and Lotta leaned heavily on each other as they crossed a bridge on the outskirts of the city and finally stepped out into the first slice of open country they had ever seen.

"It's like the fields have been rolled flat with a giant rolling pin," Milou said. She blew snow from her eyelashes and huddled closer to Lotta.

"And the c . . . canals drawn in precisely with a g . . . giant ruler," Sem said, teeth chattering.

Now they'd left the city, the air no longer smelled of stale ash and horse dung. It was so fresh it tickled Milou's nostrils. They shuffled along deserted dirt road after deserted dirt road for what felt like hours, the houses becoming shorter and wider and farther apart the farther they got from the city.

They were halfway down a painfully long, completely houseless road when Egg came to a sudden stop.

"Here's your junction, Lot," Egg said in a wheeze. He pointed down a road that ran perpendicular to the one they were on. "Milou's coordinates lead that way."

The road stretched endlessly ahead of them, flanked on either side by crisscrossing canals and a patchwork of fields, with a smattering of farmhouses that Milou could just about make out if she squinted. She had spent her entire life wanting more space, but right then she'd have given anything to not have to walk another step more.

"Have you worked out the distance?" Milou asked Lotta breathlessly.

"Of course I have." Lotta swayed slightly with exhaustion, but she shook herself and straightened up. "One thousand, four hundred, and seventy-three strides."

Four groans sounded.

Lotta took a step forward, wobbling precariously. Milou took her elbow with her free hand, careful not to get her feet in the way of Lotta's stride. They walked onward, feet dragging and breathing raggedly, as Lotta counted quietly, then silently, to herself.

As they passed a pyramid-roofed farmhouse, Milou's heart

gave a little flutter of anticipation. Further down the road, they passed another farmhouse, smoke pluming out of its chimney, and Milou's hope burned stronger.

The mist rising from the canals thickened as they walked, first curling around their ankles, then up to their knees. Then it seemed to draw inward on them from the horizon. Soon they would be able to see the next farmhouse only when they were right beside it.

"We'll be warm soon," Milou promised. "They probably have fresh, creamy milk we can heat up. And plenty of blankets and a roaring fire. I'm a little tired, so I might not be able to tell a bedtime story, but I'm sure either my mother or father will."

They passed another farmhouse. It had the same pyramid-shaped roof as the others, but instead of brown thatch, this one had a bright copper roof. Instead of the usual red and white, its shutters were a bright, bold blue. And instead of a plain wooden gate at the end of its bridge, it had a stone gargoyle on each post.

It looked both ridiculous and wondrous at the same time, and nothing like anything Milou's imagination could have conjured up after a lifetime of seeing nothing but towering town houses. Her heart sank just a little when they walked past it instead of stopping.

They didn't make it much further down the road, however.

Lotta came to a sudden halt midstep, leaning heavily on Milou.

Milou sagged beneath the added weight. "Come on, Lot, it can't be much farther."

Lotta shrugged herself free. "No. We're here." She lifted an arm and pointed weakly to the side of the road. "Your coordinates," she said breathlessly. "Right there."

Milou looked to where she was indicating and frowned.

Lotta was pointing to a tree.

❊ TWELVE ❊

TINGLES ERUPTED ALL OVER Milou's scalp as she craned her neck to look more closely. The top half of the tree emerged from the mist in long, twisting, gnarled, branches. It was leafless, frost-covered, and entirely not what Milou had expected.

Milou shook her head. This couldn't be right.

"Maybe you miscounted—"

Lotta huffed indignantly. "I did *not* miscount."

Sem sighed heavily.

"It must be the copper-roofed farmhouse," Milou said, ignoring him. "This tree is so close."

"Milou," Sem said, half impatiently, half pityingly. "I'm

sorry, I really am, but this so-called clue of yours is futile. There's nothing here."

"No!" A shiver of despair coursed through her. "You're wrong, Sem. There must be something—"

"Over here," called a disembodied voice from the mist beyond, which sounded suspiciously like Egg. "I've found it."

Milou looked to the others. Egg had been standing with them moments before. Now he was gone.

"Just carry on further down the road a little way," he called out. "Hurry, I'm freezing."

They shuffled forward, as quickly as their aching legs could manage, and found Egg standing at the canal edge, in front of a set of gates. The gates were not like any of the others they had passed, not even the ones with the gargoyles. They were, Milou decided, like the gates of a graveyard. Milou's heart felt like it was about to leap out of her mouth.

Rusted iron railings rose like spears from the ground, their painted-gold tips gleaming in the moonlight. Ivy creepers curled around the two tall posts on either side, and a heavy padlock hung from a chain that had been wrapped around the middle of the gate several times. Above the lock was a weathered wooden sign. Milou stepped closer and read: POPPENMILL. Except, the word "POPPEN" had been scratched out and replaced with "ghost." And then below that, in the same scratchy scrawl, someone had etched: DANGER! KEEP OUT!

She pressed her face up against the gates and squinted into

the gloom, but the mist was now too thick. She could not see any red and white shutters, nor a triangular roof.

"Where is it?" she asked in frustration.

"Look up," Sem said breathlessly.

Milou followed his wide-eyed gaze, to where the mist had opened slightly above them. Emerging through the gloom, further back from the road than the farmhouses had been, was the shadowy cross of skeletal sails.

A thrill coursed through Milou's aching body as she realized what she was seeing.

It wasn't a farmhouse at all.

It was a *windmill*.

The fog drew back in, and the windmill's sails disappeared again, but this did nothing to cloud Milou's delight.

The pocket watch had led her *home*.

Goose bumps danced all over her arms and neck, and her ears tingled pleasantly. Not a warning this time, she thought, but an encouragement, urging her forward.

She had a good feeling about this place.

"I have a bad feeling about this place," Lotta grumbled beside her. "It looks—"

"Old," Sem whispered.

"Haunted," Egg said, eliciting a tiny gasp from Fenna.

"Perfect," Milou breathed.

"I was going to say 'uninviting,'" Lotta said. "The gate

is locked, there are no lights on, and the sign isn't exactly welcoming."

"They've probably just gone to bed. Come on, there'll be food and warmth inside."

And my parents, she thought.

She resisted shooting Sem an I-told-you-so look and, instead, approached the thin canal that ran along either side of the entrance and underneath the wooden bridge upon which the gates stood. Hefting her coffin basket up onto her shoulder, she edged herself and Lotta toward the ice. It was too low for her to step down onto, so, hoping for the best, she jumped down, pulling Lotta with her. Their feet landed with a solid thud, but the frozen canal did not crack.

"Milou!" Sem called out. "I'm not sure this is a good idea. The sign says—"

"That sign is for other people, not family," Milou said over her shoulder. "Come *on*."

The sound of feet dropping onto the ice behind her was the only response she received. With her free hand, Milou grabbed the iron post and pulled herself and Lotta up onto the bank on the other side of the gates. Egg, Sem, and Fenna followed a moment later. Fresh snow crunched loudly beneath them as they edged almost blindly toward the mill. As they got closer, all Milou could see was the redbrick wall of the lowest level.

It took them a few minutes to find the front door. There

was a scratch and a hiss as Sem struck a match and passed a candle to Milou. She held it up. The door seemed to be made of equal parts thick oak and peeling black paint. Two lanterns, held up by iron hands, hung on either side, unlit, their glass shattered. In the middle of the door was a knocker: an iron ring, held in the mouth of a lion.

A thrill of delight ran through her.

This was the moment she had waited twelve long years for.

Her family was a mere heartbeat away.

Milou had to stretch up on tiptoes to reach the knocker. She wrapped her frozen fingers around the ring and gave three short, sharp knocks, loud in the eerily calm night. She held her breath, listening intently for approaching footsteps, trying to picture the look of surprise on her parents' faces when they opened the door and found her standing there. Would it be her mother or her father who answered? Would they recognize her? Of course they would. Just like she would recognize them.

She waited, biting her lip, but the silence rang on, long and deafening.

Milou's smile faltered. She rattled the handle, and the door swung inward, groaning as it opened fully.

Darkness greeted them.

The candle puffed out.

"I don't want to go in there," Egg whispered nervously, his and Fenna's worried faces peeking out of the top of their shared coat.

"There's nothing to worry about," Milou said and stepped forward.

"Hang on," Sem said.

Milou thought he was going to try to stop her. She readied herself for another argument, but he just rummaged in his wheat sack and produced some more matches and candles, handed them out to the others, then relit Milou's and gave her a smile of encouragement. Huddling close, they held their candles above their heads, forming a halo of light around them, and stepped inside.

They entered a small, square hallway. A row of clogs hung from hooks beside the door. Milou took another step and caught sight of a figure in the deep darkness beside a cupboard. Her candle flickered as she spun toward it, shadows dancing wildly across the stone floor.

"Papa . . . ?"

Her voice died as the shadows stilled. Milou realized it wasn't a figure at all but a coat stand, a cap balanced at a jaunty angle atop it.

She hurried onward, through a low doorway to the left that led into a kitchen that was not quite a semicircle, but almost. Against the middle wall was a stove, pots and pans dangling from hooks above it. A small table with two chairs sat beneath the window. Milou held the lantern higher. A tall wardrobe and two smaller cabinets were lined neatly along one side wall. And a cupboard bed, its doors wide open, took up almost the entirety of the other wall. Milou could see it was empty, its bright-green quilt tucked neatly in.

Milou licked her dry, cracked lips. "Papa? Mama? It's me . . . it's Milou."

She put her coffin basket down on the table and ran her finger over the back of one of the chairs. Her fingertip came away coated in a thick layer of black dust. She squinted into the deep shadows and took another step; something crunched beneath her boot. Smashed crockery littered the floor.

"What a mess," Lotta said, shivering beneath their shared coat. "I wonder what happened."

"They're probably just too busy to clean," Milou said. "They'll be thrilled to know I can help them with the house-work now that I'm back."

She walked briskly toward the next doorway, into a similarly proportioned living room. A fireplace sat within the middle wall this time, cold and empty, its mantel bare. Two rocking chairs sat opposite it, in front of another window, blankets draped over the backs and thick cushions on the seats. There were bookcases filled with tomes, and another cupboard bed, its mahogany doors closed.

Giving Lotta her candle, Milou wriggled out of their coat, ignoring the sharp sting of cold, and opened the cupboard-bed doors. She found herself staring at a red-quilted bed this time, as cold and empty as the first one.

A small gasp of despair left her lips.

"Milou," Egg said. "Perhaps we should come back—"

But Milou was hurrying through the next door, only to find herself back in the hallway they had started in, having lapped the ground floor entirely.

She looked despairingly at her friends. "They'll be upstairs, no doubt."

Then she took the candle back from Lotta, hurried toward the ladder, and climbed, breathless and swaying with exhaustion, up to the next floor. The walls were rounder upstairs, with a small landing and a single door blocking off the room beyond.

Milou pushed it open.

A white face greeted her from beyond the door, its head flopped slightly to the side.

Milou's heart seemed to stop entirely.

Then she saw that the face had a snout.

And pointed ears.

And . . . stitches all over its . . . *cotton* skin.

Milou squinted at the figure.

Its eyes were *painted*.

On the tip of its snout was a button.

There was stuffing sticking out the side of its neck, and it was wearing a finely tailored suit of soft Amsterdam velvet in a deep shade of burgundy. Lotta and Sem emerged from the stairwell to stand beside her, their faces as pale as the one before them.

"It's a puppet," Milou said, a giggle of hope bursting from

her lips. "A fox puppet." She could see strings now, suspending the puppet from a hook on the side of some shelving. "This is definitely the right place."

She stepped in and looked around the circular room. The dust was thicker up here, and Milou gagged on a cloud of it, waving it away from her candle's light to get a look at the room. Running down the middle of the room, from a hole through the ceiling, was a thick, square, wooden pole. The rounded thatch walls were covered in puppets of all shapes and sizes. There were rolls of fabric, spools of string, tools, a desk filled with paintbrushes and paint pots, and a cast-iron sewing machine.

Bram Poppenmaker's puppet-making workshop.

"We're only halfway up the windmill," she whispered, the room swaying beneath her weary legs. "They'll be upstairs."

They had to be here.

They just had to.

With renewed hope, Milou ran across the room toward a ladder that led up to a large, rectangular hole in the puppet-room ceiling. Her arms and legs ached as she hauled herself up and over the ledge, her candle nearly losing its flame.

Lotta reached for her. "Milou—"

But Milou was already scaling the next ladder up to the next floor.

She crawled through to the next level, and her head hit something hard as she tried to stand. Milou hissed, dropping to a crouch and feeling her way toward an empty place to sit.

As the dust settled and her candle stilled, Milou realized why there was barely any room to move: Huge wooden cog wheels interconnected, horizontally and vertically, in a complex array from the ceiling right down to the floor.

There was a *thud* and then another hiss of pain beside her as Lotta emerged through the hatch and crawled toward her.

"Holy Gouda," Lotta breathed, staring up at the mechanisms with her mouth hanging open.

Milou stood, carefully, and held the candle up to the domed ceiling, illuminating more shadows and more dust, but no ladders or stairwells.

This was the very top of the windmill. There were no more rooms for her to search.

Milou's shoulders drooped, as if her invisible puppet strings had been snipped clean, and her legs finally collapsed under her. Her knees hit the floor hard, but the pain of it hurt less than the way her heart seemed to be squeezing in on itself.

"Oh, Lotta," Milou said, her voice cracking. "They're gone."

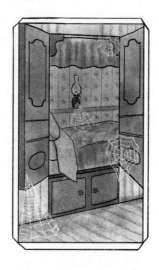

❧ THIRTEEN ❧

MILOU WAS ONLY VAGUELY aware of being led by
Lotta and Sem back down to the kitchen. Her eyes were wet,
and, despite the fur coat now draped around her shoulders,
a numbness had settled heavily over her, making it almost
impossible to walk.

Sem had been right.

She'd come all this way for nothing.

The Poppenmakers were gone.

Her friends' voices sounded muffled behind the raging
despair in Milou's mind.

"What's wrong?" Egg was asking.

"Milou needs to sleep this ordeal off," Lotta was saying. "Help me get her into bed."

Milou was ushered into the green-quilted cupboard bed by Lotta and Sem. It smelled musty, but it was softer than anything she had ever lain upon. Fenna was already in the bed. She pulled Milou close and wrapped her arms around her, resting her chin on Milou's brow. The blankets were heavy, but not scratchy in the slightest. Despite all this, Milou still could not stop shaking.

"They're gone."

That voice sounded like her own, but it was far too high-pitched and raw to be hers, surely?

Egg's face appeared above hers. "It'll be all right, Milou," he said softly. "We'll be all right. I promise."

Then Lotta was beside her too, more arms enveloped her, and Milou's tear-blurred eyes lost their battle to stay open.

Milou woke to sunlight. She'd somehow slept through the dawn bell. Gassbeek was going to kill her. Panic stole through her and she scrambled backward, blinking furiously, trying to work out why the dormitory seemed much, much smaller and her bed much, much bigger. Gone were the drafty eaves, replaced with a low, mahogany ceiling. The brown, threadbare blanket she was used to had somehow transformed into multiple layers of blanket and a bright-green quilt.

The memory of the previous night came creeping back.

Gassbeek was dead.

Milou was home.

Her family was gone.

Just as her heart began to break again, she spotted above her head, sitting on a low shelf, her cat puppet, its head sewn back on so deftly that it could only have been done by Sem. She shuffled upward to sit and pulled the pocket watch free from beneath her collar, rubbing a thumb over the inscription.

> Beneath the stars I found you.
> 52:284040, 4:784040
> Under the moon I lost you.

Even after following the coordinates all this way, Milou was still lost to them.

Fenna and Lotta stirred, looking up at her through sleep-heavy lids.

"Milou?" Lotta spoke gruffly, one pigtail sticking out vertically from the side of her head, the other loose entirely. "What is it?"

"Nothing," Milou whispered, climbing over Lotta. "I just need some fresh air."

Lotta yawned in response, her lids drooping closed again. Fenna, however, climbed out to join Milou as she peered through the doorway into the next room. The boys were still sleeping soundly in the other cupboard bed in the living room,

Sem facedown, one long arm dangling to the floor, and Egg resting his head on his carefully folded soot-stained shawl. She closed the door quietly so as not to disturb them.

Compared to the gloominess of the night before, the kitchen looked radiant. The shadows were gone, but the thick dust remained, curling around the shafts of sunlight and sticking to every surface.

Milou began opening smaller cupboard doors near the sink. There was no food; only more dust. She tiptoed over to a wardrobe and opened one door. Her breath caught at the sight of the clothing that hung inside. Men's shirts, jackets, trousers; all finely made, practical, and gentlemanly. On the other side of the wardrobe, Milou found an entire rail of dresses, cloaks, and scarves; again, finely made, but surprisingly small and . . . youthful.

Sighing, Milou gazed around the sun-dappled, debris-strewn room. Her ears, neck, and shoulders tingled in a way she had never felt before: a coldness that seemed somehow, impossibly, to warm her—easing the tightness in her chest ever so slightly.

At least she was *home*, she told herself, even if her parents were not.

"I'm going to find them, Fen," Milou whispered. "I've got a whole windmill full of new clues now. Which means I'm closer to finding them now than I was yesterday."

Milou reached into her mother's side of the wardrobe and

selected a long, green cloak—which was only slightly too big for her—and wrapped it around her shoulders. Then she found a red one for Fenna to wear and thick cotton socks to cover their frozen feet. She cast a quick look at her sleeping friends and then took Fenna's hand.

"Come on, let's search this place from top to bottom."

The mechanism room was still dark, still empty. Despite this, Milou and Fenna climbed up and around every single cogwheel to check for clues. But there were no stray midnight-dark hairs or hidden messages carved into the wood for her to find. The walls groaned, and, high up in the thatched dome, there was an unusual scratching noise.

The only thing Milou could find of any interest was a small square door on the side of the wall. She had to work at the latch with all her strength. It finally slid open, and Milou carefully pushed at the door, which opened out into the sky. Cold air rushed in, and, when Milou saw just how high up she was, dizziness overwhelmed her.

The low-lying land of the polder looked entirely different in the light of day: a milky patchwork of frostbitten fields, crisscrossed with canals. Thatched barns were dotted around between the farmhouses, cows grazed in the fields, and cyclists moved slowly up and down the road, waving to one another as they passed. Everything was so spread out and luxurious, unlike the crammed, busy city she was used to. From this distance, Amsterdam was just a line of gray with a cloud of grayer gray above it. Had they really walked all that way?

Milou closed the door, sealing the outside world away once more. She saw that Fenna had climbed to the very top of the room, her gaze fixed toward the noise above.

Scratch. Scratch. Scratch.

"It's probably just a bird's nest, Fen," Milou said. "A pigeon, most like."

Fenna sighed and nodded, then clambered back down, wiping dust from her legs.

"I think we can safely say there is nothing up here," Milou said. "Let's go and find something *useful*."

She nudged Fenna toward the ladder, down to the puppet-making workroom. She had been steeling herself to explore this room, but even so, the sight of the puppets her father had crafted sent fresh waves of despair coursing through her. Everything was left out just so, as if the Poppenmakers had merely stepped out for the day. And yet, the thick dust coating everything showed that it had certainly been much longer than a day, or a week, or even a year.

Milou approached the desk—and something lying beside it caught her eye.

A picture frame, its glass shattered. She picked it up carefully and blew the dust away.

Inside was a child's portrait of a man. His face was potato-shaped, one eye twice as large as the other. His nose was a backward L, and he was either wearing an upside-down bucket on his head or a top hat, Milou couldn't quite tell. The only thing she could see for certain about this man was that he was happy; his banana smile stretched all the way up to his plum-sized ears. Below the portrait, in scrawling printing, was a poem:

Dearest Papa,
Your smile is the stuff of which dreams are made.
Your eyes are two shimmering stars.
Your heart is my center of gravity.
And no love is as huge as ours.

In the corner of the page, in a slightly messier hand, someone had written:

By Liesel, 1872, Aged 10

Milou's ear tips prickled. Her breath hitched. The portrait was exactly twenty years old.

"I . . . I think Bram Poppenmaker has another—" Milou swallowed. "He has another daughter."

She handed the picture to Fenna, who read it silently.

"I suppose that explains the dresses." Milou bit the inside of her cheek to stop more tears from falling. "I have an older sister. A daughter he *kept*."

Once again, her ears prickled, sharply and unpleasantly. Milou rubbed them hard, determined not to cry. There would be a logical explanation for it all. Somewhere. She just needed to keep searching.

She turned back to the room and rummaged through every drawer, every shelf, every nook. There were no letters, no photographs, no personal documents at all. She dug into the stuffing of every puppet, looking for more hidden items or messages, but found nothing. She checked for loose floorboards or other secret compartments.

Nothing.

And it was as if she and her mother had never existed in the first place. No poems, no portraits, nothing at all to suggest a third person lived here. Nothing to suggest a baby—her— had lived here either. Milou's fingers shook as she wrote down the few clues she had found. Then she snapped her Book of Theories closed and headed down to continue her search in the kitchen.

By now the others were awake, and dressed in Bram and Liesel's clothing.

"I hope you don't mind," Sem said, sheepishly tugging at the collar of the striped shirt he wore. "It's just so cold."

"Of course not," Milou said, rummaging through the drawers beneath the green-quilt bed. There had to be more clues somewhere. "I'm sure my father won't mind, Sem."

"I found this," he said, sitting on the bed beside her. "Downstairs by the front door."

He was clutching a small stack of newspapers. Milou took them from him, blowing the dust off them.

"They're all dated 1880," Sem whispered. "The most recent one is December 1880," he added. "When you were . . ."

Milou nodded in understanding, her throat constricted with emotion. They'd abandoned the windmill the very month Milou had been left on the Little Tulip's rooftop.

"Thanks, Sem," Milou said, jotting it down in her notebook. "That helps a lot."

He gave her a tight, uneasy smile. "I still think you should be prepared for disappointment—"

"I've had nothing *but* disappointment up until now, Sem, so what's a little more of it going to matter? Good or bad, I *need* to know what happened. I need answers."

"There are so many books here," Lotta said from the other side of the room. "It would take me months to read all these."

"Well," Milou said, pulling herself together and standing. "You've got plenty of time to read them now that we don't have to break our backs doing chores all day, every day. Though, of course, this place does need smartening up—"

"We can't stay here," Egg said. He was sitting by the window, paper on his lap and a charcoal stick in his fingers, drawing.

"What do you mean?" Milou asked.

Egg grimaced. "I'm sorry, Milou, but we can't stay here if your parents aren't here."

"But—"

"Egg's right," Sem said. "Five orphans squatting in an abandoned windmill with no adult in sight is going to draw attention from the neighbors."

"We can just tell them that my parents—"

"They won't believe us."

"Then we'll just keep ourselves hidden," Milou insisted. "No one needs to know we're here."

Lotta shook her head. "We can't hide smoke from the chimney, and we can't stay indoors indefinitely. It's just not practical, and it's too big a risk. There may not be as many neighbors here as we had in the city, but there are enough to ask questions."

"But—"

"They might alert the Kinderbureau," Egg said. "If your parents aren't coming back any time soon, then there's no one to stop us from being dragged back to the orphanage and blamed for Gassbeek's death."

Milou didn't have an answer to that. Her parents were supposed to have been here to solve everything for them.

"There's no harm in staying one more night," Lotta said. "That gives Milou time to search for clues, time for us to gather what we can to take with us, and time to think of where on earth we can go." She blew out through pursed lips. "I suppose I can at least read *one* book in that time."

Milou sank onto the ledge beside Egg, resigned and defeated.

She pressed her cheek against the cold window and peered out at the winter-ravaged polder, which now seemed as utterly miserable and desolate as she did. The only color in sight was the bough of the oak tree and the strange copper roof of the farmhouse next door.

"It's a shame we can't stay," Egg said softly. "There are so many wonderful things to draw and paint. Like that barn. I wonder why the Poppenmakers used such grand doors for a barn. They're nothing like the simple wooden doors on all the others."

Milou looked at his drawing, then out the window, and saw that he was right. The Poppenmill barn did have unusually ornate mahogany doors, carved with swirling, flowering vines, much like the ones on the cupboard beds.

Tingles erupted all over her scalp, and, before she even realized it, she was running out the front door, the winter wind whipping at her as she hurried down the weed-ridden path to the barn. She reached the barn door, panting and shivering, and tugged on it. The hinges screeched, and dust erupted around her.

She stepped inside, her feet touching a spongy floor. Milou looked down at red carpet. She waved cobwebs away as she took another step forward, only to bump into something.

A velvet chair.

She blinked her eyes until they adjusted, then realized there wasn't just one velvet chair but many. Rows and rows of them. Milou staggered past them, down a thin aisle, and stopped in the middle of the barn, directly beneath a gaping hole in the ceiling, through which the morning sunlight streamed in. At the far end was a huge stage, its tattered, moth-eaten curtains closed.

Milou's heart skipped in double time when she realized what she was seeing.

It was a theater.

And there, behind the curtains, was the unmistakable silhouette of someone standing on the stage, arms stretched out toward her.

MILOU'S BOOK OF THEORIES

New Evidence

- My parents left me a pocket watch, engraved with a riddle and coordinates, hidden in my puppet. It led me home, but they're not here.
- Front gates chained with a rusted padlock. The sign has been vandalized, claiming that this windmill is haunted and dangerous.
- Windmill is empty of people, but not empty of their belongings.

- Clothes belonging to a man, my father, and to a girl, my sister.
- Portrait and poem made by Bram's other daughter, Liesel.
- Newspaper stack by front door, all dated from twelve years ago . . . the year and month I was abandoned.

Missing Evidence
- No hidden messages.
- No photographs.
- No hint at where they have gone.
- No sign of my mother.
- No sign of a baby (me).

Perhaps, if I solve the pocket-watch riddle, I'll know how to find them.

❖ FOURTEEN ❖

MILOU RAN DOWN THE theater aisle and leapt onto the front of the stage. The withered curtains fell from their rails as she tugged them open, raining down on her. She frantically disentangled herself from them.

A girl stood before her, feet pointed, arms held out in a ballerina's pose.

A girl with large, unblinking eyes and bright-pink rosebud lips.

A girl made of cotton and suspended on strings.

A puppet.

Milou silently scolded herself. She was a fool to have thought it could be anything else.

Or any*one* else.

Warm, salty tears slid into the side of her mouth.

"Milou!" Lotta called out from behind her. "What were you thinking? You could have been seen—Holy Gouda!"

Milou quickly wiped at her cheeks and faced the others. They were all gawking at the theater.

"This place is amazing," Egg said, turning in slow circles as he made his way down the aisle.

Sem was the only one looking right at her. "Are you all right?"

He glanced at the ballerina puppet, his worried expression transforming into a sympathetic one.

Milou blushed, then stepped around the puppet and into the shadowed area of the stage. To one side was a pile of wooden planks and half-finished set pieces—all of it stacked precariously. On the other side there was a large wooden ladder leading up to a puppeteering platform above the stage. Milou made her way toward it, then stopped.

A lump of blankets lay, crumpled and frosted over, in the far corner of the stage.

Milou's ears prickled sharply, and her heart thumped. She nudged the pile with her foot, and it rolled open, revealing nothing but more blankets.

Milou rubbed at her ears. Her Sense didn't seem to be helping much at the moment.

"Look," Sem said, his voice tight.

He pushed the blankets further aside, and Milou gasped.

Claw marks.

Just like the ones on her basket.

"What if I'm too late?" Milou said quietly. "What if they're—"

"If they were dead, the windmill would have been cleared of their stuff and sold," Sem said. "And they wouldn't have left you the pocket watch to find them, either."

Milou hoped he was right.

"It's all so . . . confusing," she said. "I need to find out what happened."

"I know you do." Sem gave her a reassuring pat on the shoulder.

"This place really is full of possibility," Lotta said, sitting down on one of the velvet chairs. "It's a shame we can't stay. I'm certain I could get the mill working again. Imagine all the things you could bake, Fenna, if we could grind our own grain."

Fenna smiled ruefully.

"I'd love to learn how to use that sewing machine in the workshop," Sem said. "I've always dreamed of using one."

"If only I'd found the pocket watch sooner," Milou said glumly. "Perhaps my father might have still been here. It's not fair that I've finally found my home, and I can't even stay in it."

Silence fell, dust motes danced, and the frost-covered marionette sparkled.

"What if Bram Poppenmaker *was* here?" Egg said suddenly. He had climbed onto the stage and was circling the puppet.

"But he *isn't*," Lotta said.

Egg grinned. "But what if he *was?*"

"Egbert!" Lotta looked up at the hole-riddled ceiling in frustration. "You're making less sense than a square cheese."

"What are you thinking, Egg?" Milou asked, recognizing the glint in his eye. It was the same look he got whenever he thought up a new project or painting.

Egg reached up and tugged on the puppet's string, making her wave. "We could *make* a father."

They all frowned up at him.

"A *puppet* father." Egg's smile turned wistful. "Do you remember that time I painted a gaping wound on Milou's forehead, and Lotta nearly fainted when she saw it?"

Lotta huffed. "It looked real."

"That's my point," Egg said. "We could create a convincing illusion."

"Like when the matron—" Sem started, then stopped.

Silence fell as they all thought back to the awful events of the previous day. Gassbeek had been so convinced by a mere shadow she'd been frightened to death.

"We trick people into thinking Bram has returned?" Milou said. "And that way, the neighbors will leave us be?"

"What about Rotman?" Sem asked. "Suppose he comes

looking for us? He's lost his workforce, and we hurt his foot—he didn't seem pleased about that."

"Rotman needs doctored paperwork to get us past the dock officials," Lotta said. "With Gassbeek gone, he doesn't have that option. And he wouldn't risk exposing their *deal*. No, I think our biggest concern is the Kinderbureau. If they ever found out what we've done—"

"There's no reason for them to doubt the paperwork," Milou said. "As long as our neighbors don't suspect anything, the Kinderbureau will have no reason to come here—they'll be far too busy dealing with replacing Gassbeek, anyway. All we need to do is convince people on the polder that Bram's come home, and that he's taken us all in."

Lotta's mouth opened as if to protest, then snapped closed again.

"That might actually work," she said finally. "We could make sure he is just visible through the windows, as long as we don't let anyone get too close a look. If anyone does comes around, we'll have to make sure they don't step foot inside the mill."

"If nothing else," Milou said, "it will buy me more time to find my parents. Once they're back here for real, we'll be safe."

"And it gives us time to work out another plan if we do need to leave," Egg added.

"We need money for food," Sem said gravely. "There's no food here and Fenna only managed to grab a stale loaf of bread, a few potatoes, and a carrot before we fled. It's all very well having shelter, but that won't stop us from starving to death."

"We could sell some stuff?" Egg suggested. "The silverware, maybe?"

"No!" said Milou. "We can't sell anything that doesn't belong to us."

"We could make something to sell at the market," Sem offered. "Some puppets, perhaps?"

"There's two problems with that," Lotta mused. "First, selling Poppenmaker puppets will draw too much attention to us. Second, the markets are in the city. If we go into Amsterdam, we risk being recognized by any adopted orphan that still lives there, or anyone else who knows us from the Little Tulip—the deliverymen, for example."

"If we dress smartly and make sure our faces are partially covered by scarves, no one will recognize us." Sem smiled. "You can leave the disguises to me. I could make dolls to sell, instead of puppets. We have all the materials for that, and we can always restock Meneer Poppenmaker's supplies as soon as we can afford to."

"So, we won't leave?" Milou asked. "I'll find my parents, and we'll sell dolls to make money in the meantime. Everyone agreed? Fen?"

Fenna nodded a yes.

"That's set then," Milou said, a thrill blooming inside her

still-aching heart. "What are we waiting for? Let's go build ourselves a father."

They sneaked back into the windmill, ducking briefly beneath the large oak tree to avoid being seen by a passing cyclist, and then filled their empty bellies with the last of the stale bread Fenna had taken from the Little Tulip's kitchen.

"Is this the only picture you could find?" Egg asked dubiously, holding Liesel's portrait of Bram.

Milou nodded. "Yes, that's all we have. Sem, you can use some of my father's long johns for the body. Egg, use whichever paints you need. I'll find him an outfit to wear."

"Fen and I will clean," Lotta said. "We can't live in all this dust. And I'm going to start a fire; I'm fed up with not being able to feel my toes."

By the time dusk settled, flames were popping and crackling in the fireplace, casting an amber glow around the kitchen, and the children's puppet-father ruse was almost complete.

Lotta hummed happily as she placed another log on the fire and held her hands up toward the heat. "Holy Gouda, that feels good," she said with a sigh, wriggling all twelve fingers. "Perhaps we could heat enough water for some baths tomorrow."

Milou's skin tingled with both warmth and delight as she stood back to examine Sem and Egg's handiwork.

"I think you got the potato-shaped face just right, Sem," Milou said. "And Egg, the eyes you painted are perfectly mismatched."

The puppet father was as tall as Sem, with limbs made of long johns filled with stuffing. Using Bram's sewing machine, Sem had stitched the head from a plain piece of cotton, and Egg had painted his features. The puppet was wearing brown wool trousers, a green button-down shirt, a woolen hat, and a black jacket made of Amsterdam velvet.

"It'll do nicely," said Milou. "If you squint, he looks real."

Lotta came to stand next to her, and Milou noticed her friend's eyes had gone slightly watery.

"He looks splendid," Lotta said, taking the puppet's hand in her own and placing a kiss on it. "It is a pleasure to meet you, Papa."

Sem lifted Puppet Papa from a hook on the wall and sat him in a chair by the kitchen table. Milou climbed onto the table and grabbed the two wooden crosses from which twelve strings were connected to Puppet Papa's limbs. She flicked one of the crosses upward, and Puppet Papa's arm lifted. With a couple of gentle maneuvers, the puppet was picking his nose.

Sem rolled his eyes as Lotta laughed.

"Can you make him walk?" Egg asked.

Milou held her arms wider, in a proper puppet-master pose, and began to jiggle the crosses. After a few moments of Puppet Papa looking like he was frantically trying to shake a spider from his person, Milou had him moving in a stationary walking position.

"Bravo!" Egg giggled.

Milou smiled. "Watch this."

She jiggled the crosses some more, until Puppet Papa was doing something that resembled a dance, arms waving above his head and legs hopping from one foot to the other.

"Where's Fenna?" Egg asked. "She's been upstairs for ages now—she needs to see this!"

As if in answer, something *clomp-clomp-clomped* down the stairs and into the kitchen. Fenna, feet decked in wooden clogs and arms cradling a bundle of cloak, was staring, open mouthed, in the doorway. Milou turned Puppet Papa to face her and lifted his head.

"*Hallo*, Fenna," Milou said, in her deepest voice. She moved the strings so that Puppet Papa made a small bow. "I am your papa."

Fenna smiled, bright and rapturous. The bundle in her arms wriggled and emitted a loud *screeeeeeeeech!*

"What was that?" Lotta asked.

Screeeeeeeeeech!

HooOOooOOoo!

Fenna opened a thin gap in the cloak bundle. A heart-shaped face appeared, the color of parchment, and two huge dark eyes blinked up at them.

"Where on earth did you find an owl, Fen?" Milou asked,

climbing down from the table to get a better look. Fenna pointed up, and Milou remembered the scratching noise they'd heard in the windmill's dome. "Not a pigeon then. Did you pull it out of the roof?"

Fenna shook her head, then made a few gestures.

"He fell?"

Fenna nodded sadly, rocking the owl gently in her arms.

Screeeeeeeeeech!

HooOOooOOoo!

Lotta stepped forward and peered beneath the cloak. "He's no bigger than a fledgling," she said. "He must have been born very late in the year. And his left wing looks malformed. I bet he was abandoned. Poor thing looks half-starved and completely spooked."

"He's an orphan?" Egg asked quietly. "Like us?"

"Well, little owl," Milou said, stroking the soft feathers on its head, "I suppose we can make room for one more orphan in this windmill."

Fenna's smile lit up the room, and Milou's heart gave a little stutter at the sight of it.

"He'll need a name, in that case," Lotta said. "How about Bartje?"

Fenna's nose crinkled, and the owl snapped its beak.

"Wouter?" Egg said.

Fenna shook her head, and the owl screeched.

"Screechy?" Milou suggested.

Fenna rolled her eyes.

"No," Sem said, looking thoughtful. "He needs a name that suits him—"

SCREECH!

All of them, except Fenna, plugged their ears with their fingers.

"How about we call him Noisy then?" Egg said.

SCREEEECH!

Sem broke out in a big, lopsided smile. "Do you remember when Gassbeek thought she might be able to get rid of us more easily if we learned to play a musical instrument?"

SCREEEEEECH!

Sem's grin widened, as the others nodded. "He sounds just like that noise Milou made on the violin."

"That wasn't *noise*," Milou huffed. "It was *Mozart*."

SCREEEEEEEEEECH!

"Well, how about we call him Mozart?" Sem asked Fenna, eyes twinkling as he gazed down at the bird.

The owl turned its head 180 degrees to look at him, then gave a little musical chirp. A giggle burst from Fenna's lips, a raspy trill that seemed to fill the room.

They all stared at Fenna, who clapped a hand over her mouth, her cheeks turning a shade of red to match her hair. A lump caught instantly in Milou's throat.

"Mozart needs a nest," Lotta said finally. "Why don't we build one above the wardrobe?"

Fenna tucked the bird gently to her chest and nuzzled it. Then she lifted her head and nodded, smiling brightly.

The lump in Milou's throat hardened as a new, unwelcome realization settled over her. If her plan to find her parents failed, if they were dragged back to the Little Tulip, then she might never see Fenna smile—or hear her giggle—that way again.

MILOU'S BOOK OF THEORIES

The Puppet Theater

Observations:

- The windmill barn has been partially converted into a puppet theater.
- Holes in the roof, tears in the seats, disintegrated curtains.
- Marionette dangling from puppeteering platform.
- Building materials and stage props piled to stage right.
- Pile of blankets to stage left.
- Claw marks next to the blankets. A match to the ones on my coffin.

Are these werewolf marks?

Did something terrible happen?

Is my family still alive?

❧ FIFTEEN ❧

AFTER A PALTRY MEAL of potato stew, the children settled down beside the fire in the living room. Puppet Papa was sitting in the bigger rocking chair, one leg propped up on his knee and a pair of thin wire spectacles balanced on his cotton nose.

"Another log for the fire, please, Sem," Lotta said in a deep voice, pulling Puppet Papa's head string to nod at the fireplace. "And Milou, *darling*, clear those plates away, would you?"

"Of course, Papa." Milou giggled.

Fenna smiled as she took off her apron and hung it on a peg on the wall. She had made a nest for Mozart out of puppet stuffing atop the wardrobe, and now she clambered up to drop him a handful of worms she'd gathered from under the barn theater's stage. Wedging herself into the chair with Puppet Papa, Milou couldn't have wiped the smile from her face if she'd tried. This was, she thought, the most perfect evening of her life so far.

No matron.

No shivering.

No fear.

Sem finished hanging a thin cotton curtain across the windows and drew it closed, sealing the rocking chairs, Puppet Papa, the fireplace, and the five of them behind it.

"It works!" Egg announced with excitement, shouting from the other side of the glass. A few moments later, he was inside again, beaming. "I could see your silhouettes, but that was all. Puppet Papa looks like a real person."

It had been Milou's idea to hang the curtain on the kitchen window, and another across the cupboard bed they would put their fake father in should anyone come inside the mill. Any passing neighbors wondering if Bram Poppenmaker had really returned would see the evidence of it clearly: smoke curling up from the chimney and light pouring through the downstairs windows. If they came closer, they would see a family of six around the fire listening to a story. That was what families did in the evenings. Milou was sure of it.

"Excellent," Milou said. "Then it's time for Papa to tell us a story."

"Ooh!" Lotta said, standing beside the bookshelf. "Speaking of stories, I found two books we could read tonight."

She dropped a huge tome on Milou's lap.

"A Medical Guide to Consumption?" Milou read the title. "I'm not sure this would make for an exciting bedtime read."

"Ugh, fine, I'll read it to myself later then," Lotta said, taking the book from Milou and placing a small leather journal on Milou's lap instead. Her eyes twinkled. "You'll like this one."

"What is it?" Milou asked.

Lotta smiled. "Just open it and see."

Milou turned to the first page, and chills erupted all over her skin. There was a pencil drawing of what looked much like the oak tree outside, except its trunk was more gnarled and its leaves much darker. The topmost branches twisted upward into two jagged lines of writing:

A Carnival of Nightmares
by Liesel Poppenmaker

Milou ran her fingers over the page, feeling the rough words her sister had scratched onto it. Liesel was a storyteller, just like her.

"There are more of her stories on the bookshelf," Lotta

said. "They're all romantic ones, though, except for this one. It seems you and your sister are both very alike and very unalike."

The next page had a single line, where Liesel had written a dedication:

For Thibault

Milou swallowed. Who was Thibault?

Whoever he was, he had known her sister. He knew what she looked like, what her laugh was like, maybe even what had become of her. Milou couldn't help but feel a sting of jealousy at the thought of Liesel writing a story for him, instead of her.

Sem and Fenna slid through the curtain and sat on pillows on the floor. Egg followed a moment later, climbing onto the other rocking chair beside Lotta.

"Milou's going to read us a story," Lotta said brightly. "Aren't you, Milou?"

All Milou could manage was a quick nod, as her fingers fumbled to turn the page.

In a shaky voice, she began to read.

When darkness falls, the nightmares come. There is no hiding from them. Once they sink their claws into you, once they have drunk from your soul and tasted your fear, they know exactly where to find you.

My own nightmare has plagued me for weeks.

I lie awake in my bed, knowing that they are waiting. My battle to stay awake is futile, of course. I am drifting down into the murky fog of sleep before I even realize that my eyes have closed. The walls of my bedroom disappear, replaced with endless dark. The warmth leaches away, and I am left shivering. Thunder roars and lightning whip-cracks above me, birthing a pale moon in the dark, starless sky.

I am standing on a tundra. The grass at my feet has shriveled and died. This bleak land stretches to the horizon in every direction, lit only by that faraway moon. I realize I am clutching something to my chest, and when I look down, I find a rusted iron cage; inside it is my own beating heart.

Thud-thud. Thud-thud. Thud-thud.

Shadows slither around my feet, pulsating in time. Tendrils reach up toward my heart cage, and I bat them away. A boom sounds, shaking the ground beneath me.

In the distance, a tall, gnarled tree rises from the barren ground. Its branches reach upward and outward like tentacles, and I have to crane my neck to see the top of it. I wrap my arms more tightly around the heart cage as the tree's ascent comes to a shuddering halt.

The Night Tree is grotesque: branches made of bones, and leaves made of talons. My feet immediately start walking toward it, as they do every time I come here. I do not control my feet anymore, the shadows do. As always, I stop after 175 steps, just a few paces from the tree's trunk.

There are faces carved into the gnarled bark. Some I know only vaguely, others are of the people I love most. All except one, of course.

"Let me be!" I yell at the shadows, the tree, the faces.

"You can't escape this any longer, Theodora." The faces speak as one monstrous voice. "The carnival awaits, and you must enter."

"No."

"Theodora."

I startle at the sound of my name, spoken so sweetly, even though I know it is coming.

A boy stands beside me. His ears have sharp points and tufts of brown fur covering both lobes. His eyes are yellow, and his nose is more of a snout. When he smiles, I catch a glimpse of his dagger-sharp teeth.

"Werewolf," the faces in the tree growl.

I clutch my heart cage tighter and shake my head. The boy's face returns to that of a normal boy, and he smiles at me, half boyish, half wolfish, but wholly familiar and comforting.

"Hendrik," I whisper, as the shadows slither ever further up my legs. "Help me, please."

As soon as his hand grips mine, the shadows loosen their grip and I am able to kick them away. Hope blossoms inside me, and soon the heart cage in my arms is wrapped in bright, flowering vines. Hendrik and I turn our backs to the Night Tree and run.

Suddenly, we are running along a path made of grave-mud. The Night Tree is gone, and there is nothing left but this vast and dark wasteland besides Hendrik and me, and my beating heart.

I count our steps. Each night, we get two steps further. Last night we made it to 663 steps. With every step the beat of the caged heart quickens. At 665 steps, we come to a halt. I blink until my vision clears, my pulse a staccato in my ears.

Just a pace away is a gate. Huge iron bars painted black, their tips a bright gold. I can see monsters beyond the bars. They are dancing, singing, calling my name. Claws, teeth, talons, snouts, whiskers . . . I see so many grotesques, they seem to blur into one horrifying being. There is music playing, but it is unlike any music I've heard before. Sounds clash together, as if each note is battling to be heard. Violins screech, drums thunder, a flute wails in agony. Shadows spill out and wrap around my ankles once more. I want to cover my ears, but I can't. I want to run away, but I can't.

This is when I usually wake up again, gasping for breath and batting away invisible monsters, but tonight I can tell the shadows will not let me go. Tonight will be different.

"It is time," the nightmares call.

Hendrik tugs on my hand, trying to pull me away again, but this time, the shadows only grip tighter, pulling me toward the gates. More appear, reaching out to the heart cage, and I realize that there is only one thing I can do.

I look up at the gates, letting my fear wash over me. Then I uncurl my fingers from Hendrik's and push the heart cage into his arms, giving him the bravest smile I can muster. He looks at me, confused and scared, but before he or I can speak, a wind rushes at me, tearing me off the ground, pushing me forward, away from him, away from my own beating heart.

I pass through the gates and

An ember popped loudly in the fireplace. Milou's friends blinked up at her, leaning forward in eagerness.

"And?" Lotta asked eagerly. "She passes the gate and then what?"

Milou turned the page, but the next one was blank. "There is no ending." She flicked through the remaining pages. "The rest of the book is empty."

"What?" Egg cried. "But it *must* have an ending."

"Fancy not finishing a story," Sem said. "Surely if you start a story, it must be easy enough to finish it?"

"It's fine." Milou smiled. "I shall just make up my own endi—"

Her ears prickled an instant before the sound of rattling at the window.

Milou jolted upright, slamming the book shut in her lap. They all peered around the curtain. A shadow passed the window.

A *person*-shaped shadow.

"Who was that?" Lotta gasped.

Sem picked up a candlestick and was across the room, into the hallway, and opening the door in just a few long strides. Milou raced after him. They stepped out into the frozen night, snow swirling down in delicate little lumps. The night was black, and the mist hung thickly above their heads, blocking out the moonlight. Sem held the flickering candlelight closer to the snow-laced ground.

Footprints. Under the window, leading off toward the gravel path. Milou followed them, tugging Sem along with her.

The prints turned, not toward the front gate, but off the path and down toward one of the smaller canals that lay behind the windmill.

"Who's there?" she called. "Show yourself!"

The only response she got was a whistling howl from the wind.

Milou bent down to examine the prints. She'd scrubbed enough shoe and clog prints from the Little Tulip's foyer floor to recognize the kind of footwear that made them. These prints were rounded at the toe, with a thick, wide heel, both of which suggested it was a man's boot.

The prints were small, however.

A boy, then.

"Show yourself!" Milou called again, anger and panic raging through her.

How much had this boy seen? How long had he been standing there, watching them? After Sem had hung the curtain to shield Puppet Papa? Or before?

She hadn't expected anyone to come trespassing right up to the window to have a look. The sign on the gate suggested people were scared of the mill; the unbroken lock showed that they kept their distance. But it seemed at least one neighbor was brave enough to venture closer.

It would only take one to ruin everything.

"Let's go back inside," Sem said.

Milou made to follow the prints. "But—"

"Whoever it was," Sem said, pulling her back toward the windmill, "they're gone now."

MILOU'S BOOK OF THEORIES

Liesel Poppenmaker

- She is a storyteller, like me.
- She writes poems for our father.
- She writes stories for her friends.
- She wears overly frilly aprons.
- She is thirty years old now.
- She is lucky to have grown up here.

Perhaps Liesel got married and moved away. Maybe my parents went to visit her and her new family and just haven't come back . . . in twelve years.

Perhaps Liesel got a job writing operas for a theater in Italy. Maybe my parents went to go and see her there and just haven't come back . . . in twelve years.

It doesn't make sense.

Nothing makes sense.

Where are they?

❈ SIXTEEN ❈

MORNING BROUGHT BOTH SUNSHINE *and* gloom. The polder was aglow with a sun-speckled frost, the main canal glittering like a long sliver of diamond. Milou, however, felt as if the world were gray and morose. She was still worried about the spy from the night before, as well as frustrated with her lack of progress in solving the mystery of her family's disappearance. Deciding that sleep was a lost cause, she climbed out of bed and curled up beside Puppet Papa, her Book of Theories open on her lap. Mozart flew down, in a haphazard spiral, from his wardrobe perch to watch her.

"Oh, Mozart," Milou whispered, as the bird stared at her from the arm of the rocking chair. "I don't suppose you have any clever revelations that will help me find my family?"

Mozart blinked. Milou sighed and went to tickle his head feathers.

Screeeeeeeeech!

Snap!

She whipped her fingers away just in time. The cupboard door opened, and a blanket with legs and a blonde head appeared.

"Morning, Milou, morning, Papa," Lotta whispered, giving Puppet Papa a kiss on the forehead. A six-fingered hand emerged from the blanket to stroke the owl. "*Hallo*, Mozartje."

Screeeeeeeeech!

Snap!

Lotta's hand retreated within the safety of the blanket.

"I think he's hungry," Milou said, closing her Book of Theories so that Lotta wouldn't see her failure of an investigation.

"He needs more meat. Gouda knows where we'll find any. We'll all be eating worms soon, at this rate."

"Sem will have some dolls ready tomorrow. I'll go with him to Amsterdam. Maybe we can buy some meat then."

Their stomachs growled in unison.

Lotta went over to the window to peek through the kitchen curtains.

"How many?" Milou asked. Lotta held up a hand. "Six!" Milou groaned. "There were only three a few minutes ago.

Nosy farmwives. Haven't they got anything better than to do than just stand there gawping?

Milou walked over and peered out of the window. Six ladies stood by the gate, their winged-bonnet-clad heads together. On the canal, several children slid to and fro on skates, making sure to remain within sight of the mill. Two men had stopped to fix their cycles on the road just a bit further down, but Milou didn't think bicycle fixing involved staring at the windmill. She had expected people to be curious about the mill being inhabited again, but she hadn't expected them to gawk quite so openly.

"We need to do something," Milou said at last.

"What kind of something?" Lotta asked.

"Something *normal*."

"Normal?"

"Yes. Normal families do not hide behind curtains. We're making ourselves stand out."

"And what is normal?"

They watched as the women by the gate pretended to chat, while sneaking glances at the mill. No doubt hoping to be the first to get the gossip on Bram Poppenmaker's return.

"Gossip!" Milou said. "Of course!"

These people might have important information that could help Milou.

"I have an idea," she said brightly.

✤

Milou opened the door leading from the puppet workshop out onto the high balcony that wrapped around the windmill's entire circumference. Icy air blew in and a clothless sail groaned just in front of her. She peered out and saw that the farmwives were still watching the downstairs window.

"Quick," she whispered to the others. "Now."

Fenna and Lotta carried out the rocking chair, upon which sat Puppet Papa. They had wrapped him up in a thick coat, hat, gloves, and a scarf that covered most of his cotton face. They set him down against the wall, under the window, and Egg added a blanket over the lower half of his body. Milou covertly fed the puppet strings through the top of the window, to where Sem was waiting.

"Oh, Papa," Milou yelled, casting a quick glance to the spectators below, who all started at the sound of her voice. "Isn't it a wonderful morning. Look, there are our neighbors. Why don't you give them a wave?"

The farmwives squinted upward. Puppet Papa lifted an arm and waved. Tentatively, the women waved back. Further away, on the main canal, the skaters came to a halt.

"Now you can watch us skate," Milou said, her voice carrying across the polder. "And the fresh air will do you such good."

Puppet Papa nodded, as did Milou to Sem, whose face was only just peeking out from behind the curtain. Then she, Fenna,

Lotta, and Egg headed back downstairs. Milou had found three pairs of skates in the wardrobe. They weren't the booted skates that Milou had seen in Amsterdam, but rather skate blades that strapped to the bottom of shoes.

As soon as the four children stepped out the front door, the gossiping ladies made a hasty retreat. The two men cycled off. Milou frowned. At least the three children on the ice hadn't run away. Milou hoped they had enough gossip to help her.

"Do you mind if I skip the skating?" Egg asked as they reached the main canal. He had his coal bucket slung over his shoulder. "We've been cooped up all morning. I'd like to map the area."

He sat on the bank and unrolled a piece of parchment. The girls carried on, wobbling toward the canal edge on skate-decked feet. The children on the ice snuck glances their way but made no move to come closer. Spurred on by a gentle ear tingle, Milou took a deep breath and jumped down, swinging her arms to propel herself forward. Her skates landed on solid ice, and her momentum sent her soaring forward.

On.

And on.

And on.

It was both terrifying and exhilarating, as if she were a marionette, being dragged forward by invisible strings. And as her scream died away, so too did her momentum.

The others were still standing at the canal's edge, staring

after her. Milou took a step and wobbled. Her right leg shot one way, the world tipped upside down, and the canal rose up to meet her back. All the air left her lungs and she lay there, gasping, for several long moments.

"That was an interesting skating technique," Lotta said with a giggle, her face blotting out the sky as she leaned over Milou.

Fenna appeared next to Lotta. They hoisted Milou to her feet. She looked to the skating spectators. They were all still huddled and gawping, hiding their giggles behind mittened hands.

"It's impossible," Milou said. "The skates just make it *more* slippery."

"It is not impossible, silly. Your mistake was throwing yourself around like a rag doll. Watching you was a lesson in how *not* to do it. Here, look." Lotta let go and slid in a circle around Milou and Fenna, swishing her feet and holding her arms out. "Keep your back straight, but lean ever so slightly forward. Find your center of gravity and it will provide you with the necessary equilibrium to stay upright."

Milou blinked at her. "You can turn everything into a science lesson, can't you?"

"That is because science is *in* everything."

The girls linked arms, wedging Milou in the middle.

"Ready?" Lotta asked.

Milou groaned, then nodded. They set off, feet sliding

from side to side in unison, up and down the canal. Lotta suddenly let Milou go and gave her a push.

"Gaah!" Milou instinctively began to windmill her arms again.

"Stop panicking!" Lotta cried.

Milou straightened her back and leaned into her wobble, holding her arms out to balance herself. She grinned, then peered over her shoulder. The other children were skating again, closer to the canal bank this time.

"I'm going to talk to them," Milou said.

Lotta nodded, then she and Fenna gracefully glided away. Milou's ears tingled. If she made a mistake, their ruse would be exposed. Wobbling much less than before, she skated over to the children.

The two girls were about Milou's age, and the boy looked to be a few years younger. One girl was short and dark-haired; the other was nearly as tall as Sem, with hair the color of honey. The boy looked like a miniature version of her, clearly a sibling. They stopped skating as soon as they saw Milou approach.

"*Goedemorgen*," Milou said brightly. "I'm Milou Poppenmaker, pleased to make your acquaintance. Those are my sisters, Fenna and Lotta."

"I'm Sanne," said the honey-haired girl, as she looked down her long nose at Milou. "This is my brother Arno, and my friend Kaatje. You don't look like sisters."

"We're *adopted* sisters."

"Is Meneer Poppenmaker really back then?" Arno asked nervously.

"Of course," Milou replied. "He's up there watching us, see?"

She waved at Puppet Papa, who waved instantly back at her.

There was a long silence as the children looked from Puppet Papa to one another, then back again.

"But my mother said the Poppenmakers were dead," said Kaatje. "She said they died of the White Plague and that their bones are lying in their beds to this day. My brother said he's heard their ghosts wailing at night."

Milou smiled through gritted teeth. "Clearly, your mother was wrong."

If this was the only kind of gossip they had, it would be of no help to her.

"That can't be right," Arno said. "My mother reckons Meneer Poppenmaker was in trouble with the law. Our father said he saw the Poppenmaker carriage hurrying away in the dead of night, years ago. It was a full moon, so he saw Meneer Poppenmaker's face clearly. He looked terribly unhappy, apparently. He's been on the run from authorities ever since; everyone knows that. Liesel too."

Milou's ears prickled in warning, but it was too late.

"You don't know *anything*," she spat.

The boy flinched. His sister, Sanne, pulled him toward her and shot Milou a furious glare.

"We *know* that Liesel Poppenmaker was a lovely, *fair-haired* beauty," Sanne said, eyeing Milou from head to toe with an incredulous smirk. "We *know* that she hung around with undesirables. We *know* she stopped my father from shooting that huge, beastly dog that terrorized the neighborhood all those years ago. We *know* this place has been much more pleasant since the Poppenmakers left, because that's what everybody around here says. And we *know* that it's not normal for a family to just disappear one night."

Milou swallowed, her ears now rushing.

"The only thing we *don't* know," Sanne continued, "is where they've been all these years and why Meneer Poppenmaker had repeatedly refused to sell the mill to decent working folks like my parents. Something suspicious *must* have happened."

Milou took a steadying gulp of air, her mind swirling with anger, confusion, and a thousand more questions. Questions she couldn't ask without rousing suspicion.

"It was nothing suspicious at all," Milou said with a forced smile. "He and my sister just decided to explore the world."

Sanne scoffed.

"My *father*," Milou said, forcing all her conviction into that single word. "My *father* decided to adopt some orphans from the city and return home to give them a better life, so here we all are. That's all you need to *know*."

Milou and Sanne glared hard at one another, the others glancing nervously between the two of them. They only broke their staring contest when Lotta and Fenna skated up beside them.

"Uhh. It's nice to meet you," Lotta said, holding a hand out for Sanne to shake.

Arno and Kaatje gasped at Lotta's fingers. Sanne recoiled. They all turned their attention hastily to Fenna, who, to Milou's surprise, held the blonde girl's gaze with a steady one of her own. She did not, however, smile.

"Who is that?" Arno asked.

Milou turned to see Egg standing behind them at the canal's edge. His head appeared from behind his map, and he pulled his shawl away from his face to offer them a small smile.

The polder children stared at him. Milou could almost hear the hinges of their jaws as they dropped.

"Where did Bram Poppenmaker find a child like *that*?" Sanne asked, not quietly in the slightest. "Clearly he's not from *Nederland*."

Egg's smile disappeared; he hid once more behind his map. Milou's anger flared.

"That's our brother Egg. He's a cartographer," she said proudly, squaring her shoulders. "Sem, our other brother, is inside, making dolls."

Sanne narrowed her eyes at Milou. "I suppose it does make sense that a man as peculiar as Meneer Poppenmaker would adopt an entire circus of freaks." She grabbed her brother's hand and turned away from them. "Come on, Arno, let's go skate further down the canal."

"Hey!" Milou yelled, ignoring the sudden prickling on her earlobes. She bent down and picked up a handful of snow from the canal bank, squashing it into a ball.

"Milou, don't," Lotta whispered.

Sanne turned. "What—"

Milou's snowball caught her right in the face.

Sanne spluttered and gasped, scraping the snow from her face. She blinked at Milou with a mixture of surprise and fury. Milou's ears tingled, but she didn't regret what she'd done. She wouldn't let anyone speak about her friends that way.

The two girls stared each other down again.

Then Arno giggled, and a snowball caught Kaatje's chin, then one hit Lotta's chest.

An eyeblink later, more were flying in every direction, hitting shoulders, heads, and legs, and punctuated by shrieks of delight. Even as Sanne started laughing and slinging snow at her friends, Milou stood rigid, her fury still gripping her tight. Something cold and hard hit her on the cheek.

"Hey—"

Milou suddenly found a snowball in her mouth instead of words.

She spat it out, coughing, and found Fenna grinning before her. Milou gathered a handful of snow from the side of the canal and launched it at Fenna's head, but she ducked just in time. The snowball flew right over her and hit Lotta on the forehead instead.

"Oops," Milou said.

Lotta charged for her, a wild grin on her face.

Milou flapped her arms in a panic trying to turn and run. She made it three desperate steps before her feet slipped beneath her. She flew forward and slid across the ice on her stomach for what felt like an infinity, snow spraying into her face.

On.

And on.

And on.

And on.

Her squeal of delight was cut short as she slammed into two adjacent lampposts.

"Oof!"

There were not usually lampposts in the middle of canals, as far as Milou was aware. Her eyes were blocked with snow and ice, so she reached out a hand and gasped when she realized the lampposts were both warm and seemed to be wearing trousers.

Milou pushed herself up to her knees, blinked snow from her eyelashes, and found herself face-to-shin with a tall figure, silhouetted by the bright winter sun. Her gaze followed the long lamppost legs up, noticing the outline of a tailcoat and a stiff, peaked cap. Milou's own hat had fallen off, and as she reached down to pick it up, she noticed the figure's boots: men's boots, small, with rounded toes and a wide heel. Her heart leapt up her throat.

The spy.

❉ SEVENTEEN ❉

THE FIGURE LOOMED ABOVE her. As she struggled to her knees, Milou noticed silver buttons on the jacket, military style, and a belt wrapped around the middle with a baton wedged firmly in it. A uniform, she realized in horror.

"I'm so sorry . . . uh . . . Meneer," Milou spluttered, staggering up onto her skates.

"I am not a Meneer," said the tall figure in a stern, but decidedly female, voice.

"Oh, *goedemiddag*, Mevrouw," she spluttered, her ears prickling steadily. "I'm so sorry I bumped into you."

Milou looked down at the woman's boots again. She couldn't be a hundred percent certain, but they looked like a match for the prints she'd seen outside the house.

"That was a remarkable impression of a dancing octopus," the uniformed woman said. "I've never seen anything quite like it."

Milou rubbed at her ears. "I, um—"

She blinked up at the woman, who gazed down at her with an amused expression. She wasn't an old woman, perhaps in her early thirties, but her eyes did crinkle in the corners, and she had a thin streak of gray in the middle of her light-brown bangs. A large gold locket hung from her neck, and in the crook of her left elbow hung a wicker basket, its contents hidden beneath a double hatch lid. The woman arched a single eyebrow high up her forehead, and Milou realized she was gawping. She shook herself and held out a gloved hand.

"My name is Milou Poppenmaker. It is a pleasure to meet you."

The woman's raised eyebrow twitched. A hand clad in soft black leather shook Milou's, firm and strong. Milou couldn't help looking at the uniform again.

"Edda Finkelstein," the woman said, tipping her peaked cap in greeting. "Polder warden for these parts. I'm sure your father has mentioned me."

Polder warden.

Was that like a police officer?

Milou gulped down a mouthful of nervousness and stretched her smile even wider.

"Of course he's mentioned you," she said, her mind clunking like a broken clock. "He's said such wonderful things about you, Mevrouw Frankenstein."

The woman's eyebrow rose higher.

"It's *Finkelstein.* So, Milou Poppenmaker," Edda Finkelstein said brightly. Milou knew a new question was coming. It was the woman's unwavering eyebrow that told her: an eyebrow of curiosity. "Where has the elusive Bram Poppenmaker hidden himself away all these years? I'm dying to hear all about it."

Milou was opening her mouth to spin her wild but convincing tale, when a warm, herby smell tickled at her nostrils. A growl thundered out from the vicinity of her belly button. The deep, rumbling type of growling that can only be made by the emptiest of stomachs.

Edda's other eyebrow rose.

Milou felt a blush burn at her cheeks. "Pardon me," she said, the belly grumble still rumbling on and on. "I'm afraid we were so excited about skating that we forgot to have lunch."

With a final gurgle, the belly rumbling stopped. The herby smell lingered, making Milou feel suddenly, overwhelmingly dizzy.

The warden narrowed her eyes slightly. "You look vaguely familiar, Milou. Have I met you before?"

Yes, Milou wanted to say, *you spied on us last night. That's why I look familiar.*

Instead, she smiled brightly and said, "I am Bram's youngest daughter. No doubt that is why I look familiar."

"I see," Edda said, the Eyebrow of Curiosity rising once more. "And the other four, are they the long-lost offspring of Meneer Poppenmaker as well?"

Four. She knew exactly how many of them there were. It must have been her. Milou's ears prickled again.

"Those are my best friends," Milou said, trying to keep her voice from shaking. "I asked my father to adopt them."

She summoned what she hoped was a confident smile, and held it in place as Edda Finkelstein cast a curious glance at the windmill. Milou took a calming breath in through her nose. If the polder warden had seen them assembling Puppet Papa, then surely she'd have arrested them by now?

"And where, um, where is Liesel?" Edda asked, her smile tightening slightly.

"Traveling," Milou said. "With her friend. She's quite the adventurer."

"Yes, of course." Edda's smile faltered and faded completely. Her gloved hand reached up to the locket, then lowered again.

Milou inhaled deeply to quell her nerves, but that warm, rich aroma was still in the air.

"Why are you dressed like a police*man*?"

Milou started. She hadn't heard Lotta skate up to them. Milou peeked behind her quickly to find that Fenna and Egg had both gone back indoors. Up on the balcony, Puppet Papa appeared to be looking at them, his head tilted toward the canal, face covered with a scarf.

"I'm dressed as a polder warden, actually," Edda said, matching Lotta's scrutinous expression.

"But you're a woman."

"Correct."

"That's impossible. They don't let women join the force."

"It's *improbable*," Edda said. "Not impossible."

"How did you convince them? Were you a soldier once too? Have you—"

"This is Lotta," Milou interrupted. "Lotta Poppenmaker."

"You're very curious, Lotta Poppenmaker. Tell me, is that oil I see on your hands? And a waistcoat over your dress?"

"It seems you're also curious." Lotta crossed her arms, but Milou could see a glint of awe shining in her friend's eyes. "As you avoided my question by asking more questions."

Edda smiled. "It seems there are lots of questions in the air today." She patted the basket in her arms. "I made some food as a homecoming offering. How about we go inside? Your father can tell me all about his wild adventures." Edda skirted around Milou. "The food won't stay warm out in this cold."

The woman's legs were exceedingly long and quick. She was halfway toward the canal bank before Milou had even managed to turn and take a single step.

"No!" Milou cried. "Stop!"

A sharp warning prickled her ears, but Milou didn't need her Sense to tell her she'd made a mistake. Edda stopped mid-stride, one leg already up on the bank, and turned. The Eyebrow rose once more.

"He's contagious," Lotta blurted.

"Contagious?" The Eyebrow of Curiosity rose higher. "Then why was he out here in the freezing cold?"

Milou shot Lotta a worried look.

"I have the situation perfectly in hand," Lotta said confidently. "He's wrapped up warm, and our brother Sem is up there with him."

"And what ailment is it Bram is suffering from?"

"Bacterial tuberculosis," Lotta said. "Or, as many laymen call it, consumption. He was seen by a fantastic microbiologist in Berlin who performed groundbreaking treatment to weaken the offending bacteria. We think he's over the worst of it and should be well again come spring."

Milou tried not to gawk. What was Lotta doing? What was she saying? Half the words didn't even make sense.

"I don't suppose you know what a microbiologist is, or the nature of bacteria," Lotta continued animatedly, "but I assure you, a little fresh air will do him good."

"It's best you don't come too close," Milou interjected. "We wouldn't want you to catch it."

Edda's mouth twitched again. "No, we wouldn't want that

at all." She sighed, then lowered her eyebrow. "Well, I suppose you'd better take this. Perhaps it will help make Bram feel better."

Edda opened the lid of the basket and held it out for Milou and Lotta to see. The smell was so intoxicating, Milou felt dizzy again. Beside her, Lotta made a low groan of longing.

"Smoked sausage with plenty of potatoes, some carrots, and an aubergine I bought at the market." She slipped the basket from her elbow and handed it to Lotta. "This is far too much for me to eat alone; you may as well have it. I live just over that little bridge." She pointed toward the copper-roofed farmhouse. "You can return the dishes to me tomorrow."

Milou responded with another belly growl. Lotta's stomach joined in. They both quickly wrapped their arms around their middles and peered in the direction Edda was pointing—at a small farmhouse, divided from their mill by a thin canal, a narrow field, and the huge, skeletal oak tree.

"Thank you," Milou said. "We'll see you tomorrow."

Edda bowed in farewell, then set off across the icy canal in a lope so long-strided it would have made a giraffe jealous.

Milou turned to Lotta. "How did you—"

"I read that medical book last night. It's fascinating. As is Mevrouw Finkelstein. A female polder warden. Isn't she splendid?"

Milou's ears tingled as she glanced back over her shoulder,

to where a line of small, wide-heel footprints followed in Edda's wake.

"Yes, splendidly troublesome."

With the kitchen cleaned, the fire roaring, and Edda Finkelstein's feast laid out on the Poppenmakers' finest crockery, the children gathered around the kitchen table. Puppet Papa watched over them from the rocking chair, wrapped in a corduroy dressing gown, smiling his banana-shaped smile, as they stared at the food.

"It's beautiful," Sem said.

He started to sit down, but Milou put an arm out to stop him.

"Maybe we shouldn't be eating this," she said.

They all shot her an incredulous look.

Sem's eyebrows crinkled. "Why on earth not?"

Milou waved her hand at the food. "It could be a trap."

Egg laid his shawl on the back of his chair and sat down. "I doubt those carrots are going to jump up and drag us back to the Little Tulip."

Milou was still unconvinced. Worry gnawed at her, despite her eerily unprickly ears. "What if she's just trying to gain our trust so she can hand us over to the authorities and claim a reward?"

"If she had seen anything incriminating last night, we'd

be back in Amsterdam by now," Lotta said. "And anyway, you don't know for certain it was her at the window last night."

"What if the food's poisoned?"

"Then we'll die incredibly happy," Sem said, sitting down beside Egg.

"But what if—"

Egg held up a hand to silence her. "What if we just ate this before it all goes cold?"

As if in answer, all five stomachs gurgled in unison, like an entire orchestra of drainpipes.

Sitting themselves down on velvet chairs borrowed from the theater, the others began to pile their plates high with food. Milou reluctantly sat down too. Fenna took her plate and filled it with sausage, carrots, potatoes, and a strange purplish vegetable she hadn't seen before.

Then her friends dived straight in, slurping, gulping, and scraping cutlery.

Milou stabbed at a piece of pink sausage. It wasn't gray like the occasional scraps of meat they'd been fed at the orphanage. She bit into the end of it, hot juice spilling all over her mouth, and groaned in relief. Warmth radiated from her scalp to her shoulders, and an unfamiliar sense of calm washed over her. Any nefarious plot Edda Finkelstein might have had in mind by offering them this food was worth it for the unrivaled joy of the flavors now dancing across her tongue.

"I could eat a hundred mouthfuls of this," Egg said, holding up his forkful of the aubergine. "Even if it does taste suspiciously of eyeball."

Fenna held a strip of sausage up in the air, then grinned in rapturous delight when Mozart spiraled down and took it from her fingers, nipping at them as he did. Fenna sucked her finger where the owl's sharp beak had caught her and turned back to her food. With a muffled *hooOOooOOoo*, Mozart flew in circles back into the shadows.

Soon, their plates were licked clean and the five of them were leaning back in their chairs, rubbing their rounded bellies.

Lotta slurped at all twelve fingers, then licked at the sauce that had dribbled out each side of her mouth. "Holy Gouda, that was good."

"This is what it's like then," Sem said.

"What what's like?" Egg asked sleepily.

"Being a *normal* family."

For the first time since meeting Edda, Milou smiled.

MILOU'S BOOK OF THEORIES

Gossip

Useful intelligence:

- They speak as if Bram and Liesel lived in the windmill alone: no mother or baby mentioned.
- Bram was seen leaving the windmill one night, in

December, under a full moon.

- Bram refused to sell the windmill.
- A cloaked figure was often seen sneaking around the mill at night.
- Liesel was a "fair-haired beauty" who hung around with "undesirables."
- A "huge, beastly dog" used to terrorize the neighborhood. Could this have been a werewolf? If Sanne's parents are as ridiculous as she is, I bet they wouldn't be able to tell the difference between a large dog and a werewolf.

Nonsense:

- Rumors about plague, ghosts, and criminal activity.
- Sanne and her silly, smirking face.
- Sanne's suggestion that Egg doesn't belong here.

What other reason would my father have to refuse to sell the mill, other than because he intends to return one day?

Perhaps they really have just gone traveling?

Or did the werewolf chase them away, despite my sister having saved its life? Why would she save its life? Perhaps, like Fenna, she is just too kind-hearted to see any creature come to harm. Maybe my parents are still hunting it down.

⚜ EIGHTEEN ⚜

THE CHILDREN WOKE BEFORE dawn, and ate
leftovers for breakfast on the windmill's balcony, all ten legs
dangling over the balcony's edge and all five sets of shoulders wrapped in thick wool blankets. Afterward, they sat and
watched the sun rise over the seemingly never-ending landscape. Birdsong drifted up to them in sweet trills, and, with
freshly licked lips, Fenna began to tentatively whistle each trill
back to them. Sem was stitching dolls, Egg was drawing, and
Lotta was gazing happily across the polder, her legs bedecked
in newly fashioned trousers inspired by the polder warden's.
Mozart nestled in Fenna's cloak, sleeping soundly.

Milou was the only one not smiling. She was watching

Edda Finkelstein's copper-roofed farmhouse, certain she could see the polder warden's curtains twitching.

"I'm glad we decided to stay," Lotta said. She waved to a passing farmer, who tipped his hat in return. "Our neighbors are lovely."

Milou knew Lotta was really referring to Edda.

"Not all of them are," Egg muttered, and Milou gave his hand a squeeze.

"Milou and I can head into the city this afternoon to sell the dolls," Sem said. "Perhaps we'll earn enough for a feast like the one we had last night."

In his lap was a duck doll, wearing a pale-blue puffed-sleeve dress and a lacy winged bonnet. Sem was stitching the bottom of its left foot closed, with Fenna tucking the stuffing in as he went.

"First we'd better return these dishes," Lotta said gleefully, getting to her feet. "We should all go over and thank Mevrouw Finkelstein."

"That woman is far too curious," Milou said. "We should just leave the dishes by the front door."

"That's not how *normal* neighbors behave," Lotta said. "It would only encourage her inquisitiveness."

Milou sighed dramatically. Lotta was, of course, right.

No matter how much Milou wished to, there was no avoiding Edda Finkelstein.

❧

They dressed neatly. Fenna plaited Milou's hair, and Sem wore one of Bram's bowler hats to cover his ears, which Milou snatched right off his head again.

"There's nothing wrong with your ears, Sem."

Cheeks reddening, Sem nodded. "I just thought . . . well, you said we needed to appear more normal."

"Milou's right," Lotta said. "But I'm not sure bringing Mozart is going to help us appear normal."

Milou turned to find Fenna tucking the owl into the front of her cloak. Her friend responded to Lotta's statement by clutching Mozart more tightly and narrowing her eyes in a decidedly defiant manner.

"Suit yourself," Lotta replied. "I suppose there's only so much normal the five of us can realistically get away with. Just don't let him out of your cloak if you can help it."

Fenna smiled and nodded.

They set off to Edda Finkelstein's house, passing Sanne and Arno, who were skating on the canal again. Egg pulled his shawl up to cover his face, trying to hide from their outright staring, which only soured Milou's mood further. She linked arms with him and marched past as if the two siblings didn't exist.

They passed under the oak tree and skirted around a raised flower bed rimmed with a stone border. Milou led them over a little bridge, and stepped onto a neat stone path that wound its way toward Edda's farmhouse. The two pigs in the pen were snuffling at the frozen mud, and clucking noises emanated from the chicken hut just beyond.

"It's really quite inspiring to see a woman have all this on her own," Lotta was saying. "I didn't see a wedding ring on her finger, so she must be a spinster."

Milou looked to her friends and was disappointed to find they were all looking impressed.

Fenna's smile was almost touching her ears as they approached the polder warden's brightly painted front door. The doorbell was a small brass peacock. Fenna giggled softly, then pulled the peacock's legs, and a tinkling of arpeggiated chimes sounded. Milou scowled as a traitorous bubble of awe tickled at her insides.

"Um, Milou," Egg whispered, tugging her arm urgently. He nodded toward a metal plaque on the front door, upon which was written:

E. FINKELSTEIN
CLOCKWORK ARTISAN

Her friends turned to her, mouths agape, then looked at the pocket watch dangling from her neck. Milou clutched it tightly, suddenly feeling dizzy.

"Do you think she's your—"

"*No*," Milou said, the mere thought of it twisting her insides. "It must be a coincidence. She can't be—"

"Poppenmakers!" Edda's voice projected suddenly, from nowhere.

They all jumped, and Fenna made a small gasp of surprise.

"Where's her voice coming from?" Egg whispered.

"Speaking tube," Edda's tinny voice singsonged. "Next to Lotta's elbow."

Lotta let out a half gasp, half squeal. She put her face close to a round metal grill. "I've heard about speaking tubes," she shouted. "But I've never seen one!"

"Ow," Edda said. "Clearly not. Come in, the door is unlocked."

Lotta pushed the door open, and they stepped inside.

Tick-tick-tock-tock-tick-tick-tock-tock.

It sounded like a thousand tiny metal feet dancing a chaotic rhythm. They walked into the middle of a square hallway surrounded by clocks. They were nothing like the plain grandfather clock in the Little Tulip; nor were they like the fancy mantelpiece clock in Gassbeek's office. Each one was an intricately built sculpture in the form of an animal.

A metal bear, head fashioned from an old saucepan and body made of bicycle parts, loomed in the corner closest to the door. Its jaw was open in a silent roar, and nestled in its mouth was a clock face. A row of metal cats hung in a line along a wall, their metal tails swishing and swooshing and their eyes ticking left and then tocking right.

There were ducks with tiny clocks for eyes; an octopus

whose eight arms pointed toward the year, month, day, hour, minute, second, mealtime, or bedtime; a pig in a copper top hat with a clock for a snout; and a windmill, as tall as Milou, whose sails whooshed at a dizzying speed around a clock face made of a metal polished to such a shine she could see her own dumbstruck face reflected right back at her.

"Holy Gouda," Lotta said, spinning in a slow circle. She and Fenna collided mid-spin as they took in the strange sight. Mozart let out a disgruntled *hooOOooOO*.

"That's an odd lamp," Egg said, pointing to a glowing glass orb that hung from the middle of the ceiling by a thick wire. "It's like fire, but . . . not."

"Electricity." Lotta breathed the word out like a prayer.

"Indeed, indeed." Edda's tinny voice sounded from a large speaking tube located in the middle of the bear clock's belly. "Now close the door, would you; the bear's cogs squeak most unpleasantly when it gets too cold. Take the first doorway on your right and up the stairs."

Behind the door was a staircase, lit by more electric bulbs all the way up. Lotta took the lead eagerly, climbing up and around until they finally emerged into a large, open room. More clocks, in various stages of assembly, lined the walls and counters. Tools were scattered on every surface. There was so much stuff everywhere that Milou didn't notice Edda immediately. Then she saw the familiar streak of silver through light-brown hair, bobbing behind a metal elephant head. Edda peered around the side of it, her face appearing just below its curved trunk.

Milou quickly shoved the pocket watch under her collar. It pressed, cold and seemingly heavier, against her racing heart. She stared at the polder warden, a thousand questions bashing against her skull, though one was much louder than the others:

Could Edda Finkelstein be her mother?

She wasn't old enough to be her mother, surely?

"Ah, *welkom.*" Edda's left cheek had a thick smear of oil across it, and her bangs were sticking up behind a pair of goggles that rested on her forehead. "You have arrived at a most fortunate time. My sleeve is caught in a cog, and I can't let go of this sprocket or the whole thing will collapse."

Edda raised one of her eyebrows, which were far lighter than Milou's black ones.

Not to mention, Milou did not possess the ability to raise a single eyebrow at a time.

"Cogs . . . sprockets . . ." Lotta spoke fervently. "This . . . wow."

Milou had never seen Lotta look so flabbergasted.

Edda's bright-*blue* eyes danced in delight at Lotta's awed expression.

You look vaguely familiar, Edda had said yesterday.

Milou stared at her, examining every inch of her face.

There was nothing familiar about Edda Finkelstein.

"This is Sem, Egg, and Fenna," Milou said croakily.

"We're just here to return your dishes. We'll be immediately on our way, so as not to disturb you."

Milou set the dishes on a countertop and pulled on Sem's elbow, intending to drag them all straight back to the windmill.

"Oh, don't be silly," Edda said. "You're not disturbing me at all. In fact, I could do with an extra hand here."

Lotta was suddenly elbowing her way past Sem and Milou, in a hurry to help Edda. Milou reached out to grab her but missed.

"I think I've dropped a cog," Edda said. "If I hold this, can you reach in and find it?"

Lotta nodded enthusiastically.

A large tabby cat was curled up on the windowsill. Fenna used her Mozart-free hand to scratch the cat's forehead, provoking a grumpy yowl from the beast.

"Ah, Fenna," Edda said. "That is Meneer Catticus. If you scratch behind his left ear, you'll earn his adoration very quickly. That's it, Lotta, that cog just there."

Fenna beamed.

As did Lotta.

Sem and Egg wandered wide-eyed around the room. Milou stood just stood there, trying to keep the questions from bursting from her lips. She couldn't just ask Edda outright, not without the polder warden immediately realizing Milou hadn't been telling the truth about who she was. If she wanted answers, she'd have to ask *careful* questions.

Milou gave Edda a bright, dimply smile. "Do you make these clocks for your children?"

The Eyebrow of Curiosity shot upward.

"There are no children here."

"Elsewhere then?"

The clock maker sighed.

"I do not have any children," Edda said. "How's your father feeling today?"

Milou hid her frustration at Edda's deflection by brightening her smile further.

"He's resting in bed with a book."

"I'm glad to hear Meneer Poppenmaker is feeling well enough to read," Edda said, the left side of her nose twitching slightly, as if she were trying to stop a sneeze. Or a sneer. "Perhaps if he's well enough tomorrow, I could visit—"

"Got it!" Lotta said, holding a small metal cog.

"Excellent work," Edda said. "You have twelve exceedingly nimble fingers! You would make a fine clock maker."

Lotta grinned so delightedly it made Milou grimace.

"Do you make watches too?" Egg asked, with a pointed look at Milou. "I only see designs for more clocks."

"Hmm? Oh, no. I've always preferred making larger pieces of clockwork— Oh dear. I seem to have torn my sleeve again. I never seem to learn."

This time it was Sem hurrying across the room to Edda's

rescue, a needle and thread already in his hands. "Here, let me."

"Oh no, really, it's—"

"It's the least I can do after the wonderful meal you cooked us."

"In that case, you are my hero, Sem. My sewing abilities leave a lot to be desired, if I'm honest. My, you're very adept. I have plenty of mending work for you, if you wish to earn some extra coin?"

Sem beamed.

Milou turned away, walking up and down the narrow gap between the work counters. She picked up a small clock face and pretended to examine it, trying to think of what questions she could ask Edda without it sounding like she was asking questions.

"That's an interesting shawl you have there," Edda was saying to Egg. "Such an unusual shade . . ."

"It's . . . uh . . . a little stained," Egg said, clutching it protectively. "Charcoal—"

"Ah yes," Edda said. "Quite a nasty stain, too. As someone who works with various oils and grease, I've seen my fair share of those. I have a special cleaning concoction I could try, if you'd like?"

"Oh," Egg said, clutching the shawl more tightly. "No, really—"

"I promise I won't damage it," Edda said gently. "Wouldn't

it be wonderful to see it restored to its former glory?"

Milou set the clock face down a little too hard. It rolled off the edge and clattered to the floor.

Everyone looked at her.

"Sorry—"

She bent down to pick it up, crawling under the worktable as it continued to roll away from her. As she finally managed to grab it, something sharp caught her finger. She stifled a hiss of pain as she plucked a splinter out. Then she saw what had caused it.

Four deep, large lines had been gouged into the wooden floorboards.

Claw marks. Far too big to be from Meneer Catticus.

And as with the ones in the theater, Milou was certain they were a match for the gouges on her coffin basket.

She looked a little further along the floor, noticing more and more of the scrapes. Along the skirting boards, up the workbench legs, and poking out from beneath various clocks.

They were everywhere.

Milou swallowed hard and shuffled backward out from under the worktable, crashing into a coat stand. It fell down beside her, its contents covering her. Cheeks flaming in embarrassment, she scrambled to her feet and set the stand right, gathering the coats and hanging them back up. She looked up at Edda, who looked back at her with a small frown.

"Are you all right?" the polder warden asked. "You seem a little . . . flustered."

Milou's heartbeat matched the *tick-tick-tock-tock-tick-tick-tock-tock* of the clocks around her. Edda was still staring. As were her friends.

Milou forced herself not to look at the claw marks.

Edda was connected to the Poppenmakers somehow.

Milou's Sense prickled in agreement.

She wasn't entirely certain what a werewolf would look like in human form, but Edda Finkelstein's gentle appearance was not what she would have expected.

"I feel sick," Milou lied. "Let's go."

She turned and fled, down the stairs and out the door. She was halfway to the canal that separated the windmill and Edda's house when Fenna and Egg caught up with her. She looked over her shoulder and saw that Lotta and Sem were still hovering on the doorstep, talking to Edda.

"Hurry up!" Milou yelled to them.

Lotta's shoulders seemed to sag in defeat.

"What was that all about?" Sem whispered when they'd caught up. "Are you really feeling ill?"

Milou hurried toward Poppenmill. "Of course not—"

"Wait!" Edda called, suddenly just a few paces behind them.

Milou silently cursed those long lamppost legs of hers.

"Egg," Edda said breathlessly. "Your shawl . . . ?"

Egg blinked at her. Then, he hesitantly unwrapped it from around his neck and handed it over.

Edda smiled. "I'll bring it back soon, I promise. And Lotta, I need an apprentice. I could do with a pair of hands as nimble as yours."

Lotta's grin stretched out toward her pigtails. "Oh, I'd love—"

"We'll have to ask our father," Milou said, grabbing Lotta's hand and pulling her away. "Goodbye, Mevrouw Finkelstein. Thank you again for the food."

Dragging Lotta along with her, Milou sped toward the mill.

MILOU'S BOOK OF THEORIES

Edda Finkelstein

- Approximate age: early thirties.
- The local polder warden—even though she's a woman.
- Lives alone and works—even though she's a woman.
- A clock maker, but not a watchmaker.
- Unmarried and says she's never had children.
- Claw marks all over her workroom.
- Is far too curious about us. Probably spying on us too.

Is far too *kind* to us. What does she want?

She doesn't seem to like Bram much, despite what she says to the contrary. Every time his name comes up, there's a little twitch in the side of her nose. An almost-sneer that she never quite stops in time for me to notice.

She's connected to my family's disappearance. I just know it.

The claw marks and the clockwork—it's too much to be a coincidence.

Perhaps they discovered she was the werewolf, and she tried to kill them?

Perhaps it is her they are hiding from?

❧ NINETEEN ❧

"WHAT ON EARTH WERE you thinking, agreeing to work for her?" Milou growled. "We should be keeping our distance!"

"She's nice," Lotta snapped back. "You're being paranoiac."

"No, I'm not. She knows more about my family's disappearance than she's letting on. I found claw marks *all* over her workroom floor."

Lotta shrugged herself free. "If you try suggesting she's the *werewolf* from your Book of Theories—"

"What other explanation could there be? The claw marks

were *huge*. There's no way that cat of hers could have made them."

Lotta opened her mouth, then shut it again.

"We need food," Egg said. "We can't survive forever on the small amount we took from the Little Tulip. If she's offering to pay Lotta . . ."

Milou growled inwardly. She should be focusing on finding her parents, not arguing with her friends. "I'm trying to keep us safe."

"It's a calculated risk," Lotta said, softening slightly. "And I'm sure there's a logical reason for the claw marks, Milou. If I work for her, I could ask her—"

"No," Milou said. "You're definitely not asking her any questions. If she realizes we're on to her, we could be in even bigger danger. And we already have a plan to make money. Sem and I are going to Amsterdam right now to sell the dolls. We don't need that woman's help."

Before Lotta or Egg could argue the matter any further, Milou marched into the kitchen toward the wardrobe, rifling through Liesel's dresses until she found something that no one would recognize her in: a lilac dress with an obscene amount of frills on the apron. She chose a matching bonnet, tucking her ebony hair into it, then covered the bottom of her face with a silk scarf, just as Sem walked into the room.

"Have you come to tell me off as well?" Milou asked. "I'm only trying to keep us safe."

"No," he said. "I just came to say we should take Puppet Papa. That way, no one will mistake us for orphans."

Milou and Sem took a three-wheeled cargo bicycle that had been stashed at the back of the puppet theater. It had a large crate at the front, perfect for carrying fake fathers.

"Do you know how to ride this thing?" Milou asked.

Sem shrugged. "We've watched millions of people cycle," he said. "It can't be that difficult."

It took Sem a few attempts to get the pedals going, but the extra wheel helped to keep the bike from toppling over. They sat Puppet Papa in the front crate, his face swaddled in a thick scarf, with a hat that covered most of the rest of his head. They positioned him carefully, making it look like he was reading a book. Milou squeezed in the crate in front of him.

It was far quicker, it turned out, to cycle to the city than it had been for them to walk. As it was, they had to go only as far as the outskirts, discovering there a market street full of shoppers and traders. They found a small space next to a cheese stall, in the shadow of a tall oak tree that Milou felt was perfect. They parked the cargo bike under a branch, and Milou covered Puppet Papa with a blanket, right up to his hat, giving the impression of a sleeping figure. Then, arranging the dolls on a blanket on the ground, the two of them sat and waited, hoping to make their fortune.

But hours passed, and they sold only one doll. The cold was seeping into every inch of Milou, making her irritable. The crowds kept stepping over them, trampling their blanket and pushing them farther back toward the oak tree.

"People keep just walking past," Milou complained, wrapping her cloak more tightly around her shoulders. "We need a table."

"We can't very well carry a table all this way," Sem replied. "Perhaps we need to ask Egg to make us a fancy advertising board or something."

A small girl wearing a winged bonnet and with cookie crumbs around her mouth suddenly appeared at Milou's feet, sitting down in a rumpled mass of skirts. She grinned up at Milou expectantly.

"What's her name?" the girl asked, pointing toward a mouse doll. "And why is she dressed like a pirate?"

"Her name is Theodora," Milou said, smiling. "And, actually, she's dressed like a werewolf hunter. See this sword? It's made of solid silver, forged in moonlight. All it takes is a single nip"—Milou slashed the doll mouse's sword at the girl's nose, eliciting a giggly shriek of surprise—"and it will turn a werewolf's blood into solid stone."

Two boys sat on the ground in front of Milou, their

mittened hands cradling hot, oozing stroopwafels.

"What happened next?" asked one boy, licking a glob of syrup from his wrist. "Did the werewolf eat her?"

Milou smiled, the cold suddenly gone as she picked up another doll and made the two face each other.

"Oh, he certainly tried to eat her," Milou said softly and menacingly. "But let me tell the story from the beginning."

Clink-clunk-clink-clunk-clink-clunk.

Milou's unexpected audience, now twenty-something strong, began to throw coins into the bucket Sem had set out to collect their doll-selling earnings. Milou grinned as Sem carried the bucket back to the bicycle.

"Puppet shows, Sem! That's how I could earn money for us," she said. "Did you see how I made them jump and squirm? I'm telling you, audiences love to be scared. I think I might add some decapitations next time . . ."

"You did very well," Sem said. Then he peered into the bucket and frowned. "You made thirty-four cents, three buttons, a fingernail, a used handkerchief, and a half-eaten cookie."

Milou's smile faltered slightly. "It's a start, at least," she said. "I could come back tomorrow, and the day after. It'll soon add up."

"I sold two more dolls while you were performing. It'll keep us going for a while. Maybe another good meal will cheer everyone up, so you, Lotta, and Egg can make up. I just need to fix a spoke on the back wheel, then we'll go."

As Milou bent down to put the money bucket in the crate next to Puppet Papa, a familiar smell tickled the inside of her nostrils. An oily, smoky smell.

She stood, heart kicking against her rib cage, and scanned the market street. She'd made a half turn when she spotted a familiar swirl of pipe smoke rising about the heads of the crowd. A gap appeared amongst the sea of people, and Milou saw a gray wool suit and sealskin boots.

Rotman.

Milou froze, the backs of her legs pressing tightly against the bicycle, as Rotman limped past. She quickly pulled the scarf right over her nose and kept still as the sugar merchant ambled her way, smiling toothily at those he passed and stopping to say "*hallo*" to a baby in a perambulator. Milou lowered her eyes, hoping she'd be invisible enough that he would walk straight past her.

She felt his gaze land on her a mere instant later.

Instinctively, she looked up through her lashes. He was still smiling that big, fake smile: all teeth and no soul. But he did not appear to recognize her.

Heart galloping, she ducked her head in greeting. Rotman's smile remained fixed, then looked past her to Puppet Papa. His eyes narrowed.

Then he dipped his head again. "*Goedemiddag, Meneer.*"

Milou's heart came to a shuddery stop—she watched in surprise as Puppet Papa returned the nod, and then a familiar, slightly squeaky, not-quite-baritone voice said, "*Goedemiddag.*"

Without a second glance, Rotman leaned on his cane and disappeared into the bustling crowd, a cloud of fishy pipe smoke trailing behind him. Sem appeared from behind Puppet Papa, his face paler than the moon.

With a *thud—thud—thud*, Milou's heart slowly started to beat normally again, but her palms were sweaty, and her legs felt like they might crumple beneath her.

"Let's go home."

Dusk seemed to be creeping in from all directions by the time Sem pedaled over the bridge to Poppenmill. Edda Finkelstein emerged from her house, dressed in full polder warden uniform once more, and waved to them.

Milou mustered up a small smile, then lifted Puppet Papa's arm to wave back.

Edda nodded once, then set off down her path toward her own gargoyle-gated canal bridge. Milou waited until the polder warden was walking down the road, her back to them, before stumbling wearily from the cargo bucket. She helped Sem carry Puppet Papa quickly into the mill.

Fenna was standing on the kitchen table, dangling a worm from her fingers, her lips pursed.

Milou frowned. "What are you——"

Fenna let out a sudden sharp whistle, in response to which there was a loud screech and a flash of white. Milou ducked as Mozart spiraled over her head, his wing flapping past her forehead. He swooshed down to Fenna's outstretched arm, took the worm, then landed on her shoulder and swallowed it in one gulp.

Standing at a safe distance by the walls, Egg and Lotta clapped. "Bravo!"

Fenna's responding giggle sent delighted shivers down Milou's spine.

They all turned to Milou and Sem, who set Puppet Papa down in his rocking chair and then presented the basket of food they'd bought.

Their smiles brightened.

"You did it," Lotta said.

"It's not all good news," Milou said, as Sem set the food down on the table. "Rotman's still in Amsterdam."

Egg frowned. "But I thought you said he had a tight shipping schedule to keep to?"

"He has no *crew*," Sem spat. "And I don't suppose he's very happy about that, or the fact he's still limping after our last encounter."

"Rotman's not our problem anymore," Egg said. "Not if we keep out of his way."

Milou sighed, every inch of her filled with weariness. "I'm sorry I was so awful earlier. I'm just scared that this will all be taken from us. And I'm scared Edda will be the one to take it from us."

"We're all scared," Lotta said softly. "But look at how far we've come already. It was a risk to leave the Little Tulip like we did. But we're making it work, and we'll continue to do so."

"You're right," Milou said. "I think I'm going to go to lie down before dinner. My head is spinning."

She climbed into Puppet Papa's cupboard bed, too tired even to make it to the next room. She'd just settled in when there was a sharp rap at the front door. She heard footsteps, then the creaking of hinges, followed by four startled gasps.

Milou peered through the cupboard-bed doors. Sem was standing by the windmill's entrance, and she could tell by the way his left leg was shaking that something was wrong. A woman stood on the threshold, and Milou could tell right away that it wasn't Edda Finkelstein.

"*Goedenavond*," Sem said overbrightly. "How can I help you?"

Milou squinted at the visitor. She was tall, wearing a long red coat, and her blonde hair was pulled into a tight bun on top of her head. In her arms she carried a large leather book and she seemed to be struggling under the weight of it.

"*Goedenavond*," said the woman, as she peered into the

gloom of the windmill. "I'm sorry for the late hour, but it took me a while to find this address."

The woman didn't look like a farmer, Milou decided. She was far too tidy looking; Milou doubted that her clothes had ever gotten within sneezing distance of a cow. Additionally, she doubted that farmers were known for carrying unusually large books around with them. Milou tried to read the writing on the cover. It looked familiar.

"We are not quite prepared to receive visitors *at this hour*," Sem said, leaning over slightly in an attempt to block the woman's wandering gaze.

"I am here to speak to Meneer Poppenmaker," she said. "Is he in?"

"Might I ask what your business is with our father?" Sem said curtly. "He is not feeling very well at the moment."

The woman tapped a gloved hand on the book. With the lettering no longer obscured, Milou's heart stuttered. The book *was* familiar. Egg had written in it just a few days ago.

"My name is Rose Speelman," the woman said. "And I am here on behalf of the Kinderbureau."

❄ TWENTY ❄

MILOU SHUFFLED BACKWARD AND peered over the edge of the half-closed cupboard-bed door. Her friends were all frozen to the spot, and Milou didn't need to see their faces to know they were as horrified as she was. Why was the Kinderbureau here? Had they made a mistake with the paperwork?

"Is Meneer Poppenmaker in?" the woman said, trying to peer over Sem's shoulder into the kitchen. "It's awfully cold out here." She made an exaggerated *brrrr* noise to emphasize her point.

"I, um . . . you," Sem stuttered. "He . . . you . . . well . . ."

"Good evening, *Mevrouw*," Lotta said, bumping Sem aside with her hip. "I am Lotta Poppenmaker. How may I help you?"

"Ah, yes," Speelman said, peering down at a sheet of paper in her hand. "Lotta. The clever one with more fingers than is usual. It is a pleasure to put faces to names. I do not usually get to see the faces. Yours is particularly pleasing. Now, if you wouldn't mind, I need to speak to your adoptive father urgently."

"Father is asleep. How about you come back another—"

"Is that him there? Meneer Poppen—"

"Shh. You'll wake him."

"I'm afraid I must insist on speaking with him."

Rose Speelman pushed past Lotta and Sem. Milou reached out and pulled the corner of the curtain they'd hung above the cupboard bed, hiding Puppet Papa fully behind it.

There was a sharp whistle, followed by a *screeeeeeeeeeeeeeeeeeech!* Mozart flew from his nest, spiraled down to block Speelman's path, and grabbed a piece of meat from Fenna's outstretched fingers before swooping back into the shadows.

"What is *that*?" shrieked Rose Speelman, clutching the record book tightly to her chest.

"That is Mozart," Lotta said. "It is his hunting time. He's hungry."

Speelman's eyes widened behind her glasses. She sidestepped cautiously toward the kitchen table and sank into a chair. "How peculiar," she said, eyeing Mozart's wardrobe-top nest warily. "Does he bite?"

Fenna smiled sweetly and nodded, holding up a bloodied fingertip.

HooOOooOOooOO!

"I really must speak with your father," Speelman said, keeping her gaze fixed firmly on Mozart's hiding place. She waved a hand in Milou's direction. "Please wake him."

Milou groaned silently. The woman wanted to speak to Bram. There was clearly only one way to get rid of her. Quietly and carefully, Milou took Puppet Papa's cross strings and lifted his head slightly.

"Lotta, *liefje*," Milou croaked as deeply and huskily as she could. "What is all the commotion about?"

She fake-coughed, heaving, wracking coughs that burned her throat. Peeking over the door, Milou saw Speelman hastily cover her nose and mouth with a handkerchief. The Kinderbureau agent shuffled her chair farther away from Puppet Papa.

"Meneer Poppenmaker," Speelman said, her voice slightly muffled by the handkerchief. "I'm awfully sorry to disturb you, but I am here on official orphan business." She tapped the record book again. "I was sent to audit the Little Tulip's adoption records and found an anomaly."

"But the paperwork was perfect," Egg cried. He was sitting himself in the chair beside the cupboard bed.

Milou grimaced; Egg did too. Speelman gave him a curious look under her spectacles.

"I mean," he spluttered, "Matron Gassbeek always prides herself on perfect paperwork. She says it's ever so important."

Milou let out another stream of coughing. She shook Puppet Papa's strings, making his shoulders shake. "And what—*cough*—anomaly—*cough cough*—would that—*cough*—be?"

Over the top of the door, she watched Rose Speelman curl her lip.

"It seems you did not pay the adoption fees."

Milou's blood turned to ice.

In their haste to leave, they had forgotten all about the fees.

Balancing the record book on the table, Rose Speelman flipped it open, shook her head until her spectacles fell onto her nose, and then cleared her throat.

"The items payable are as follows. Five orphans at a rate of ten guilders each. Payable upon receipt of the goods, which was *several* days ago. That means the final outstanding sum is fifty guilders, sir."

Rose Speelman snapped the record book closed again.

Fifty guilders.

That was more money than Milou had ever seen. How on earth were they going to get that sort of money together?

"I apologize for your having to come all this way," Milou

said gruffly, coughing. "However, the matron and I had an understanding—"

"Elinora Gassbeek is . . . um . . . no longer at the Little Tulip Orphanage," Speelman said. "I am afraid that we really do need to settle this affair right here, right now. Perhaps one of your new children can go and fetch the money. I will wait a while to rest my feet."

Milou's heart stuttered. Lotta looked up at her with wide eyes of panic. The others were trying their best to not look at anything.

"Um . . ." Milou said, clearing her throat. Her mind was racing, but she knew she had to keep talking. "I am afraid to say that I do not have the money just yet. This sickness, it has stopped me from—"

"With all due respect," Speelman said sternly. "You have taken five children without paying. Raising orphans is an expensive business, and we must recoup the costs if we are to keep the orphanages running. Business is business, Meneer Poppenmaker, and our records must be updated and in full order, or I wouldn't be doing my job properly, would I now? Regardless of your current condition, I must insist that you pay me today, or I will have no choice but to take the children back with me."

Lotta gasped. Fenna curled into a tight ball on her seat. Sem's left knee began to shake. Egg shot Milou a panicked look. Careful not to jostle the puppet strings, she opened a small wedge of curtain so that only Egg could see her. Then she pointed, with her nose, to the paper and quill beside him. Egg looked confused.

Speelman leaned forward, squinting at the alcove. "Did you hear what I said, Meneer Poppenmaker?"

Milou's stomach twisted painfully. She tried to speak but couldn't. This was it; there was no way out of it.

Lotta stepped in front of Speelman. "Forgive my manners, Mevrouw Speelman, for I have not offered you a refreshment. Can I get you a drink of water? Or perhaps some warm milk?"

"No thank you, dear," Speelman said, waving her away. "Not with this sickness around. Meneer Poppenmaker?"

Screeeeeeech!

Speelman shrieked in surprise, covering her head, and Milou used the distraction to whisper to Egg.

"Write a letter from Gassbeek saying she gave us more time to pay," she hissed. "And sign it with her signature. Can you remember it?"

Egg's eyes grew round and frightened, but he took the paper and turned his back to the rest of the room to do as Milou had asked. Milou took the puppet's strings again and lifted Puppet Papa's left arm, just as Egg shoved the paper onto Puppet Papa's lap.

"Lotta," Milou rasped. "Be a dear and pass Mevrouw Speelman this letter, would you?"

Speelman stood. "I can—"

"No, no," Lotta said, pushing Speelman's shoulders down to make her sit again. The agent landed on the seat with an "oof." "Honestly, you do not want this sickness. Poor Papa, it's not been pleasant for him."

Lotta hurried over, squeezed carefully past the curtain, and took the note from Puppet Papa's lap.

"Matron Gassbeek assured me that it was fine to settle the outstanding balance, once I was convinced these orphans would actually be suitable adoptees," Milou croaked. "Matron Gassbeek said she was happy to wait for the money—"

"As I said, Elinora Gassbeek is . . . uh . . . no longer in charge." Speelman said, eyeing Mozart warily. "It is not at all usual to make such an arrangement with adoptions."

"Yes, well, these children are anything but usual," Milou said hoarsely. "Matron Gassbeek was adamant that they were unadoptable. She said I would be doing the orphanage a favor by taking them off her hands. And I have to say, they are very useful around the mill, despite their peculiarities."

"I suppose they are a little peculiar," Rose Speelman said, glancing at each one in turn.

Lotta met her with a cold stare, Sem smiled unconvincingly, Fenna and Egg dipped their chins, and Milou wanted to roar in the woman's face but bit the inside of her cheek instead. Speelman drummed her fingers on Egg's letter. There was a long pause. She stared at Puppet Papa for so long that Milou was certain she'd realized something was amiss.

"Oh, I suppose I can just add this to the file for now," Speelman said at last, tucking the letter into the record book. "I should have my audit finished in a week or so, and as long as the fees are settled then—assuming you want to keep these peculiar children—then I see no harm in honoring Matron Gassbeek's offer."

"That is most kind," Milou croaked.

"It was a pleasure to meet you, Meneer Poppenmaker. I shall return in ten days for the fees."

"Ten days it is," Milou rasped. "Have a pleasant journey back to Amsterdam."

Speelman was only one step from the doorway when she turned, her brow furrowed. "Where is the fifth orphan?"

Lotta flinched.

"Milou is fetching medicine for me," Milou said gruffly.

"I see," Speelman said. "I'm sure you're taking as good care of her as she is of you. Anyway, I must be off. I have a long ride back with this beast."

She heaved the record book onto her shoulder and slipped out into the night.

❧ TWENTY-ONE ❧

THE FRONT DOOR CLOSED behind the Kinderbureau agent with a wind-slapped *thunk*. Milou dropped Puppet Papa's strings and let out a long breath. She joined the others at the window above the table, and they watched as Speelman stuffed the record book into the front basket of her bicycle, then pedaled off through the gates, over the bridge, and off down the darkened road.

Edda Finkelstein was still sitting by the flower garden, pulling weeds from the low wall as she watched the Poppenmill. The polder warden dipped her peaked cap as Speelman cycled past, and, even from this distance, Milou could see the Eyebrow of Curiosity raised high and indomitable.

Milou growled. "That woman just can't let us be, can she?"

Lotta let the curtain fall closed again. "If Edda were on to us, Speelman would have had more suspicion about Puppet Papa. No, Milou, this is our fault. We were careless in forgetting about the fees."

"Fifty guilders," Sem said, his voice small and hollow.

Mozart let out a sharp *screeeeech*.

"You could probably buy a small house for that," said Lotta.

"Or some tickets to Asia," said Egg.

"Or five *peculiar* orphans," Milou added.

No one spoke for several long minutes. Outside, the wind was picking up, howling and wailing, much like the despairing thoughts in Milou's head.

"We're going to have to buy our freedom then," she said finally. "We have ten days to work it out. We'll raise the money, pay her, and be rid of the Kinderbureau once and for all."

The others all looked at her as if she'd said something utterly stupid.

Milou's ears tingled softly. "I realize it's an improbable feat, but—"

"No," Lotta said, and Milou could almost see the cogs of her mind scrambling for a solution. But then she shook her head. "It really is *impossible* this time."

"But—"

"We should get some sleep," Sem said. "We should make the most of these warm beds in the few days we have left. We can talk about where to go next in the morning."

Milou looked at each of them in turn, unbelieving that they could give up so easily. "You want to *leave?*"

Egg shook his head. "We *have* to leave."

One by one, they turned away and headed to bed, except for Sem and Milou.

They sat at the kitchen table, feet meeting in the middle, and stared out the window, watching the frost glisten.

Neither spoke.

Weariness gripped every inch of Milou.

She couldn't let all this be taken from her. She *wouldn't*. She just had to be as brave and as clever as her parents and sister undoubtedly were, wherever they were.

There had to be a way for the five of them to stay.

The others were soon asleep, thin plumes of breath mist rising out of the blankets.

"That theater . . . it's the kind of thing you've always dreamed of, isn't it?" Sem said eventually.

"Almost," Milou replied.

She didn't need to mention that it was missing one vital thing: her family. Sem would know how she felt. He *always* seemed to know how she felt. They sat there silently for several long minutes, watching the dust motes swirl and the frost glisten.

"Do you want to know what my dream was?" Sem said quietly.

Milou's head snapped toward him.

"Cirque du Lumière," he said, smiling wistfully.

Milou frowned. Three years ago, a Parisian circus troupe had come to Amsterdam. The five of them had risked Gassbeek's cane by gathering on the street outside to watch the troupe parade down the street on their way to the park. They had each been given a poster for the show by a clown. The very same poster that was now one of her most treasured possessions: a keepsake of a moment of joy in an ocean of gloom. She still remembered the looks on all their faces that day. It was the first time she had ever seen Fenna really smile.

"You want to be a clown?"

He rolled his eyes. "Of course not. Though I'd probably make a good one."

"Well? What then?"

"A few days after the parade, when I was cleaning the gutters out in the front, a few of the acrobats were walking past. They had long cloaks over their outfits, but I recognized them right away. One of them, a woman with skin darker than Egg's, got the hem of her cloak torn by a passing tram. I ran over immediately and offered to stitch it up for her. We talked about the circus, and she said their costumes were always getting ripped; that there didn't seem to be enough thread in the world to keep up with their costume-repair needs."

Sem's voice trailed away. Milou waited quietly for him to continue, wondering why he had never told her any of this before. When he started speaking again, his expression had darkened.

"When I told her about some ideas I had for their costumes, she offered to take me on as an apprentice costume designer," he said quietly. "She wanted to go into the orphanage that very moment and arrange it with Gassbeek. The circus was due to leave for Denmark the following day."

Milou tried to swallow, but found her mouth was completely dry. "What happened?"

Sem gave a tight-lipped smile but refused to meet her gaze. "I told her I couldn't go, of course."

"Sem! Why on earth did you tell her that?"

Milou realized she already knew why he hadn't gone.

"I couldn't leave you four. I wanted to wait until each of you had a family before I left. And, well, I guess some things just aren't meant to be." He gave her a rueful smile. "You weren't the only one trying *not* to get adopted, you know. Although, to be honest, I didn't have to try very hard. These ears did most of the work for me."

All Milou could do was stare at him. Sem had given up his dream for them?

"I'm telling you this because you need to decide what's most important to you," Sem said. "We followed you here because it was our only chance at getting out of that place. Now we all risk getting sent back in ten days. Perhaps your family *will* come back for you one day, but the rest of us don't have that hope to cling on to. The freedom we have now is the only thing we've ever had that belongs to us."

"My family—"

"Your family *abandoned* you, Milou." Sem squeezed his eyes closed for a moment. When he opened them again, he looked nothing short of weary. "I'm not sure I'll ever understand why you are so fixated on finding those people. I couldn't care less if my birth family left me because they couldn't stand the sight of me or because they had other reasons. The fact is they left me, in a bucket no less, to live in the most miserable orphanage imaginable. The last thing I'll ever do is set foot in that place again."

"I won't let Speelman take you back there," Milou said.

"Then you agree that we will probably have to leave this place?"

Milou looked from Sem to the flickering flames in the middle of the room, at the five pairs of boots Fenna had hung neatly along the wall beside the front door.

This was her home.

It was *their* home.

Then she looked back at Sem, the boy who had given up his dream to stay with them and make sure they were looked after.

"I promise I will do whatever I must to keep all five of us safe," Milou said, wiping at a warm tear. "Even if that means leaving."

MILOU'S BOOK OF THEORIES

THEORY REANALYSIS

Werewolf Hunter Theory

New clues: claw marks in the theater and in Edda's workroom. A story, written by my sister, which includes a werewolf boy.

Theory viability: still possible.

Spy Theory

New clues: no sign of my mother, unexplained desertion of the windmill, no photographs or personal documents; my family was reclusive and clearly very secretive.

Theory viability: still possible.

Baby-Phobia Theory

New clues: no sign of a baby or any baby stuff.

Theory viability: still possible.

Unthinkable Theory

Clues: no dead bodies, no ghosts, no bloodstains.

Theory viability: There is still no point thinking about this one until the others are disproven or further evidence comes to light.

❊ TWENTY-TWO ❊

MILOU WOKE SHIVERING. SHE was still lying on the
kitchen table, cheek against the window frame, with a blanket
that Sem must have wrapped around her now tangled around
her ankles. She pulled it up to her shoulders and peeked out the
curtain.

Despite the frosty morning, the fields, canals, and main
road were still bustling with activity. Her gaze settled on one
particularly tall, long-legged figure that was weaving around
the bonnet-clad farmwives, nodding to passing cyclists, and
looking all too officious.

Edda Finkelstein.

There was a shuffling noise from the room next door, then

Egg appeared, his raven hair sticking up at all angles and his dark eyes squinting at the morning light.

"We should be packed and ready to run at a moment's notice," he said, rolling his polder map carefully and tucking it into his coal bucket.

"You're right," Milou said glumly, turning her attention back to the polder warden, who seemed to be keeping within eyeshot of Poppenmill at all times.

Egg continued to scour the kitchen for items to pack. "I've been thinking, perhaps we could head south, to France or Spain. At least it'll be warmer down there."

"Hmm-mmm."

Edda had paused to talk to the same group of women who had stood at the gates of Poppenmill just a couple of days previously. They huddled together. Sly glances were cast to the mill, eyebrows were raised, and Milou groaned and let the curtain fall closed.

"You're having second thoughts about leaving, aren't you?" Egg asked flatly.

"Surely you understand why I can't just leave here with nothing, Egg," she whispered. "You've always wanted answers just as much as I have. You want to find your family too, don't you?"

Egg sighed. "For me, it's never been about finding out who my parents are. It's about finding out who *I* am; it's hard to know for certain when I've never even met anyone else who looks like me."

"I know who you are. You're Egbert Poppenmaker, a boy destined to be the greatest cartographer the world has ever known. What does it matter if you look a little different from the people around you?"

"It matters a great deal," Egg said. "Because knowing where in the world I come from is just the first of the many answers *I* need."

Milou swallowed, then nodded in understanding.

"Perhaps we could head east to Bavaria," Egg said, changing the subject. "They have huge, ancient forests there we could hide in."

"I don't suppose it matters much where we go," Milou said glumly.

If they really were going to have to leave, it would mean she'd come all this way for nothing.

As they ate more potato stew for breakfast, the others discussed where they could go, how they might find food and shelter, and when they should leave. Milou nodded and hmm-mmmed along to the discussion, but her ears were tingling and rushing, her mind whirling with despair, and she didn't really hear them. After clearing the dishes, she slipped quietly away to the upper floors.

If they had to leave the windmill, then Milou was determined to find something, anything, that might help her eventually locate her family.

Milou spent the afternoon scouring the windmill from top to bottom, then from bottom to top and back down again, certain that her mother or father or sister must have left a clue hidden for her somewhere; anything that would tell her where the three of them had disappeared to. But all she had to show for her efforts several hours later was hair full of cobwebs, three fingers full of splinters, and a heart full of growing doubt.

Perhaps they didn't want to be found.

Perhaps Gassbeek had been right all along.

Perhaps her parents really hadn't wanted her.

By the time night fell once more, and despite the roaring hearth and warm blankets, Milou was shivering with unease, her ears prickling incessantly.

As the others got themselves ready for bed, Milou curled up once more on the kitchen table, peering carefully out the window as the polder warden continued her reign of scrutiny outside, if not on the road talking to their neighbors, then in her garden or tending to her pigs and chickens, but always within eyeshot and always looking as curious as ever.

"Here," Egg said, suddenly on the table beside her. He put the Carnival of Nightmares notebook in Milou's hands. "We should travel light, but I don't see why you couldn't take this."

Milou's ears tingled as she ran a hand over the etched drawing of the Night Tree. "Thank you."

He peeked through the other end of the curtain.

"Once we leave, you'll never have to worry about her again," Egg said, looking very worried. "Though she . . . she still has my shawl. I can't leave without it."

"If she doesn't return it tomorrow, I'll get it back for you," Milou promised. "Even if I have to knock her door down to get it."

Egg smiled. "That won't draw attention to us in the slightest."

They watched silently as Edda handed a basket of eggs to Arno, then waved goodbye. She crossed the little bridge over the canal, her eyes never leaving the mill. Then, halfway down her stone path, she stopped, turned, and walked up to the oak tree.

Milou pressed her face a little closer to the glass.

The polder warden stood in front of the tree, placing one hand against the trunk. Her shoulders seemed to sag slightly. Then, just as abruptly, she dropped her hand, stood up tall, and walked all the way to her house without a single glance back at the mill. Milou was still frowning in confusion long after Edda's front door had closed behind her.

"Hmm," Egg said.

"What?"

"I hadn't noticed before, but this tree"—he tapped Liesel's book, lying beside her—"looks an awful lot like that tree." Then he tapped the window.

Prickles spread from her ears down her back.

Egg was right.

The oak tree *was* the Night Tree.

Milou waited until all the lights in Edda's house were out before slipping out the front door and hurrying toward the tree. She didn't light the lantern she'd brought with her until she was safely hidden beneath the oak's skeletal canopy.

The tingling on her ears intensified the closer she got, spreading to the back of her neck as she reached out, just like Edda had, and touched it. Goose bumps erupted all up her arms.

This tree must have heard at least a century's worth of secrets.

Maybe, just maybe, it had a secret only for her.

Lotta must have been right about the coordinates after all; Milou's parents wanted her to find this tree, she was certain of it.

Her ears tingled as if in agreement.

Holding the lantern up to the gnarled bark, Milou made a lap of the tree's trunk, running her fingers over it. Halfway around it, she found her first clue.

Claw marks.

They were hard to make out since moss had grown over them in places, meaning they must have been there for quite a long time, but Milou was certain they were the same as the ones on her coffin and the ones in Edda's workshop. She spread her fingers out over the marks, their size confirming her suspicions.

Her heart racing, Milou glanced back at the polder warden's house, which was dark and still. Edda was *definitely* connected to all this somehow. Whatever role she'd played in the Poppenmakers' disappearance, Milou would find out.

Setting the lantern on a branch above her, Milou stepped onto the flower garden wall and hoisted herself up onto the first branch. In the glow of her lantern, she found herself staring at more marks gouged into the tree.

Names. Tens of them. Some covered over in moss, others—like Sanne's and Arno's—carved more recently. Milou read them all. It wasn't until she got to the second branch that she found one that started a fresh wave of ear tingles.

Edda

Milou stifled a growl and climbed higher.

More names, none of which she knew.

She wasn't even halfway up yet, but already she could tell why the polder people liked to climb this tree. The only view that rivaled it was from the windmill's rooftop hatch.

Arms aching and chest heaving, Milou finally got to one of

the topmost branches. It was a long drop to the ground below, and for a moment, she sat there hugging the branch with her eyes closed, trying to stop the world from spinning. When the dizziness eased, she opened her eyes again.

There, right in front of her, were two names she recognized.

Thibault and Liesel

Her ear tingling turned into a storm of tiny, icy-cold prickles, and Milou rubbed at her ears grumpily.

"Thibault," she whispered, the foreign-sounding name feeling funny in her mouth. It was the same name she'd seen in Liesel's book. Milou felt an unfamiliar twist in her belly, as if she'd eaten something too sour or too hot. It should have been her name there, not Thibault's. It should have been her sitting up here with her sister, sharing secrets and telling stories, gazing out across the polder and up at the stars, but this boy, Thibault, had been there instead.

Milou carefully clambered across to the next branch, using the glow of the moon to see by now. She had to climb across two more, then one higher, before she found another carving, etched just beside a small hollow.

Her fingers shook as she traced each small line.

Br—m and An——ese

Milou wiped at the moss, but the carving was so old that her scrubbing at it made little difference in its legibility. Still, Milou was certain it said Bram. And the name beside it must have been her mother's name.

Her ear tips became a maelstrom of prickles.

Milou let her hand drop to her side, then her gaze settled on the hollow.

Wedged inside was a small red bundle, half the size of her fist.

Milou pulled it out and held it in her open palm. Upon closer inspection, she realized it was a carefully folded handkerchief. Squeezing it, she could feel something small and hard inside. She turned it over and lifted one edge. Milou's stomach lurched, and a small gasp left her lips.

In the corner, embroidered in white silk thread, was a name:

A. Poppenmaker

Finally, she had proof of her mother.

An initial, if not a whole name.

She carefully unrolled the age-crusted handkerchief completely.

Two golden rings glinted up at her.

Wedding bands.

Milou tilted one of the rings up toward the moonlight.

In the very same tiny type font as on her pocket watch was an inscription.

Beneath the stars I found you

Her ears rushing wildly, Milou looked up, at the bright constellations that twinkled above her, at the way the moon shone down, turning everything below it a silvery gray.

Her parents had climbed this tree to watch the night sky.

And here she was, twelve years later, sitting in the same spot they had. From this height, she could see straight through the theater's hole-pocked roof to the marionette on the stage, who stood, haloed by the moonlight, as if ready to begin her dance beneath the stars.

Milou gasped.

The solution seemed so obvious now.

She wasn't meant to find *them*.

They were supposed to find *her*.

They had lost her. Now Milou had everything she needed to let them know that she had made it home.

And maybe, just maybe, it would also get her the money they needed to get Speelman off their backs at the same time.

❊ TWENTY-THREE ❊

THE THEATER STILL SMELLED moldy, despite the fact that they had left the door open for days now. Dust motes floated in the columns of moonlight that streamed in through the hole in the roof, illuminating every cobweb and every bit of grime. The ballerina puppet was coated in a new layer of frost, its strings like stalactites. Milou sat her friends down on the front row of the theater as she explained her money-making, parent-summoning plan.

"A puppet show?" Egg asked, incredulous. "In *here*?"

"Yes!" Milou beamed. "It's such an obvious solution, isn't it?"

"Not really . . ."

"A grand reopening will be the talk of Amsterdam and the answer to *all* our problems. Not only will it make us the money we need, but as soon as my parents hear about the show, they'll know I've returned and hurry home to me."

Mozart, who was awake and sitting on Fenna's shoulder, let out a loud *screeeeech*.

"It will be a huge task to get this place looking like it once was," Lotta said. "And it will cost money too."

"On the contrary," Milou said, feeling increasingly pleased with her idea. "This place already looks fabulously horrendous."

Sem shook his head. "People will expect a certain kind of quality where this theater is concerned. This looks like the scene of a horror show."

"But that is my point, Sem Poppenmaker." Milou grinned. "Use those big ears of yours to listen properly. The mystery of the Poppenmakers' disappearance has been the source of gossip and intrigue for years. Everyone, except Edda, of course, is too scared to even set foot on this land."

"You're not convincing us yet," Egg groaned.

"Egg could paint a few monsters on that wall over there," Milou mused. "We could tear the velvet seats up a little bit more and add some dirt to the carpet. Oh! And we should do the show at night, when it's dark and cold like it is now."

She realized her friends still looked unconvinced.

"Haven't my stories shown you that people *love* to be

scared?" Milou said. "We will *terrify* them, and they will pay through the nose for the experience."

Lotta's eyebrows began to unfurrow. Fenna nodded. Even Mozart let out a *hooOOooOOoo* of seeming agreement. Sem's face broke into a huge, crooked grin.

"You truly are an evil genius, Milou Poppenmaker," he said.

Milou grinned back. "I know."

"It'll still cost money to set up," Lotta said, though her expression was more thoughtful than dubious. "We'd need to make more puppets, and we'd need to add some lighting to the room. You can't operate more than one puppet on your own, so I could mechanize some of them. And perhaps we could install some speaking tubes, so your voice can be projected. We have some of the materials we need. I could ask Edda for some of the other bits; that way, it shouldn't be too expensive. I'm sure she won't mind lending it to us, were I to accept her offer of apprenticeship."

Milou opened her mouth to protest, then shut it again. She gave Lotta a short nod; they would need more money than they could make selling dolls if her plan was to work.

"We should be saving any money we earn for our escape plan," Egg said. "Not throwing it away on a plan that has no guarantees of success."

"I promise," Milou said, "if my plan doesn't work, we will have everything in place for fleeing. Please, Egg, give this a chance. We have the opportunity not only to get the Kinder-bureau off our backs for good but to really make something of ourselves."

"We have *nine* days left, Milou."

"Then we will hold our show in eight days and have one left over should it not work out the way we hope. It'll be tight, but *not* impossible."

Egg stared at her hard for a few moments, then nodded. "Fine."

Milou resisted the urge to hug him, since his expression hinted that he was still apprehensive. She gave him a grateful smile instead.

"What show will we put on then?" Lotta asked. "'The Princess and the Werewolf,' perhaps?"

"No," Milou said, dropping her voice to a raspy growl. "I'm thinking something *much* more terrifying than that."

She climbed up on the stage and did a pirouette, her cloak flying around her.

"Welcome, ladies and gentlemen," she said, loudly and gruffly, "to the Theater of Terrors. Prepare to be spooked, prepare to tremble in your seats, prepare to be awed. I give you . . ."

She paused dramatically, then, in her best werewolf voice, said:

"*A Carnival . . . of Nightmares!*"

✴

February arrived the very next day, with a nose-numbing frost that drove most of the inhabitants of the polder indoors. Mist hung thick and low over the canals, refusing to lift. Milou hoped it would stay this gloriously gloomy until the night of the puppet show in seven days.

Lotta set off to Edda's house with her toolbox, a firm promise to not ask questions, and a glint of delight in her eyes, as soon as the sun had risen. The others headed to the theater, to begin the arduous task of preparing the stage for their show. By the afternoon, they had new curtains hanging from the rails, a huge Night Tree painted on the stage's back wall, and rumbling stomachs all around.

That night, as Fenna and Sem prepared dinner from the last of the food they'd bought at the market, Liesel's book lay open on the table in front of Milou, a blank page staring up at her. She needed an ending for the tale, but for the life of her, Milou had no idea how to finish Theodora's story. Every time she tried to think about what might lie beyond those carnival gates, her mind drifted to her family.

Would they come to the show?

Two days later, they had Theodora and Hendrik puppets, needle-pricked fingers, and a rumble of excitement that they might actually pull this show off. Except for one irksome thing. Milou still couldn't think of an ending.

"My hands are going to fall off at this rate," Egg said,

setting a poster aside to dry next to a teetering stack of more posters. "And we need more ink . . . again."

"Lotta will be back soon," Milou said. "She can give you some more money for ink."

Fenna set a tray of steaming-hot stroopwafels out in front of them. Sem immediately put down his sewing and tucked in. From her apron, Fenna pulled a strip of dried meat. She held it up and whistled softly. Wings fluttered from the cupboard top, and Mozart swooped down in a loose spiral, taking the meat from her fingers.

"He's getting better at flying," Sem said, syrup dribbling down the side of his mouth.

Fenna's responding smile was bright enough to light up the dark side of the moon. Milou had even, that very morning, heard Fenna humming quietly as she baked. It seemed that this puppet show was working magic in more ways than she'd expected: It was making them happy.

The kitchen door opened with a howl of wind, and Lotta stumbled in, stamping her clogs loose of snow. "You need to come to the theater," she said. Her nose was bright pink from the cold. "Right now."

"It's too cold," Egg said, shuddering.

"Trust me," Lotta said. She hurried over to the table, grabbing two stroopwafels. "What Edda and I have done is worth a few frostbitten noses. Come on!"

"Edda?" Milou asked, frowning. "What is Edda doing in the theater?"

"Just come," Lotta said.

It was no warmer inside the theater than it was outside it. Edda Finkelstein was standing by the stage, holding a strange metal box. Milou bristled at the sight of her, the unease she felt around the clock maker refusing to shift. Especially now that the Kinderbureau was suspicious of them.

"Aha!" Edda said, her voice muffled by her scarf. "You're just in time. Watch this."

Edda pressed a button on the top of the metal box. There was a low hum, then a crackle. Edda grinned at them as the stage erupted with the light of hundreds of little bulbs, twinkling like stars.

Milou couldn't help it: Her jaw slackened. "Is that . . . ?"

"Electricity?" Lotta said. "Yes. And Edda also thinks we should open the theater with a fireworks display. Just imagine!"

"There is a fireworks stall in the city market," Edda said, putting the metal box on the stage. "I should get back home; Meneer Catticus needs feeding. Thank you for your help this morning, Lotta."

"No, thank *you*," Lotta said, beaming at Edda. "Your help means the world to us."

"You are most welcome," Edda said, her eyes meeting

Milou's. "Do send my regards to Bram, won't you? I hope this weather isn't making him feel worse."

Milou felt another twinge of unease. She nodded.

"Oh," Edda said, reaching into her satchel. "Egg, I almost forgot. Here is your shawl. I managed to get most of the charcoal off it, but not all, I'm afraid."

She held out a folded bundle of bright red, orange, and yellow silk. If not for the familiar egg-shaped pattern and sooty patch, Milou wouldn't have believed it was the same shawl.

Egg just stared at it.

"It's Javanese batik, I believe," Edda said, unfolding it and wrapping it carefully around his neck. "Though I can't be a hundred percent sure. If you could find someone who has traveled to that part of the world, they might be able to confirm it."

"Thank you," Egg said, his voice choking with emotion. He rubbed at a tear. "Thank you."

Fenna shuffled up to him, wrapping an arm around his middle. Edda smiled kindly, then she gathered her toolbox and left. Lotta trailed along, talking excitedly about the chemical compounds of fireworks. Milou followed them to the theater door.

"Why are you scowling again?" Lotta asked, when Edda had disappeared around the side of the building. "You're not going to start on about Edda, are you?"

"There's just something about her," Milou said. "Something that makes me feel like that woman will be our downfall."

Lotta raised an Edda-like eyebrow. "Are your magical danger-sensing ears telling you this?"

Milou flinched. "No. Logic is. Nothing about her makes sense."

Lotta was quiet for a moment. Milou avoided her gaze for as long as she could, worried she'd see smug satisfaction in Lotta's eyes at her admission, but when she looked up, Lotta just looked thoughtful.

"I think Edda had a husband once," Lotta said finally. "I found a pair of men's boots by the back door. Far too big for her."

"Maybe he died?"

Lotta shrugged. "Maybe. There's a sadness about her that she doesn't let show very often. The kind of sadness I imagine someone might have when they miss someone dearly." She turned back to Milou. "I honestly think she'll do us no harm, even if she did learn the truth about us. She's nothing like Gassbeek was. She's good. I don't know how I know that, but I do. Deep down in the pit of my belly, I know it's true."

"That sounds like a very unscientific hypothesis."

Lotta smiled. "Maybe I have magical goodness-sensing guts."

"I'm still not convinced."

"Will this convince you?"

Lotta grabbed Milou's hand and dropped a drawstring pouch into it. Milou squeezed it. It felt like it was filled with coins. Lots of coins.

"What's this?"

"An advance from Edda, for you to place an advertisement in the national paper."

"An advertisement?"

"Your father isn't likely to be in Amsterdam, is he? If you want him to hear about the show, then you need the message to be spread farther than just the city. It costs two guilders to place a weeklong ad. Edda said I could borrow the money from her."

Milou felt tears prickle in the corners of her eyes. "Two guilders . . . don't you want it to go toward the adoption fees?"

Lotta shook her head. "Not if it can help you, no."

"Thank you," she whispered.

"Tomorrow then," Lotta said brightly.

"Tomorrow what?"

"Tomorrow we go to Amsterdam and let everyone know that, for one night only, the Poppenmaker theater is open once more."

MILOU'S BOOK OF THEORIES

Beneath the stars they'll find me

Here is the advertisement I plan on placing in the newspaper. I've even left a hidden message in the underlined words. My family is clever enough to work it out.

Bram Poppenmaker presents . . .

"A Carnival of Nightmares"

Meneer Poppenmaker requests the honor of <u>your</u> presence at the Theater of Terrors. "A Carnival of Nightmares" is a deliciously monstrous story, written by Bram's <u>daughter</u>, that <u>is</u> sure to have you squealing in delighted horror. The show will be brought to life with full-sized puppets, mechanized contraptions, projected acoustics, and electrical lighting! Goose bumps guaranteed, or your money <u>back</u>.

This Saturday, dusk

Poppenmill, near Amstelveen

Tickets: 50 cents per person

❧ TWENTY-FOUR ❧

THEY SET OFF FOR Amsterdam at first light, all five of them on Bram Poppenmaker's cargo bicycle. Milou was squeezed into the back of the crate, clutching a bagful of posters and trying not to choke on Fenna's hair as the wind whipped it around her face. Behind her, Sem panted as he pedaled at speed toward the city. The polder air tingled with the smallest promise that spring was on its way, and hope as she'd never felt it bloomed in Milou's chest. Today was the day that she would send the secret message to her parents. Soon they would know that she had come home.

"The canals are thawing!" Lotta yelled from the front of the bicycle. "Look!"

Milou pushed aside a handful of Fenna's red curls and peered over the edge of the crate. Sure enough, the ice was patchy. Grass was poking free from the blanket of frost, and the everlasting mist shimmered like spun gold.

"It won't be too much longer until the tulips are out," Lotta said. "That would be a sight worth painting, don't you think, Egg?"

Wedged near Milou's other knee, Egg was staring silently down at his shawl, running one hand over the pattern.

"One day soon," she said, more softly, "when we're finally safe from Rotman and the Kinderbureau, we'll find someone who can tell us more about Java."

Egg frowned up at her. "There's no reason I can't try to find someone today."

"Yes, there is. We have an important mission. It'll have to wait, Egg, I'm sorry."

Egg gave her an odd look, then turned his face away from her.

Milou felt a sharp stab of regret in the pit of her stomach, recognizing his pained expression for what it was: a desperate hunger for answers. That same desperation gnawed at every inch of her too. She'd help Egg find his answers soon enough, in any way she could, but right now they all needed to focus on their mission.

There was too much at stake to worry about anything else.

That's what she told herself, over and over, as Sem pedaled them onward and as Egg slumped down further into himself, burying his face in his shawl.

Less than an hour later, they arrived at the outskirts of the city and tumbled, stiff-legged and aching, out of the crate as Sem propped the bicycle against a railing. Lotta had equipped them each with a bag of posters, a hammer, a pouch of nails, and a hasty lesson on how not to squish their fingers. Two of Milou's fingers were still throbbing, but she barely noticed. Her stomach was full of jittery impatience.

"Milou and I will put posters up in the inner ring of the city," Lotta said. "Sem, you do all along the Prinsengracht canal. Egg and Fenna, you will do all along the Keizersgracht canal. One poster every ten meters. Avoid the Little Tulip, and wear your scarves up high over your nose at all times, just in case. We will meet by the clock tower in Sophiaplein at four and then stop off at the newspaper on our way home."

"Don't be late," Milou added, her fingers seeking the reassuring presence of the coin pouch in her pocket. "The newspaper closes at five."

Still refusing to meet her gaze, Egg nodded, grabbed Fenna's hand, and disappeared into the crowd. Sem dipped his cap, then set off with a jaunty lope toward the nearest bridge. Hefting their bags over their shoulders, Milou and Lotta set off toward the busy market square on the other side of the canal. They rounded a corner and emerged among a rippling tide of walking canes, winged bonnets, clogs, boots, cloaks, wicker baskets, and smiling faces. Milou had never seen so many people in one place before. It seemed that the whole of Amsterdam was out to enjoy the first snowless day in months.

The market stretched out in front of them, stalls lining both sides of the street. The air smelled of a thousand wonderful fragrances. Each new gust of wind carried a new scent: spice, smoke, caramel, fruit, fish, shoe polish. It wasn't just food and clothing being offered, though; there were Bavarian broom sellers, an umbrella repairman from London, a man selling artificial limbs, children selling ribbons, carpet beaters, and a woman with very few teeth offering mustachio-trimming services. In the middle of it all was a huge street organ, decorated with a row of dancing wooden swans. A lively symphony burst from its pipes, and a smiley-faced man stood beside it, shaking a money tin to the rhythm.

"It's so noisy," Lotta yelled, her smile gone as she dodged around a circle of dancing children. "And cramped."

Milou was too busy gawping to respond. Her eyes settled on a bell-shaped tent, wedged between a clog stall and a tram stop. The tent's curtains, Milou noticed, were drawn tightly closed. She had to squint to read the hand-painted sign attached to the side.

It read: **SPIRITUALIST FROM BOHEMIA—SEANCES AND FORTUNE-TELLING.**

A shiver ran down the back of Milou's neck, and she found

herself walking toward the tent—until six fingers closed on her forearm and pulled her back.

"Who in their right mind would buy rabbit's feet?" Lotta said, nodding toward a peddler in a fur coat. She handed Milou the hammer and some nails, then uncurled a poster and held it up against a wooden signpost. "People's silly superstitions can be so cruel."

"I bet Gassbeek would have loved those," Milou said, bringing the hammer down. "She'd have probably worn them as earrings— Ow!"

Lotta caught the hammer as it fell, and rolled her eyes. "How can you miss the nail so often?"

"Uhh dunnuuh," Milou said, sucking a new lump on her thumb.

With three short *tack-tack-tacks*, Lotta drove a nail into the top of the poster. She added another to the bottom and then stepped back to examine their handiwork. "Just another ninety-nine to go."

They walked ten stretched-leg paces down the street, and Lotta tacked another poster to some scaffolding, and then another one to the back of an advertisement for lace doilies. Milou's gaze kept drifting back to the spiritualist's tent, wondering who was inside it. A sudden bell-tinkling made her jump. A tram was negotiating its way through the market, and the bay-colored horse pulling it snorted at Milou as she staggered out of its path. Milou turned to find Lotta watching the tram with pure mischief glinting in her eyes. She grabbed Milou's arms, and they followed it to the tram stop.

"I'm going to nail a poster to the back of it," Lotta whispered. "That way, our advertisement will travel all over Amsterdam. Keep an eye out, would you?"

She disappeared around the side of the tram as people began climbing out of the carriage. Milou crossed her arms and tried to look inconspicuous, looking lazily up and down the market. Once again, her eyes were drawn to the strange tent, now right beside her. Then, before she knew what she was doing, she reached up to touch it, the curtains drew back, and a girl emerged.

She wore a long green cloak, the hood pulled up over her head; long wisps of white-blonde hair spilling out the sides of it. Her eyes were painted in a way that made them look almost cat-like, and her lips were stained bloodred. Milou's gaze dropped to just below the girl's chin, where a white, round object dangled from a chain. It was, Milou realized in horror, not a pendant but a human eyeball.

"Gah!" Milou pulled her arm to her chest and staggered backward a step.

The girl's eyes snapped to hers. Long, ring-bedecked fingers reached up to touch the eyeball on her neck. Then a slow smile crept onto those blood-red lips.

"It's porcelain," the girl said in a heavily accented voice. She held it up for Milou to see more clearly, then tapped with a long nail to show it was as hard as stone. "See? It's an artificial eye. It belonged to a boy one hundred years ago. He lost his right eye in a sword fight with his little sister."

"Oh," Milou said. And then she frowned. "How could you possibly know all that?"

The girl's smile twitched at both corners. "Because his spirit told me."

Milou felt a tiny pinch at her right earlobe. She gasped, but before she could even reach up to her ear the sensation was gone. The girl was squinting over Milou's shoulder, holding the eyeball over her right eye. Milou followed the girl's gaze, but there was no one behind her. She could just about hear the quiet *tap-tap-tap* of Lotta's hammer. When she turned back, the girl was staring intently at her. Milou wondered how old she was; certainly older than she and Lotta, but it couldn't be by much.

"Let me read your fortune," the girl said, pulling the tent curtain open behind her. She lowered her voice. "I could give you the answers you most crave."

Milou opened her mouth to respond, but her ear tingled. She looked up and found the girl squinting past her shoulder again. Once again, Milou found nothing at all behind her.

"Thank you, but no," Milou said. She touched the coin pouch. "I already know what I need to know about my future."

"But what about your past—"

The girl snapped her mouth closed, again looking past

Milou. This time, Milou turned to find Lotta standing there, hammer in hand and scowling hard.

"We should get going, Milou," Lotta said, taking her hand and pulling her away.

"Do your ears ever—" the girl whispered as Milou brushed past, but Lotta increased her pace and dragged her away before she could hear the rest.

"Try to keep away from the kooks, would you?" Lotta said.

"She said she could read my fortune."

"Honestly, Milou!" Lotta groaned, stopping at another signpost. "Palmistry is such a sham. There is no scientific evidence whatsoever that the future can be predicted. You shouldn't waste your money on that nonsense."

"She doesn't read palms. I think she uses the eyeball of a dead boy."

Lotta stopped, mid-hammer strike, and gave her a disgusted look.

"Forget it," Milou said, not wanting to start an argument. "Let's just hurry up. I don't want to miss the newspaper. And you're right, I don't need to resort to silly superstitions to find my family."

"Good," Lotta said. "Now let's get those fireworks, so we can hurry back to meet the others."

Milou glanced back behind her. The tent curtains were closed again, the girl nowhere in sight.

Sem was already waiting at the rendezvous point when Milou and Lotta arrived just before four o'clock. He was sitting on a bench, covered in pigeons.

"I tripped over a bag of grain," Sem said with a lopsided shrug. "I managed to scoop most of it back into the bag, so they didn't charge me."

Milou stifled a smile and wiped some grain from his hat into her hand. She held it up to a gray pigeon. Lotta dug a hand into her bag and pulled out a squashed bread roll. They watched the clock tower as they ate, swiping away greedy pigeons. At quarter past four, there was still no sign of Egg and Fenna.

"What's taking them so long?" Milou said, her patience waning with each tick of the grand clock.

"They probably just lost track of time," Lotta said. "They'll be here soon."

Another five minutes ticked by achingly slowly.

"I'm not waiting anymore." Milou stood, brushing crumbs off her chest. "You can stay and wait if you like. You can tell Egg I'm not happy. He knows how important this is."

"He wouldn't do this on purpose," Sem said.

"He's angry at me. Maybe he's trying to make a point."

Sem shook his head, looking up and down the square with worried eyes. "No, something's not right."

Milou opened her mouth to respond, but then caught a

glimpse of a figure running across the other side of the square. An embroidered silk cap bobbed through the crowd, and then Fenna emerged just ahead of them, panting and panic-stricken, tears streaming down each cheek. Sem was on his feet and bounding toward her in an instant. Milou and Lotta hurried after him.

"What's wrong?" Lotta asked at the same time as Sem asked, "Where's Egg?"

Fenna's fists were balled up, and she was gasping and gulping. Lotta took Fenna's hands in her own and rubbed them. "Take a deep breath," she said.

Fenna shook her head. She pointed behind her.

"Did he get lost?" Milou asked.

Fenna groaned and shook her head again.

"Is he hurt?" Sem asked. "Did something happen to him?"

Fenna squeezed her eyes closed and took a few steadying breaths.

"What happened?" Lotta asked. "Where is he?"

Fresh tears spilled out of Fenna's eyes. Milou reached up and wiped them away with shaky fingers. Then, in a quiet voice, Fenna spoke:

"Rotman."

❊ TWENTY-FIVE ❊

THE CLOCK TOWER STRUCK the quarter hour, but
it was Fenna's raspy voice that rang as loud and clear as church
bells in Milou's ears. It took a few stunned moments before the
significance of what she'd said finally sank in.

"Did Rotman snatch him?" Sem asked finally.

Fenna opened her mouth as if to speak again, then bit her
lip and shook her head no instead. Tears streamed down both
of her cheeks.

"But you saw Rotman?" Lotta asked.

Fenna nodded.

"Did Egg go up to him?"

Fenna nodded again.

"You must have seen where they went."

Fenna waved at the crowds, miming a frantic search and a hopeless defeat.

"So you don't know where they went?"

"No."

Her voice was no more than a whisper, and Milou wasn't sure if she'd imagined it or not. Fenna collapsed onto the bench and buried her face in her hands.

Sem pinched his brow. "I'll go and ask around, see if anyone knows where we can find Rotman."

He was loping off into the crowds before any of them had a chance to respond. Milou's fingers clenched hard around the coin pouch in her pocket. She and Lotta sat on either side of Fenna on the bench. The three of them huddled together, silent and morose, minds racing. What was Egg thinking?

Sem appeared in front of them, grim-faced and panting. "No one has heard of Rotman," he said, breathlessly. "Nor his ship. I asked in every shop along the square. We're going to have to search every dock, one at a time."

"The port of Amsterdam is roughly roughly twenty-five kilometers long," Lotta said. "One thousand, five hundred acres of waterway. Nearly five thousand acres of landmass. There will be hundreds of ships across eleven major docks." When they all stared in amazement at her, Lotta added softly:

"It took me and Egg over a week to estimate that."

"That would take us hours to search," Milou said, her stomach twisting with worry and regret.

This was her fault. She should have known it would be too tempting for Egg to follow the clue Edda had given him. He'd been waiting over twelve years for something, anything, after all. And Milou had insisted he wait *longer*.

"We don't have hours," Sem said. "Anything could happen to Egg in that time. We need to find him quickly."

"Perhaps we should split up," Lotta said. "Cover more ground."

"No," Sem said. "No more splitting up. If we'd stuck together earlier, perhaps we could have stopped him from going in the first place."

Fenna stiffened. Milou wrapped an arm around her. "It's not your fault, Fen. You couldn't have stopped him."

The clock tower chimed the half hour. Milou got to her feet and took her coin pouch out of her pocket. "Let's go," she said. "We've wasted enough time."

"Milou," Lotta said crossly. "You can't really be thinking about the newspaper—"

"No. We're going to use this money to find Egg. There's only one person I can think of who might be able to find out where he is."

❧

The market was almost deserted when they arrived; half the stalls had been packed away as a dreary dusk settled over the city. Milou sprinted over the cobbles, the cold air burning her lungs. The others followed. Milou noticed with relief that the bell-shaped tent was still there. She slowed to a jog, a stitch beginning under her ribs, elbowing her way past a few peddlers and around wagons to get to it. The tent's curtains were drawn closed, but a thin strip of light spilled out around the bottom.

"Milou," Lotta said, her voice full of protest.

"Have you got any better ideas?"

Lotta fell silent, but her expression remained fixed. Beside her, Fenna eyed the tent with obvious apprehension. Sem's face was shadowed beneath the brim of his hat, but Milou could just about make out the tight line of his mouth.

"I just don't like this," Lotta grunted.

"I can go in alone," Milou said. "I won't be long."

"No," Sem said sternly. "I'm coming in with you."

There was a rustle and then the tent's curtains opened. The girl stood there, smiling pleasantly, her catlike eyes glinting in the lamplight. "Ah, there you are!" she said. "I'd almost given up waiting for you to come back."

Goose bumps rose all over Milou's neck. In the distance, the clock tower struck the fifth hour, and Milou tried to ignore the knotted lump of disappointment that sat heavy in her stomach. All that mattered was finding Egg.

"Are you all here for a reading?" the girl asked. "Four fortunes might be a little more than I can manage at this hour. Perhaps—"

"No," Milou cut in. "We don't want our fortunes told." She tried to keep her voice strong-sounding, but it came out all rough around the edges. "We've lost someone. Can you . . . can you find people?"

The girl stopped smiling. "Is this person alive or dead?"

"Alive," Sem said. "He went missing about an hour ago. Not far from here."

"I can pay you," Milou added. She uncurled her fingers from the pouch and held it up. "Please. It's urgent."

"I'm much better at finding the dead than the living."

Sem let out an angry breath. "Can you tell us where he is or not?"

The girl was silent for a moment, then nodded her head once. "Probably."

"Good." Milou grabbed her hand, shoved the coin pouch into it, then pushed past into the tent.

The inside was just big enough for a table and three chairs. There were animal skulls hanging from the frame above their heads. Candlelight flickered and incense burned, making a hazy effect that left Milou feeling somewhat dizzy. She collapsed into one of the chairs and took off her gloves. Sem followed. He took off his hat and stared openmouthed around the room. Milou fidgeted nervously. How many more minutes had it been now? Would Egg be locked away somewhere dark and cold and alone? Was he frightened? Was he hurt?

The girl sat opposite them and dropped the coin pouch on the table. "It's mostly for show," she said, as Sem continued to gawk. "People only seem to believe me if I add all this theater and pomp."

Milou sucked in an angry breath. "Is this all just an act then?"

"I think you *know* it's real, or you wouldn't be here."

"I don't *know* anything about any of this," Milou spat, her voice cracking.

The girl gave a pointed look over Milou's shoulder, like she had done earlier that day, and cocked her head. "Don't you?"

Milou glowered, her ears tingling unpleasantly, but she didn't look behind her this time. She knew there wouldn't be anyone there. Doubt gnawed at her. Had she just handed over their money to a charlatan? Was she wasting precious time that Egg didn't have? Milou didn't know what to believe anymore. Had it been any other time, she would have wanted to ask this girl a thousand questions about ghosts and fortune-telling and that long-dead boy's eyeball. She'd have marveled at the theater and pomp, filled with curiosity and intrigue. But in that moment, Milou didn't feel curious or intrigued. She felt scared and desperate, because Rotman had Egg, and this strange, unsettling girl might be the only hope Milou had of getting him back again. The air seemed to chill as the two girls stared at each other.

"What's your name?" Sem said nervously. "We never introduced ourselves properly."

The girl reached up and pulled her hood down, shaking her long silvery hair loose. "My name," she said, "is Emiliana."

Sem's nose turned bright red. "I'm S . . . Sem Poppen-maker. This is my . . . uh . . . this is Milou."

"The puppet makers. Yes, I saw the posters you put up. Everyone seems very excited about it. If I weren't leaving Amsterdam tomorrow, I would have loved to come see your show. It sounds like just my kind of thing."

"I'm sorry, but we really are in a hurry," Milou said gruffly. "How does this work? How can we find Egg?"

"Have you got anything that belongs to him?" Emiliana asked. "It might help me to locate him."

Milou reached into her own cloak to where her Book of Theories was nestled. She rifled through it until she came to a page with a charcoal sketch of two people fighting a were-wolf.

"He drew this for me," Milou said. "Will that work?"

Emiliana took the book from Milou, her eyebrows raised as she looked at the picture, then at the scribbled notes of her werewolf-hunter theory. "I guess we'll find out," she said finally. Then, reaching into her collar, she pulled out the eyeball necklace and held it over her left eye.

Sem let out a cry of surprise. Milou covered his mouth with her hand and shook her head at him. Emiliana began to speak again, but in no language that Milou recognized. Her words were hurried and clipped; she kept pausing for a few moments, then starting up again. It was almost as if she was talking to someone.

An *invisible* someone.

The hairs on Milou's forearms stood on end. She snuck a subtle glance around her, but other than the three of them, there was no one else in the room. Sem began to fidget, scrunching his cap in his fists.

"Just sit still, would you?" Milou whispered. "You're making me nervous."

Sem looked taken aback. "*I'm* making you nervous? She's speaking in tongues!"

"Shh!"

They watched Emiliana for several long minutes. A draft whistled in through the gaps in the tent's fabric, making the skulls rattle. One candle puffed out, its smoke curling upward.

"He's on a ship," Emiliana said at last. "A big one." She squinted behind the eyeball. "But also . . . old and battered. Sorry, the image I see is somewhat blurry. It's . . . eighth . . . no . . . *ninth* along the dock."

"Which dock?" Milou asked.

Emiliana spoke a quick fire of that foreign tongue again, then smiled. "There are locomotives nearby. Lots of them. Cargo trains too."

"The eastern docklands."

Milou started. It hadn't been Sem or Emiliana who had spoken, but Lotta. She and Fenna were standing in the tent's entrance.

"The eastern docklands are a short distance from Amsterdam Centraal Station," Lotta said. "It's not that far. Let's go. Now."

Milou grabbed her Book of Theories from the table and tucked it back in her breast pocket. Its familiar weight felt reassuring. "Thank you, Emiliana," she said. "Truly."

She and Sem stood. Lotta and Fenna were already outside, waiting. Emiliana picked up Milou's coin pouch and followed them to the doorway, grabbing Milou's arm just as Sem stepped outside.

"A shadow follows you, Milou," Emiliana whispered, her face grave and those catlike eyes full of seriousness.

"What kind of shadow?"

"The dead kind."

Milou's breathing stopped; her pulse roared in her ears. She tried to shake her arm free, but the girl held it firmly.

"I hope you find all that you are looking for, Milou. Not just your brother."

Emiliana let go of her elbow, and Milou noticed the coin pouch was no longer in her hand. Most likely, she had stashed it in the folds of that strange green cloak. Still, if Emiliana's directions really did lead them to Egg, and even if it meant she had to wait longer to get that message to her parents, it would be worth the sacrifice.

Milou hurried out into the darkening dusk, trying not to think of dead things lurking in the many shadows that surrounded her. It was only when she and the others were halfway down the road that she realized Emiliana had called Egg her *brother*.

The thought of what Rotman might do to him sent a fresh wave of despair coursing through her. It was more terrifying than anything Milou could have imagined. Worse than anything the matron had ever inflicted upon her. As bad, even, as not knowing where her own family was.

Was this what it felt like to love a *brother*?

Perhaps. But right then, the only thing Milou knew for certain was that she would set the world on fire if that's what it took to get Egg back.

Her fear mingled with something new, something both fiery and sharp, something like fury.

Fury at Rotman for taking someone so precious to her.

And fury at herself for letting it happen.

❈ TWENTY-SIX ❈

THEY ARRIVED AT THE eastern docklands just as the sun had finally dipped below the watery horizon. Steam billowed from huge smokestacks, giving the impression that the dusk-reddened sky was melting into the vast expanse of the North Sea Canal. Milou's eyes darted in every direction as she tried to take in the sight of it all. Men in woolen coats and flat caps carried sacks up and down planks and walkways. Horses and mules pulled carts piled high with crates. Cargo was hoisted up by steam-powered cranes onto ship decks. Dogs barked, horns blew, and the smog-thickened air reeked of burnt oil and smoked fish.

"Holy Gouda," Lotta breathed, her wide eyes reflecting the fiery red glow. "Those are paddle-wheel steamships. Edda told me they were big, but . . . wow."

"That smaller ship," Milou said, extending a gloved finger toward a more shadowy area further down the dockyard. "The one with all the sails and the questionable mast." She counted its position. "It's the ninth along."

Compared to its neighbors, *De Zeehond* really was the runt of the litter. And, aside from the canal barges, it was the only vessel made of wood rather than steel. It looked, Milou decided, like a pirate ship that had been hauled up from the bottom of the ocean floor.

"A clipper, I believe," Lotta said, squinting. "It must be at least a hundred years old and have been battered by a thousand storms. If Rotman really is a wealthy sugar merchant, then I'm a three-legged peacock. The witch girl was right then."

"*Milou* was right," Sem said darkly. "Everything Rotman told us really was a lie." He flexed his fingers. "The ship looks unguarded. Let's get this over with."

He started to step out of their hiding spot beside a warehouse, but Milou grabbed his arm. "No," she said. "We need to be careful."

"But there's no one anywhere near the ship!"

He and Fenna looked ready to burn a path through anything that stood in their way.

"I want Egg back too," she said softly. "But we can't help him if we get caught, and we can't walk along the dock without being seen."

Lotta frowned. "Perhaps we could wait until there's fewer people—"

"Egg could be hurt," Sem seethed. "It's already been over an hour. We need to get him now."

Milou studied the shipyard again. Each ship had a warehouse at the end of its dock, but the gap between each warehouse was wide open and well lit. The only cover they would have was the odd crate or wagon. They'd have to be very quick, and very careful.

"We're cold and tired," Milou said. "If Rotman sees us and gives chase, we won't make it far. Stealth is the key. We need to be long gone before Rotman even realizes we've taken Egg." She pointed toward a ramshackle shack within throwing distance of Rotman's ship. "We need to get to that warehouse and assess the situation from closer up."

Fenna led the way, crawling under wagons, leaping over fences, and slipping through uncomfortably tight spaces between stacks of crates. They paused behind a stack of burlap sacks filled with eastern spices, waiting for a nearby dockworker to finish smoking. Milou tucked her face into her scarf to still her ragged breathing. They had reached the last of the sprawling warehouses and needed to cross an almost empty patch of ground to make it to the shack opposite *De Zeehond*'s mooring. After what felt like an age, the dockworker flicked his cigarillo into the shadows, where it soared over Lotta's head and landed in the dirt.

"Go!" Milou whispered, as soon as he disappeared around the corner.

Fenna was up on her feet in an instant. Like a circus acrobat, she rolled three times beside a low wall, sprang to her feet, and was across the empty clearing within seconds. Lotta went next, crawling like a panic-stricken spider. Milou copied Lotta's approach. Then, from the shadows behind the shack, they waited nervously for Sem to follow. Milou half expected him to trip over and knock over one of the teetering sacks, but within a few long-legged, determined strides, he had made it across the wall and into the cover of darkness beside her.

Rotman's warehouse was larger than it had appeared from a distance, with a window that not even Sem could reach. It glowed dimly from within, and, as they tiptoed underneath it, muffled voices drifted out.

"I think Rotman's in there," Milou whispered, looking up at the window. "With any luck, that's where he'll stay."

She and Fenna moved to carry on, but Lotta tugged them both back.

"Wait. We should listen."

"We don't have time," Milou whispered.

"Lotta's right." Sem sighed, then crouched down beside Milou and patted his shoulders for her to climb on. "We need to know what we're up against. Come on, hop up."

"Why do I have to climb up there?"

"Lotta's too short, and Fenna can't tell us what she hears. Just hurry, would you?"

Milou clambered up, managing to get a firm hold of the window ledge with her other hand and heave herself up enough to look inside. The window was practically opaque from a coating of grease, but Milou found a small hole through which to peer. She pressed her eye against it.

A single oil lamp hung from the middle of the ceiling, illuminating a room stacked full of crates. In the middle was a small space, in which there were a desk, two chairs, and two men. Rotman sat behind the desk, his forehead wrinkled in a frown. He was wearing an expression of utter disdain, as if his nostrils were under attack by an unpleasant smell. His eyes were as cold and angry as black ice. Opposite him, with his back to Milou, sat his apprentice, Pieter.

Milou put her ear to the hole.

"Has the boy spoken yet?" Rotman said.

"No sir," replied Pieter, in a voice so quiet Milou could barely hear it. "He won't give them up."

"We'll see if he still feels that way in the morning. A cold night in the hold under the watchful eye of Dolly should convince him how serious I am."

"Yes sir."

"Don't give him any food or water either."

"No sir."

"Is he securely tied up?"

"Yes sir."

"Good. I want to be out of this stinking city by the week's end, and I intend to leave with the crew that woman promised me. One way or another I'll find them."

There was a brief pause, then Pieter spoke another quiet "Yes sir."

"I have these blasted logs to finish," Rotman said. "Get my cabin ready for me. I'll be aboard shortly. Maybe I'll have a word with the boy myself . . ."

A chair scraped noisily across the floor. Milou quickly put her eye back to the peephole, just in time to see Pieter leaving through the warehouse door and Rotman returning to his paperwork. Milou tapped Sem's shoulder, and he bent to let her down.

"Egg is tied up. He's in the hold," she whispered. She turned to Lotta. "What does that mean?"

"Belowdecks," Lotta replied quietly. "It's where they store the cargo."

Milou told them the rest of what she had heard. The children looked at each other in quiet despair.

"We'll just have to be clever about this," Lotta said. "First of all, getting onto the ship will be tricky. We can't go up the main plank without the entire dockyard seeing us, so we'll have to see if we can climb up the mooring ropes on the other side.

There are portholes all along the hull. Perhaps one of us can draw this Dolly person away from the hold so that another one of us can free Egg."

"At least one of us will have to stay by the shack and keep watch," Sem added. "We should have a signal in case Rotman leaves the warehouse, and some way of causing a distraction to give us time to get off the ship again."

Lotta smiled suddenly and rummaged in her bag, pulling out one of the fireworks she'd bought earlier that day. "Will this work? A signal *and* a distraction all in one."

"Perfect," Milou said. "Okay. Sem and I will go aboard and get Egg. Lotta, you'll be on lookout and distraction duty. Fenna, you'll draw Dolly away. Everyone agreed?"

They all gave a curt nod, then crept along the side of the warehouse, into the waiting shadows.

❋ TWENTY-SEVEN ❋

THERE WAS ONLY ONE rope tied to the rear walk-way of *De Zeehond*, and it was as thick as Milou's arm. Sem went up it first, like an upside-down squirrel. Milou watched as he reached the side of the deck, then turned and gave her a thumbs-up. She peered down at the black water lapping just a few inches below. She could feel the iciness radiating off it. It held her there, like a statue, unable to move.

Fenna gave her a little nudge and a small, sympathetic smile.

"Egg," she rasped gruffly.

And that was all it took for Milou to reach up to the rope,

with her hands and then her legs, and start shimmying up. Hanging upside down, she found herself watching the cloudless, star-bright sky instead of the water. And then Sem's strong hands were hauling her onto the deck. They crouched behind a barrel and peered around either side of it.

The ship's sails were rolled up tightly, and the masts looked like giant crosses. The deck reminded Milou a bit of a graveyard. Cold, dark, windy, haunting. Every shadow seemed as if it might contain a monster. Every ghostly creak and groan of wood sent uncomfortable shivers up her spine. And the way the ship swayed gently from side to side made Milou feel as if the world wasn't quite substantial. There were lights on inside the cabin under the poop deck and the occasional thin silhouette of Pieter as he prepared Rotman's abode. Other than that, the deck was clear.

"There's a hatch there," Milou whispered, pointing toward the bow of the ship. "That should take us belowdecks."

Milou and Sem made their way to it. Hinges squeaked as Milou lifted the hatch, but the sound blended in with the whistling wind. She looked in and, seeing nothing in the gloom, stepped onto the ladder, which groaned loudly under her weight. She descended as quickly as she could. Sem followed, pulling the hatch to a squeaking close above their heads and plunging them into complete darkness.

The air was thick with the smell of oil and salt, which clung to her skin and throat. Milou's pulse roared loud in her ears, and her breath stuttered. She reached out to steady herself on the wall, only to find it was greasy with grime.

"Light," Milou whispered.

Sem struck a match and held it up.

They were in a big, long room. Two rows of hammocks hung suspended on either side. In the center of the room was a large, horizontal wheel, with five poles sticking out of it. It reminded Milou of the cogs that Lotta had shown her in the windmill mechanism room, but there was no other cog connected to it, so Milou assumed it was turned by hand. Empty crates were piled everywhere, secured with rope. There were mops and brooms, buckets and barrels. Having spent most of her life doing hard chores, Milou recognized this as a room in which elbows were greased and backs were bent.

Sem's match fizzled out, so he struck another one as Milou found a candle for him to light. There was a knock on one of the porthole windows. Fenna's face appeared by the glass, hanging over the side of the ship by one of the guide ropes. She was waving frantically at them. Milou hurried over and opened the window, taking in a deep lungful of the fresh air as it rushed in.

"Have you seen Egg?" she whispered.

Fenna gave a curt nod, her chest heaving. She reached in through the window and pointed to a door at the far end of the room.

"He's in there?" Milou asked.

Fenna nodded again, smiling brightly.

"Did you see the guard? Dolly?"

Fenna shook her head, her smile stretching.

"So Egg is alone?"

Fenna nodded again.

Milou turned to Sem, who was frowning. "Rotman said Dolly was in there. I heard him."

"Maybe she's gone on a break?" Sem whispered, eyeing every shadow around them. "Or perhaps she's gone to bed already. We should just count ourselves lucky. Come on."

Milou turned back to Fenna. "Wait by the nearest window, okay?"

Fenna gave an eager nod and disappeared.

Milou left the window slightly ajar and turned back to the room. Sem was holding the candle high over his head, peering around with a look of concern.

"Dolly might come back at any moment," he whispered, grabbing a broomstick with his free hand. "Be ready."

Milou nodded and seized a mop. Not the most impressive of weapons, but they would have to do. As they crept forward, Milou's pulse was so loud in her ears she could no longer hear the groaning of wood or the slapping of water on the hull.

The door Fenna had pointed at was firmly shut. Milou pressed her ear to it. Beyond the whooshing of her pulse, she was certain she could hear the rattling of chains. Sem raised the broom higher, ready to wield it, and Milou moved her shaking fingers to the door handle . . . and pushed it open. The door emitted a creaking groan, and Milou and Sem found themselves staring into another long room, filled with even more empty crates. It was almost pitch-dark, except for the thin columns of moonlight that spilled in through the porthole windows.

Two round, frightened, familiar eyes stared at them from the end of the room. Egg was huddled between two beams, ropes bound tightly around his wrists and waist, and his mouth stuffed with cloth. He blinked up at them, and his eyes grew wider and more panicked. He groaned, shaking his head vigorously.

He didn't look happy to see them. He looked horrified.

Confused, Milou took a step into the room, the floorboards creaking beneath her. A low growl made her stop.

The noise had been so quiet she'd barely heard it. She peered into a gap between several crates but saw nothing at all. To her other side was a dark storeroom. Egg made a loud, muffled moan, shifting his eyes in the direction Milou had just looked. He shook his head again. Milou took another tentative step forward.

Another growl.

Both Sem and Milou stopped in their tracks. This time, as she squinted into the storeroom and Sem held the candle higher, Milou thought she saw two glowing eyes.

The eyes blinked.

Another growl.

Like the first roll of thunder in a storm, it started off quiet and got louder, deeper, more menacing. The tip of a snout appeared from the darkness. Its lips were pulled back as the monster growled once more, revealing two rows of deadly, toothy fangs.

❈ TWENTY-EIGHT ❈

MILOU STAGGERED BACKWARD, BUMPING into Sem, fear stabbing at her stomach. The monster stepped fully out from the shadows, snapping at the air. Its claws scraped across the hardwood floor, its pointed ears pinned back. A hand landed heavily on Milou's shoulder and yanked her backward.

"Dolly," Sem said, pushing Milou behind him.

The huge dog stalked toward them, looking for all the world as if it might tear Sem and Milou to pieces with just one bite of its snapping jaws.

Holding the broomstick in front of him with one hand, Sem wedged the candle atop a crate with the other.

"Free him," Sem rasped, nodding toward Egg. "Quickly."

He raised his broom and lowered his brow. Milou had never seen him look so determined.

"But—"

"Now!" Sem cried, just as Dolly launched forward.

Milou watched in horror as the dog's jaws latched on to the broom handle, sending Sem crashing to the floor.

"Quick!" he groaned, twisting the broom every time Dolly tried to snap at him. "I won't be able to hold her off for long!"

Milou staggered to the end of the room and sank to the floor beside Egg, yanking the cloth from his mouth.

"Are you crazy?" Egg cried, his voice quivering. "Why did you come here? It's too dangerous."

Milou reached for the rope that bound his wrists. Her hands were trembling.

"Why wouldn't we have come?" She tugged at the knot, her fingers slipping, and growled in frustration. "Why aren't my hands working properly?"

She didn't dare look behind her, where she could hear Sem still wrestling with Dolly. The beast was growling and Sem was grunting in exertion, but there had been no cries of agony yet.

"Just take a deep breath," Egg said softly. "Just take a deep breath. You can do it, Milou."

She shook her hands and tried again, managing to wriggle one end of the rope out of the knot. Egg wriggled his wrists out of their binding and smiled gratefully at her.

As Milou reached for the rope around Egg's waist, Sem yelped in pain. She scrambled to her feet, darting across the room to him. Dolly had snapped the broom in half and was gnawing on one piece as Sem stood, wobbling, clutching at a gash on his leg.

"Sem!" Milou skidded to a stop. Dolly blocked her way. "Are you all right?"

"Stay back!" Sem cried, his voice full of pain. "I'm okay, it's just a scratch—"

"No, it's not!" Milou cried, anger brimming. "Leave him alone!"

She picked up the nearest object, a scrubbing brush, and bashed it against the hold's wall to get the dog's attention. Dolly's giant head turned toward her, lips pulled back in a vicious snarl. Huge claws scraped the floor as the dog stalked toward Milou, fangs so sharp they could likely tear through her skin as if it were paper.

"Hey!" Sem cried, banging the mop on the floor. Milou could see his leg was causing him pain, but he held the broken mop firm and his fierce expression even more so. "Leave her alone."

Dolly ignored him entirely, snapping her teeth just inches from Milou's stomach.

"*Hey*!" Sem called again.

Dolly turned to him, her growl trebling in volume. She barked, loud enough to wake the dead and certainly loud enough to be heard abovedeck. Milou watched in frozen terror as Dolly's back legs braced to jump. Sem took a wobbly step forward, but his injured leg buckled beneath him. He fell, defenseless, as Dolly launched herself into the air. Milou could only watch in horror, a scream building in her throat.

Sem twisted on the ground, swinging his good leg around. As Dolly soared over him, straight through an open doorway, landing with a thud in the empty storeroom she had come out of, Sem moved more quickly than Milou had ever seen him. He scrambled to the door and slammed it shut. There was a muffled growl, then a loud bang as the dog threw herself against it. More barking. Another bang. But the door held firm.

Milou ran over and helped Sem slide a crate across the door to hold it closed. He grinned lopsidedly at her.

"Well, that was—"

His words died away as a strange whistling sounded just outside the porthole window. Sem hopped over to it, Milou holding on to his elbow. The sky exploded with color.

Lotta's warning firework.

"Milou!" Egg called urgently. "Sem!"

Egg was still struggling to free himself, staring across the room with a look of pure panic on his face. Milou followed his gaze. A figure emerged from the darkness. Pieter stepped into the room, wielding a large wooden mallet above his head.

"What are you doing?" he yelled, eyes darting between the three of them.

Sem bristled beside her. He reached for a nearby cargo hook but fell, clutching his leg again. Milou stood over him and grabbed the broken broomstick.

"What does it look like?" she said, holding the sharp point out toward Pieter. "We're taking Egg home."

Pieter frowned, lowering his mallet slightly. "Where's—"

Dolly chose that moment to bash against the storeroom door again, right next to Pieter. He shrieked in surprise and staggered across the room.

"She's in there?" he shrieked, his face pale. "How did you—"

Milou watched his hands shake. She realized he was younger than she had first thought. Young and terrified of the consequences he'd face if he let them leave. She lowered her weapon.

"Help us," she said softly. "You don't have to do his bidding, you know."

Pieter shook his head.

"Please," Milou said. "We don't deserve this any more than you do."

Pieter's nostrils flared.

"Help us. Please."

"He'll kill me."

"Then leave with us."

Pieter shook his head again. "I can't. You don't know what he's like. He'd find me. He'll find you too, even if I did let you go."

There was another whistle, another crackle, and a colorful glow flickered across the room. Lotta had set off another firework. Which could only mean that Rotman was now on the ship. Milou realized she couldn't wait any longer for Pieter to change his mind. She needed a new tactic. A faster one.

In three quick steps she was next to the storeroom door. "I'll open this, and let her out," Milou said. "She's not happy."

Pieter paled. "Don't."

"Please," Sem said. He was standing now, but only barely. Sweat glistened on his face. "You can come with us. We'll be safe together, I promise."

Pieter made one more indecisive noise. Then he dropped the mallet to the ground.

Milou's heart leapt up to her throat in relief. She took a few steps toward Egg, but then stopped as her left ear tingled sharply. Pieter stared at her as she took slow, silent steps backward. There was the unmistakable creak of a floorboard under pressure, coming from the hallway. The smell of oil and smoke drifted in through the doorway, then the tips of two sealskin boots.

"Well, isn't this a delightful surprise?"

Meneer Rotman emerged fully from the gloom, cruel-eyed and stormy-faced, aiming a pearl-handled pistol at Milou's chest.

❧ TWENTY-NINE ❧

MILOU STARED AT THE pistol, hardly even daring to breathe. Her ear now tingled so much it felt like it was on fire.

"My darling little *kindjes*," Rotman crooned, cocking the pistol's hammer with his thumb. "I've been so worried. Papa is so pleased to see you."

Milou couldn't speak. Out the corner of her eye, she saw Sem slump to the floor and Fenna's frightened face disappear from the other side of the porthole. Pieter was whimpering, pressing himself against the storeroom door, despite Dolly still scratching at it from the other side.

"And Pieter!" Rotman said. "I'm surprised. You saw what

these brats did to that poor old matron of theirs. Do you think they care about anyone but themselves?"

Milou looked down. Her shadow pooled at her feet, thicker and darker than any shadow ought to be. Instinctively, she took a step backward, the floor groaning in protest beneath her boots.

"Do. Not. Move. Girl."

Milou froze. The merchant's cruel grin was replaced with a look of pure menace. His mustachio twitched. Dolly barked, slamming into the door. Rotman's eyebrows rose.

"My, my. You lot really are full of surprises. Pieter, I'm of half a mind to put you in there with Dolly, to remind you of where your loyalties lie."

"Please, no. I'm sorry. I didn't mean—"

Rotman limped forward and elbowed his apprentice in the face, sending him staggering backward. Blood spurted from the boy's nose, spraying across Milou's cheek. He fell to the floor beside her, curled up and whimpering.

"We should have left this port over a week ago," Rotman roared. "Do you have any idea how much money you've cost me! Not to mention the medical bills for my foot, you little—"

"That's not our problem," Milou seethed.

Rotman scoffed. "Oh, it very much is your problem, child." He limped toward her. "And you are very much going to repay what you owe me."

"Our father is waiting for us nearby," Milou said. "He'll come looking for us if we don't return soon. He is not a man you wish to anger."

"Father?" Rotman's smile slipped, then he shook his head. "Never mind that, we can be on our way within minutes."

"You don't have the paperwork to take us."

"I'll risk sneaking you out of this harbor in these barrels if I have to—"

"Hey, cheese face!" cried a shrill voice from the porthole.

Lotta had half-crawled through the window, and in her hand was a long tube, sparks spewing out the end of it. Rotman swiveled his gun toward her, but Lotta was quicker. The firework shot from her hand, hitting the floor by his sealskin boots. The room exploded with light.

Milou threw herself to the ground, covering Pieter with one arm, as the firework ricocheted, whistling and screeching, from wall to wall. It knocked the candle over, then bounced from every surface, fiery sparks flying in its wake. Smoke plumed, filling the room. When Milou waved the smoke from her face, she saw flames erupting in patches all over the hold. Rotman was lying in the doorway, coughing and spluttering as flames licked at his boots.

As Milou pushed herself up, her hand connected with something cold and metal on the floor. The pearl-handled pistol. She locked eyes with the merchant. Rotman took one look at the pistol by Milou's hand and staggered, hand over his mouth, out the hold door, slamming it shut behind him and leaving them trapped with the smoke and fire.

"Milou!" Lotta yelled. She and Fenna were holding Sem between them, trying to get him out through the window. "Hurry."

"You're going to help my friends get Sem to the dock," she said, pulling Pieter to his feet and pushing him toward the porthole. "And then we'll help you get far away from him, I promise."

He nodded dumbly.

"We're not going without you," Sem said to Milou, then began to choke.

"I'm going to free Egg, and then we'll be right behind you," she said.

She didn't wait for Sem to argue, merely gave him a gentle shove toward the window and turned away, coughing as smoke crawled up her nose and down her throat. She staggered across the hold to Egg, who was still trying desperately tugging at the knot behind him.

"I'm coming, hang on."

There was a *creeeak* and crash behind her as a wooden beam broke from the ceiling, blocking their route to the window through which Sem and the others had just left. Milou cursed, but her hands were surprisingly still as she untied the rope. The moment he was fully free he wrapped his arms around her, squeezing the last of the air from her lungs. She pushed him gently away. There wasn't time.

They heard a crash and a long howl from the storeroom. Dolly was still trapped.

"Wait here a moment," Milou said. "Put your shawl over your mouth."

She skirted around a burning barrel. She opened the hold door, then, using the tip of the broom, pushed it through the flames and hooked it under the storeroom door handle. With a flick of her wrist, the door opened, and a dark shape shot out. Dolly yelped at the flames, then turned and bounded out the door. Milou made her way quickly back to Egg, who was staring at her in disbelief.

"I couldn't let her perish," Milou explained. "Fenna would never forgive me, even if that beast did try to eat Sem. Right, let's get out of here."

She pushed a porthole window open and peered out, sucking in a lungful of fresh air. They were much further down the ship than the window through which the others had escaped. The walkway was out of reach and there was no anchor line in sight. She couldn't see past the smoke to tell if the others had made it to land. Looking the other way, all she could see was a long stretch of endless water.

"Come on," she said, climbing out and pulling Egg with her.

They clung to the porthole ledge, nothing but black

water beneath them and no anchor lines within reach.

"We're trapped," Egg gasped.

Milou's grip on the ledge nearly slipped. She cast her gaze around in panic. There were shouts and barking from the dock. The wind was stoking the fire, and thick, black smoke was curling around the ship. The flames had reached the ship deck, spreading up to the folded sails at sickening speed.

"Our choices are *up*," Milou choked, "or *down*."

"We can't swim," Egg replied grimly. "And we're not fire-proof."

"How about sideways then?"

One of the crossbeams of the mast groaned, snapped, and plummeted down past them. It hit the river with a hiss of steam, and a spume of icy water slapped at their legs. Milou and Egg pressed themselves against the side of the swaying, burning ship. Egg clasped her hand, looking resigned and defeated.

"Milou, I am so sorry—"

"Egbert Poppenmaker. Now is *not* the time for apologies, of which I have plenty of my own to make. Now is the time to *not die*."

Egg nodded. Milou turned her attention back to the ship's side, looking for an escape route. Suddenly, the image of Lotta sliding down that rope from the laundry-room window came to her. If she and Egg were going to survive, they would have to start thinking like Lotta. There were plenty of loose ropes dangling down the side of the ship. Milou grabbed the nearest one with both hands.

"Here," Milou said. "Hold on tightly to this with me. We're going to have to swing ourselves to the next rope over there. If we can make it to the front of the ship, we can climb that anchor line down to the dock. Ready?"

Egg nodded once, his expression grim. Pushing their feet against the hull, they swung themselves sideways, hitting the next porthole hard. Milou only just managed to clasp her hand around the next rope and haul herself and Egg onto it.

They hung there for a moment, panting heavily. Another piece of flaming debris fell past them. The fire was roaring so loud now that Milou could barely hear the dockworkers' shouts. A loud bell began to chime; a fire cart had arrived.

"Seven more portholes to get past," Egg said with a forced smile.

They swung twice more, with faltering success. Milou's hands were beginning to burn, and her shins and ankles were battered. Milou hoped that the others had gotten to safety. Her eyes were streaming, and she couldn't stop coughing. Beside her, Egg was struggling too. If they didn't hurry, they'd suffocate.

"Come on," Milou rasped. "We can do this."

They made for the next rope, only for it to suddenly fall away loose before Milou could reach it. She and Egg swung back the way they'd come, hitting the side of the ship with such force most of the air left her lungs. Her ears gave a sudden, agonizing pinch.

"Up!" Egg gasped.

Wheezing in pain, Milou looked up. Above them, leaning over the side of the ship, haloed by firelight, was a large figure. Despite the cloth that covered his face, Milou recognized the small, beady eyes.

Rotman.

Their eyes met, and his murderous expression made her heart stop. Dizziness skewed her vision and she blinked furiously to see what he was doing. Rotman held a sandbag over the railings, right above Milou's head. He smiled cruelly before launching it off the edge.

Milou's stomach dropped to her knees, but before the sandbag made contact with her upturned face, she was pushed sideways. She watched in horror as the sandbag hit Egg square in the chest, knocking him away from her. She reached out with one hand, her fingertips grazing his shawl as he flew backward.

Egg landed in the water with a heavy splash, his limbs splayed out and his eyes and mouth open wide in shock. The water seemed to hollow out around him, then the waves changed direction and swallowed him whole.

He was gone so quickly, Milou scarcely had time to process what had happened.

Egg had pushed her out of the way and taken the hit for her.

Smoke clung to her hair and her face. Milou was growing dizzier. She looked up, but Rotman was gone. She looked down again. Egg didn't reappear. Bubbles erupted from where he had sunk; his shawl bobbed on the surface.

Egg couldn't swim.

But neither could she.

Something pinched at her ear, and a shadow wrapped around her hand. As she readied herself to jump, a voice, made only of the breeze, spoke to her in a desperate plea.

NO!

It was so quiet and insubstantial she would probably have never heard it, had it not spoken right into her tingling ear. The shadow around her hand swelled.

"I have to," she rasped.

And then her fingers uncurled from the rope. A heartbeat later, her feet hit the canal, and the icy water closed over her head, sucking her down into the darkness.

❦ THIRTY ❦

MILOU DIDN'T NOTICE THE cold straightaway. It struck a few heartbeats later, constricting her body from head to toe. She thrashed and kicked, but that just seemed to make her sink faster. The darkness left her blind, so she could not tell which way was up. Bubbles rushed in her ears. Again, she thrashed and kicked, praying for the surface, but the icy water held her firm. She was going to drown, she realized. Then, in her left ear, that insubstantial voice once more said: *NO!*

A hand clasped around Milou's leg, and she stifled a scream of surprise. Egg. He pulled her toward him, and they held each other tightly. She'd taken a deep breath of air when she'd jumped, but already her chest was burning to let it out.

She kicked her legs with what little energy she had left. The voice returned, quiet and garbled.

STOP.

A bubble of air left her lips, tickling her cheek.

STOP.

Milou stopped kicking.

GOOD.

Beside her, Egg was thrashing just as wildly. She squeezed his hand until he calmed. Her chest was burning now. Another bubble escaped, tickling along her cheek toward her ear. They were sideways, she realized. Using weak arms, she pushed at the water until the next bubble tickled up around her nose, to her hairline. Toward the surface.

YES.

Milou began to kick her legs again, small, controlled movements. Her head was spinning and the pressure in her lungs building into agony. Still, she kicked. Slowly, painfully slowly, she and Egg began to rise.

She broke the surface. The cold winter air felt blissfully warm as she sucked in a lungful. Beside her, Egg was doing the same. His hair was plastered down his cheeks, and his eyes were barely open. He looked as ill as she felt.

They floated on their backs, clasping each other's hand tightly, looking up at the smoldering wreckage of *De Zeehond*, listening to the clamor of the panicked dockworkers. Her vision was blurred and her eyelids felt heavy. The burning in her chest faded as her consciousness started to drift. She was only vaguely aware of Egg's grip on her hand loosening. Even less aware of the water that slowly lapped over her face.

She was sinking again.

NO!

Water sloshed up her nose, then up over her eyes. This time, however, she didn't have the strength to fight it. All she could think was that now her family would never find her. It wouldn't occur to them to look at the bottom of the North Sea Canal for her. Perhaps she'd wash ashore, but no one would know who she was.

NO!

She'd die a nameless orphan.

MILOU!

Egg's hand disappeared from hers completely, leaving her entirely alone as the water swallowed her once more.

MILOU!

It was warm now. Gloriously so. Milou's eyes were open only a thin slit, but the water seemed clearer this time.

MILOU!

There, just out of reach on the canal bed but growing steadily closer, was a gate.

Just like the one in Liesel's story.

Milou sank toward it.

NO!

The water began to darken, until once again she was completely blind.

MILOU!

Milou's arm was suddenly yanked hard, nearly wrenching it from her socket. The water over her face disappeared, and then she was in the air. Her vision showed little more than a speckled haze, in which she could make out the shape of a round head with slightly wonky ears.

Her back collided with something hard, and water erupted from her lips. It burned her throat. Someone was coughing loudly, as if their lungs were trying to escape out through their throat. She realized it was her.

"Milou?" The voice seemed both familiar and new, raspy and quiet.

"Milou?" The next voice was more recognizable, sweet and soft.

"Milou?" The last voice was like home.

The voices merged as they called her name again. They blurred together until Milou couldn't tell where one started and one ended. The only thing she knew was that the combination sounded like a lullaby. Her eyes closed and she fell into a deep, restless sleep.

Milou woke to the world swaying and rocking. The first thing she noticed as her eyes blinked open was that there was a bright night sky above her, a smattering of stars twinkling in the glow of the not-quite-full moon. The next thing she noticed was the moving silhouettes of trees in her peripheral vision. She blinked. Like floating wraiths, they continued to glide past.

Her heart stuttered. Her body remained frozen and heavy.

Had she entered Theodora's nightmare?

A pale face loomed over her; a wonky frown, disheveled blond hair, and crooked ears.

"Milou?" Sem asked, his frown easing as he smiled down at her in relief. "Oh, thank goodness you're awake."

Milou let out a groan as a shiver shook her shoulders. She was still wet and cold. Lotta's woolen coat was draped over her, shielding her from the wind, but it wasn't quite enough to remove the chill in her bones. With Sem's help, Milou sat up. They were in a paddleboat. Lotta and Fenna were each holding onto a notched axle, rotating it in synchronization to power the two paddle wheels on their side of the boat, propelling them down the canal at a steady speed. At the front of the boat, wrapped in Sem's velvet jacket, Egg slept fitfully. Beside him, drying on the boat's edge, was his soggy shawl.

"What—"

"Pieter showed us to a lifeboat," Sem said quietly. "I thought we'd lost you both."

Milou blinked. "Where is Pieter?"

"We dropped him off halfway out of the city," Lotta said.

"He climbed onto a barge heading south. He said his family is in Rotterdam."

"Where are we?" Milou asked weakly.

"Look," Sem responded with a tiny smile.

Milou rubbed her eyes. She realized they were passing Edda's house. Just ahead was their windmill.

They had made it home.

Her gaze flicked back to Egg. The reflection of moonlight from the water sent a rippling glow over his sleeping face.

They had *all* made it home.

❧ THIRTY-ONE ❧

MILOU SPENT THE NEXT day in her cupboard bed, being force-fed herbal concoctions by Fenna. Her wracking cough eventually abated, but her chest was still sore. In the cupboard bed on the other side of the room, Egg was in a similar state. He'd woken only a few times since they'd returned. Every now and then, he would mutter her name, apologizing and weeping, reliving the trauma of *De Zeehond* in his fever-laced dreams.

Milou had the same problem.

Whenever she drifted off to sleep, without fail, she dreamed of smoke and darkness, of sea creatures trying to pull her to the dark, murky depths of the ocean and toward those ghastly iron gates. And no matter how much she kicked her feet, she could never find the surface. It was an Ocean of Nightmares. And so Milou tried her best not to sleep, instead staring at the blank pages of Liesel's still-unfinished story. If she didn't find an ending soon, and they couldn't begin rehearsing it, their entire plan would crumble—opening night was in just three days.

The kitchen door opened with a creak, and Lotta and Fenna walked in.

They each held a mug of steaming liquid in their hands, and Milou could smell the nauseating herbal mixture from the other side of the room.

"It smells like old socks and cheese," Milou groaned, pushing herself as far away from Fenna's mug as she could get.

"Drink," Fenna said, in a quiet, raspy voice that nevertheless sounded like music to Milou's ears.

Fenna reached forward, pinched Milou's nose, and pushed the mug to her lips. Milou's mouth opened in protest, which gave Fenna the chance to pour the warm liquid in.

"Ugh," Milou groaned, coughing and gagging. "It *tastes* like old socks and cheese too."

Fenna smiled, then took Lotta's mug and turned her attention to Egg.

Lotta looked grave. "At least you're both alive."

"I guess Emiliana earned all that money I handed over . . ."

Lotta frowned. "You didn't give her all your money."

"Yes, I did. And I don't regret it."

Lotta shook her head. "No, you didn't. I found the coin pouch in your pocket. Sem used it to place your advertisement this morning."

Milou opened her mouth, then closed it again. Emiliana must have slipped the money back into her pocket when she'd given her that strange warning about shadows and spirits.

There was a spluttering noise from the other bed.

"That's disgusting," Egg groaned.

Milou slowly got to her feet. The ground no longer wobbled quite so much underneath her, but her head still felt a little dizzy as she hobbled over toward Egg with Lotta holding her arm.

"I've had enough of this," Egg said, scrambling out of his own cupboard bed, only for his legs to fold beneath him the moment he tried to stand.

Lotta and Fenna each grabbed one of his arms, hoisting him up. Egg shrugged them off and pitched forward again, but this time his arms went right around Milou's neck, and he pulled her into a fierce hug.

"Gah!" she spluttered around a mouthful of his hair. "You're surprisingly strong for a nearly drowned person."

"Oh, Milou," he said, squeezing her tighter. "I'm sorry I almost got us all killed."

Milou tried not to wheeze as she squeezed him back. "And I'm sorry I made you feel like your quest wasn't as important as mine. All four of you have helped me so much, and I should have been there to help you. You have just as much right as I do to find answers about your family."

"I know, but it was reckless to go straight to Rotman. I wish I'd made a proper plan."

"Why *did* you go to Rotman?" Lotta asked.

Egg leaned against the bed and grimaced. "He was the only person I knew who had traveled widely. I just wanted to know for certain if Edda's theory was right . . . if my shawl really did come from Java. I thought I could pretend to want to go with him, ask him about my shawl, and then run away again."

"I probably would have done the same thing," Milou admitted. "Or something equally as reckless, no doubt."

"I was desperate," Egg said, reaching into his cupboard bed for his shawl. He wrapped it around his neck and looked down at it. "And I still have no idea where to start."

Milou's heart twisted painfully. "As soon as Speelman is off our backs, we'll sit down and work it out. Together. If we have to knock on every door in Amsterdam to find someone who can tell us more about your shawl, we will. I swear it."

"Together," Egg repeated with a small smile. Then he swayed.

Lotta looked at him sternly. "You should get back into bed."

"I want to get up for a bit."

He cast a nervous glance at the wooden walls of the cupboard bed, and Milou knew it reminded him of the ship's hold.

"Why don't we get some fresh air," she suggested.

Lotta and Fenna narrowed their eyes. Then Lotta sighed.

"If you two are determined to ignore all medical advice, then you might as well come and see what we've been doing while you've slept."

The sun was so bright, Milou and Egg were temporarily dazzled as they hobbled out the front door. Lotta led Milou by the hand, and Milou led Egg, and they walked down the path to the barn. The theater door opened with a delightful creak. It sent shivers up Milou's spine and made Egg shudder beside her. Lotta grinned wickedly.

"I degreased the hinges a little more." She beamed, leading them inside. "For atmosphere."

Milou stood on the threshold and gaped. Sem, Lotta, and Fenna had transformed the interior. There were ghosts, made from thin white gauze, suspended from the rafters on rotating wires, floating across against the night-sky backdrop in a whisper of fabric. The carpet had been cleared of mud and dust; the seats had been straightened and their holes sewn up with thick stitches. The stage was hidden behind two new curtains, made of black Amsterdam velvet with the words "A CARNIVAL OF NIGHTMARES" written in elegant swirls across it. Fenna was dangling from the roof of a wheeled booth at the far end, painting the words "WARM STROOPWAFELS" in bright red across the roof.

What made Milou's skin tingle the most, however, was the large skeletal Night Tree that sprouted from the left side of the stage, its black branches creeping along the floor and ceiling to wrap around the stage like a frightening frame. Sem was halfway up the tree's trunk, attaching claws and bones. His hair was sticking up, and bits of gray web dangled from his left ear.

"What do you think, Papa?" Lotta asked Puppet Papa, who was currently reclining on a seat at the back of the theater, watching them work. "Splendid, isn't it?"

"It's amazing," Egg said.

Milou was speechless.

"Come and sit in the front row," Lotta said. "The best is yet to come."

They followed her down the aisle and sat quietly, dumbfounded, in front of the stage. Lotta disappeared through the curtains. Sem and Fenna came to sit beside them.

"You'll like this—" Sem started, but his voice was drowned out by a sudden loud voice that made Milou jump out of her skin.

"WELCOME, FIENDS AND GHOULS."

Lotta's voice blasted through the room, tinny and impossibly loud. The curtains opened, and Milou found herself staring at the giant fangs of a monstrously large puppet spider. Its legs twitched, and its pincers snapped. There was a creaking sound, and then the puppet spider started walking off the stage and over Milou's head. She ducked and squealed as the beast went sailing over her head and over the rows of seating, suspended from a cable she hadn't seen until just then. It wriggled to the back of the barn, then reversed all the way back to the stage, the curtains closing behind it.

A moment later, Lotta reappeared from the side of the stage, grinning maniacally. "Well?"

Milou and Egg shared a look of awe.

"It's perfect," Milou said finally, her cheeks aching with the smile that wouldn't leave her lips. "Absolutely perfect."

"I found a barrel organ too!" Lotta said, pulling back a smaller curtain at the side of the stage. "It was under all that junk at the back of the barn."

The organ was the size of a handcart, with lots of brass tubes erupting from the top. A pile of concertinaed paper was stacked on a ledge next to the ivory keys, one end protruding from a post-box-type slot. Lotta turned a crank on the side and organ music filled the room. As soon as she stopped turning the crank, the music disappeared.

"Have you finished the story?" Sem asked.

Milou's smile faltered. She'd spent all the previous day wracking her brains for ideas to end the story, but she'd been too consumed with thoughts of her underwater nightmares. Each time she'd drifted off to sleep, the nightmare returned, and Milou felt as if she were dying. It was hard to concentrate on writing stories when you were scared of falling asleep and never waking up.

"Well," she started, wondering whether they would be disappointed with her, and fearful that she would spoil the mood. All their efforts would go to waste if she didn't do her share of the work. "I—"

"It looks just like how I imagined Theodora's nightmare world," Egg said suddenly. Then his voice turned quiet. "It's quite a bit like the nightmares I have, as well."

Milou snapped her attention to him. He was right. Theodora's nightmare world had dragged her in every time she fell asleep too, like Milou's had. Theodora had been scared to fall asleep. Perhaps Theodora's nightmares had been about her fear of—

"Milou?" Sem asked.

Milou looked up at the ghosts and the cobwebs. Like Lotta's talk of cogwheels, the answer to her problem was slotting into perfect place.

"Milou?" Sem repeated.

"Yes," said Milou, her heart fluttering like the wings of a bat. "Yes. I know how the story will end."

The others grinned at her.

"Then the Poppenmakers are truly all set to go," Lotta said. "The Theater of Terrors will be ready."

Milou smiled. "And our *own* nightmare will end."

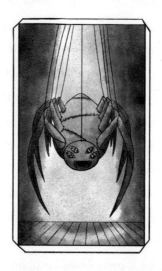

✳ THIRTY-TWO ✳

TWO DAYS LATER, THE night of the show arrived, heavy with a low-lying mist that curled up the canal banks and wrapped around ankles. The full moon hung like a giant opal in the star-dappled dusk, and the sky had turned a ghostly shade of purple. Halfway up one of the windmill's sails, Milou drew the frigid air in through her nostrils to try and calm her nerves, but her heart refused to slow to anything less than a gallop. She watched, breathless, as a procession of swaying lanterns wove its way toward Poppenmill. The neighing of horses and scraping of carriage wheels mingled with the hum of voices. Behind the iron gates, a crowd was swelling.

Their audience had arrived.

Milou wondered which one of those flickering lanterns belonged to her parents. Just thinking about being reunited with them made her hands shake so much she nearly fell from the sail twice. She gave the moon one last nervous smile and then hurried down to join her friends at the windmill's front door. They all wore matching blue cloaks, spattered with silver paint, and identical expressions of panic-stricken excitement.

"It's time," Milou said. "Let's open the gates."

Lotta's eyes widened in eagerness above the top of her scarf, and she nodded. They all put their hoods over their heads, their faces disappearing into shadow, and hurried to the gated bridge. Milou heard several gasps of surprise from beyond the iron bars, then a few more as the five of them heaved the protesting gates open. Metal groaned and scraped, then the crowd surged forward, a sea of curious faces and red-tipped noses.

"Milou," Lotta whispered. "Meet me at the theater in no more than five minutes, all right?"

Milou barely registered her words but nodded anyway. Lotta and Fenna disappeared, leaving the boys and Milou to sell tickets. The first couple stepped up to Milou and smiled. They were smartly dressed and bright-eyed. The man had a tidy mustachio under his long nose, and the woman had dark curly hair, tied up elegantly atop her head. They were, however, far too young to be her parents.

"Fifty cents each, please," Milou said impatiently, trying not to snatch the silver coin they offered her. She gave them two tickets and a forced smile. "Follow the lantern trail to that tree over there." She pointed to the oak tree, which was twinkling prettily with lanterns hung from every branch. "You'll be able to buy warm stroopwafels while you wait. The theater will open shortly."

"Thank y—"

But Milou had already nudged them along, eager to see who was waiting behind them. She snuck a glance at Sem's customers, but they looked nothing like her. Neither did the small family buying tickets from Egg.

The line slowly made its way in through the gates, ticket after ticket leaving Milou's hands. Her money pouch began to grow heavier and heavier. There were more people arriving than she'd have dared dream. Young families, old couples, ladies wearing silk bonnets, men in tall top hats, children with nervous smiles. Milou's smile slipped slightly with each person who did not have midnight-dark hair or eyes that were almost black. Her ears tingled slightly, but she ignored it. Her family would be here somewhere. She'd find them.

"You should go and help Lotta," Sem whispered after a few minutes. "Egg and I can handle this."

"Just one more minute," Milou replied as another figure stepped toward her.

It was a tall cowled figure in a bright green cloak, with a face just as hidden in shadows as her own.

"Fifty cents, please," Milou said, holding up an open palm.

There was a pregnant pause. Milou had the feeling she was being stared hard at, but it was too dark to see even the faintest outline of the person's face. Then a white glove emerged from the green cloak and dropped a guilder into her hand.

"Follow the lanterns to that tree," she said, rummaging through her coin purse for change. "The theater will open in just—"

She looked up to find the cowled figure had swept past her and disappeared into the crowd. Lotta emerged, scowling hard.

"It's been twelve minutes," she said crossly. "We're behind schedule. Fenna's nearly run out of waffles, and everyone is cold and growing impatient."

Milou looked back at the line, which still meandered out of the gate and onto the main road. Lotta tugged at her arm.

"I'll keep an eye out for them," Sem whispered. "I promise."

Milou let out a shaky breath and nodded, following Lotta down the crowded gravel path to the theater, which stood tall and dark and empty-looking in the distance.

It was too dark to see people's faces clearly, and Lotta tugged Milou too quickly for her to get a closer look. They snuck around the side of the theater to where Lotta had installed a smaller side door. Next to the door, on the wall, was a brass mouthpiece. One of Edda's speaking tubes. Lotta pushed Milou toward it.

"We need them sitting in their seats in four minutes,"

she said. "It will only work if we time things perfectly." She tapped Milou's pocket watch pointedly. "Four minutes *exactly*. Be ready."

Lotta slipped off around the back of the theater barn. Milou stood there, trembling in the cold, trying to quell her growing panic. Her parents would come. Wouldn't they?

She checked the time; a minute had passed already. She was going to ruin the entire show if she didn't pull herself together. All these people would demand their money back, and all their hard work would have been for nothing. They'd have to leave the windmill.

Milou cleared her throat. Sem would find them and it would all be fine, she told herself. She pressed her lips to the mouthpiece and, in the deepest, boomiest voice she could summon, she addressed her audience.

"LADIES AND GENTLEMEN!"

Her voice projected loudly outward in a tinny crackle. Out of the corner of her eyes, she saw the shadowed mass of people straighten.

"BOYSSSSS AND GIRRRRLS."

The hum of voices dropped completely.

"IT IS MY DELIGHT TO WELCOME YOU TO THE GREATEST, MOST GHOULISH EVENT OF THE CENTURY."

Milou heard a small child whimper.

"WELCOME, FIENDS, TO THE *THEATER OF TERRORS*!"

There was an earsplitting screech of hinges as the theater doors slid open. The sound stretched upward in pitch. Milou saw hands reach up to cover ears, and several people clung to each other. A thrill ran through her.

"STEP INSIDE . . . IF YOU DARE."

No one moved. Milou could picture what they were seeing, because it was exactly as she and the others had planned it: a large open doorway that appeared to lead into nothing but foreboding darkness.

A sudden, dramatic discord sounded from the barrel organ inside the barn. Egg had clearly taken his place. Milou checked her watch. She had one minute to get into position, and yet the crowd was still staring at the theater in apprehension.

"TICK TOCK. YOUR DOOM AWAITS YOU."

A giggle rose. Then another. And another.

She was about to speak again when the crowd surged forward into the theater. Counting down the seconds in her head, Milou allowed herself a small smile, then slipped in through the side door, emerging in the small space behind the stage. The curtains were tightly closed, and the area was drenched in darkness. She felt her way to the ladder that led up to the puppeteering platform above the stage, still counting down.

Thirty seconds left.

She heard the side door open and close, then Sem appeared on the platform next to her. They each shuffled on their bellies to take the cross-sticks of their puppets.

"Ten seconds," Sem whispered.

Through the small grill next to their faces, which looked out into the main seating area, they could just about make out the shadowed lumps of people settling in.

"Well?" Milou asked, her voice full of pleading. "Did you see them?"

She couldn't see Sem's face, but she heard him sigh softly, and her heart dropped to her stomach.

"No—"

A long whistling sound came through the large hole in the barn's roof, then the theater exploded with color and light. Lotta's fireworks lit up the night sky in bright bursts and wriggling lines. The audience all gaped upward, their faces glowing red, yellow, blue, green. Milou pressed her face against the grill, searching each illuminated face. She spotted Edda by the door, and that strange cowled figure, which still had its hood up and white-gloved hands folded neatly on the lap.

No midnight-dark hair, though.

And no eyes that were almost black.

A lump climbed up her throat and lodged at the back of her mouth.

The audience cheered as the fireworks display came to a loud, dramatic end. Then Egg's harsh, discordant organ music began again, as pleasing as nails on a chalkboard. Milou felt like she might be sick, but for a very different reason. Why hadn't she seen her family? Why hadn't Sem seen them?

Lotta's mechanical ghosts began to swirl across the ceiling, trailing ripped cloth over the heads of the startled and delighted crowd. They circled the room once and then came to a stop. Below her, Milou felt the clunking of cogs being turned, and the stage curtains squealed open. Several electrical lights popped into life on the stage ceiling, illuminating a life-sized girl puppet. In her arms was a rusted cage, a blood-red heart suspended in the middle of it.

A particularly loud chord sounded, Milou's cue to start, and the sound echoed. The crowd's cheers died away, and they all looked on expectantly, waiting for the show to begin. In the light that spilled up from the stage, she saw Sem smile encouragingly at her.

Egg repeated his cue chord, and Milou put her lips to the speaking tube set up beside her.

All that came out of her mouth, however, was a deep, strangled croak.

❊ THIRTY-THREE ❊

MILOU SQUEEZED HER EYES closed. The deathly silence crackled in her ears. Panic clung to her skin with tiny, ice-like needles. She'd never frozen like this before, not once. And yet, despite the urgency of the situation, there was nothing she could do to get words to leave her lips. She just couldn't do it.

"Milou?"

Sem's voice was quiet but enough to make Milou's eyes snap open again. Lotta's head had appeared at the end of the puppeteering platform. They both looked at her in urgency.

Another discord rang out.

More awkward silence followed, winding its way around

Milou's throat and squeezing tight. Someone in the crowd booed. Again, Milou tried to speak into the speaking tube but couldn't form words.

Where were her parents?

One person stood to leave, and Sem gave her a little shake.

"Milou," he urged. His face was lined with worry. "Please—"

Milou felt a hot, sticky tear slide down her cheek. Her chest was too heavy.

Then a whistle sounded; high and melodic, like birdsong. Through the gaps in the platform, Milou saw Fenna standing on the stage, one hand held up in the air.

Milou's breath hitched at the sight. She didn't have to look at the audience to know that all eyes were fixed on Fenna, who just weeks ago would have been more likely have jumped into a pit of hungry snakes than to stand on a stage in front of over a hundred strangers.

She could tell by the stiffness of Fenna's shoulders that her friend was anything but comfortable. And yet, there she stood, as brave as a warrior, with the sole purpose, no doubt, of giving Milou a moment to gather herself before their entire plan fell to bits.

Fenna whistled again, the opening two bars of *Eine Kleine Nachtmusik*. Although her new voice was rough and wary, her whistling was smooth and assured, as if she were part songbird herself. She whistled the tune once more, and as soon as the last note tapered off, a *screeeeeeeech* responded from the theater barn's hole-riddled rafters.

A collective gasp sounded around the audience, and then Milou heard the rustle of wings. Mozart emerged against the night sky, spiraling down into the theater. He *screeeeeeched* as he flew, making his way to Fenna's outstretched hand.

Mozart *hooOOooOO*ed from the stage, and the crowd clapped. Fenna cast a glance upward, and even though Milou knew she couldn't see her, she nodded down to her friend and pressed her lips to the speaking tube once more.

She banished all thoughts of her parents and sister, holding the faces of her friends in her mind's eye. They were counting on her, and she refused to let them down.

"EVERY NIGHT, THE NIGHTMARES COME."

Her voice was raspy and dry, but steady. She kept her eyes locked on Sem, who smiled in encouragement.

"THERE IS NO STOPPING THEM. NOT WHEN THEY SINK THEIR CLAWS INTO YOU, ONCE THEY'VE DRUNK FROM YOUR SOUL AND TASTED YOUR FEAR."

Milou tilted the puppet's head, so that Theodora looked out across the audience. Egg had painted her face in eternal sadness; her long red hair hung limply down her cheeks, and her knees were drawn up to her chin.

A soft tinkling of music emanated from the barrel organ,

and the ghosts dropped on invisible strings to glide in circles over the audience once more. Under Milou's deft control, Theodora walked to the front of the stage, her limbs moving oddly but somehow elegantly, matching the beat of the sad symphony that filled the barn.

"MY NAME IS THEODORA TENDERHEART, AND TONIGHT THE NIGHTMARES WILL COME FOR ME ONCE MORE."

The plain backdrop fell, revealing the gnarled and twisting Night Tree on the back wall.

"THEODORA TENDERHEART," the Night Tree said, in Milou's raspy voice. "IT IS TIME."

"LEAVE ME BE!"

Sem's werewolf puppet walked onstage, lunged forward, and grabbed Theodora. Milou howled into the speaking tube.

"ARROOOOOOOOOOOOOOOOOOOOOOOOOO-OOOOO!"

The audience's gasps turned into strangled yelps.

Milou and Sem guided the puppets on their journey through the nightmare realm. Even though she didn't look at the audience, Milou could hear their gasps and cries. As the iron bars of the carnival's ghastly gates slammed down onto the stage, Milou couldn't help herself; she leaned forward to get a peek at the crowd. Their eyes were wide and unblinking. Milou smiled, puppet sticks dancing in her hands.

"YOU MUST GO THROUGH THE GATES!"

Egg's music started again. This time it was livelier, though still tuneless, as if someone were dancing on the keys of an organ. More puppets appeared onstage, behind the iron gate. Monstrous ones. Mechanical, like the ghosts. They danced and frolicked behind the gate, calling Theodora's name again and again, as Milou dragged the puppet toward the gate, seemingly against its will. Theodora was just one step away when the curtains whipped closed and the oil lamps extinguished simultaneously, throwing the theater into sudden darkness. But before the audience had a chance to respond, the curtains squealed open again, and a single electric light bulb lit the stage.

It was time for Milou's ending to Liesel's story.

It was time for Theodora Tenderheart to die.

That, Milou had realized, was what the nightmares represented: Theodora's fear of dying. It was why Milou had had nightmares herself, about drowning beneath Rotman's burning ship. Milou had not stepped through those ghastly gates, but Theodora *had*. She had entered the carnival, but that didn't mean she had to suffer. Milou knew there was only one antidote to nightmares.

Theodora was back in her bed, her head in her hands and her shoulders heaving. Slowly, she climbed out of the bed and walked to the edge of the stage.

"I CANNOT REFUSE THE CARNIVAL MUCH LONGER." Milou paused for a long moment, keeping the audience waiting and wanting. "NEXT TIME I FALL ASLEEP, THE NIGHTMARES WILL HAVE ME. I WILL BECOME ONE OF THEM: A SPIRIT BOUND TO THE SHADOWS. I WILL BE LOST . . . FOREVERMORE."

The crowd was silent, except for the creaking of seats as they leaned forward. Milou adjusted the puppet's strings. A steady *thud-thud-thud* filled the room as Milou tapped the speaking tube's mouthpiece.

Theodora's heartbeat slowed.

Thud—thud—thud.

And slowed.

Thud. Thud. Thud.

And slowed.

Thud . . . Thud . . . Thud.

"I AM DYING," Theodora said quietly. "AND I AM SCARED."

There were sniffs from the front row and a wail from the middle. Milou heard the distant clunking of a crank being turned. The curtains closed once more, then opened again to reveal Theodora standing in front of the carnival's gates. Hendrik emerged from stage left; a cotton wolf's head on cotton boy's body. The audience gasped as Sem guided the puppet in a creeping walk toward Theodora.

"THEODORA," Hendrik said, stalking ever closer. "THE CARNIVAL AWAITS."

The monsters danced to the wailing organ, their grotesque

shadows swaying behind them. Their faces were terrifying: blood-red eyes, long teeth emerging from hideous snarls. And the music . . . it set teeth on edge; each clashing discord was like listening to the screaming brakes of a steam train. The music came to an abrupt halt.

"IT IS TIME," Hendrik Longtooth said, holding out a cotton hand to Theodora. "THERE IS NO NEED TO BE SCARED."

"NO NEED!" Theodora cried. "THOSE MONSTERS WILL EAT ME! THEY'LL TEAR MY FLESH FROM MY BONES. THEY'LL SLURP MY EYEBALLS. THEY'LL—"

"MONSTERS?" Hendrik said, quizzically. "WHAT MONSTERS?"

An unpleasant, high-pitched minor chord punctuated his sentence.

"THOSE MONSTERS," Theodora said, nodding toward the gate.

"WHAT MONSTERS?" Hendrik repeated, looking behind him and then back at Theodora.

Milou smiled at Sem. She moved her mouth away from the mouthpiece. "Any moment now," she whispered to him.

"Behind you!" someone shouted.

Milou's grin widened, and she nodded to Sem. It was just as they'd rehearsed.

Sem twisted Hendrik Longtooth's head to face the audience.

"WHAT DID YOU SAY?" Hendrik said, cocking his cotton head.

Someone giggled. "The monsters are behind you!" a girl cried out.

"Behind the gates!" shouted another.

More shouts and laughter erupted from the crowd. The music rose with it. Hendrik Longtooth leapt to the front of the stage in one huge jump and snapped his teeth. The shouts and laughter stopped, and so did the music.

"MONSTERS, YOU SAY?" He turned and approached the gate. It swung open, and the monsters behind it stopped dancing. "YOU THINK THERE ARE MONSTERS IN THERE?"

"I CAN *SEE* MONSTERS IN THERE!" Theodora shouted. "AND I WON'T LET YOU FEED ME TO THEM!"

"FEED YOU?" Hendrik said. "TO MONSTERS?" He shook his cotton head. "THEY ARE NOT MONSTERS, THEODORA."

"LIES!"

"COME NOW, I'LL SHOW YOU."

He held out a hand. Theodora clutched her heart cage to her chest.

"NO!" she cried out.

Members of the audience began to repeat her cries. Theodora Tenderhart took a wobbly step toward the gate. She moved forward, her limbs moving in a disjointed way.

"No!" someone called out again.

Theodora stepped inside the gate, and the shadow monsters lunged for her.

The lights blinked out and the stage was swathed in utter darkness. The organ fell silent. The shadows were so deep that no amount of squinting or leaning forward would help the crowd see what was on the stage.

And then a *screeeeeech* sounded at the back of the barn. Milou saw the audience twist in their seats. Standing atop a crate was Fenna, red curls spilling out from the shadows of her hood. Her left arm was outstretched, with Mozart perched up on it.

The owl's head turned mechanically around the room. Milou whistled, just as Fenna had taught her. Mozart flapped his wings frantically for a few moments and then launched into the air, a piece of string dangling from his claw. The bottom of the string was sparking, tiny little flames shooting out of it. As Mozart spiraled toward the stage, small sparks sprayed over the crowd. He flew over the stage and dropped the string. It fell like a feather, but as soon as it hit the stage floor, more silvery sparks erupted, and then what seemed like a thousand tiny oil lamps erupted into light. The stage shimmered brightly, revealing that the monsters were gone. Mozart settled on the platform beside Milou, chewing happily at the piece of meat she'd just handed him.

"WHERE ARE THEY?" Theodora Tenderhart asked, performing a shaky pirouette.

"SHH," Hendrik said. His head had twisted around in a half rotation, revealing an entirely plain-looking face. "LIS-TEN."

There was a squeak from the side of the stage, and then music began to tinkle into the room. Edda's music box emitted light, flighty notes, projected through another hidden speaking tube.

"BUT . . . THE NIGHTMARES . . ."

Hendrik shook his head. "THERE ARE NO NIGHT-MARES HERE."

More stars appeared, lowering down from the stage ceiling, and twinkled merrily.

"AM I DREAMING?" Theodora asked.

"YES," Hendrik replied. He caught a star and held it out to her. "A DREAM THAT WILL NEVER END. NO MORE FEAR, NO MORE PAIN. A DREAM IN WHICH YOU CAN BE HAPPY AND AT PEACE. FOREVER."

Theodora took the star from him and held it to her chest, where her heart cage had been.

Then the curtains fell closed.

Silence settled like a blanket over the crowd.

Nervously, Milou peered through the grate to see their reaction. A woman three rows from the front was on the verge of bawling, snot bubbling from her left nostril. Edda's cheeks looked damp. The cowled figure sat more rigidly, gloved fingers entwined tightly together. A man in a bright-blue tailcoat stood and began to clap. Another person stood and did the same. Then another. Milou felt the lump in her throat loosen as the entire audience got to their feet to clap and cheer.

She did not notice the cowled figure slip quietly away.

❊ THIRTY-FOUR ❊

THE POPPENMAKER CHILDREN PEERED through the closed curtains as the crowd slowly made its way out of the theater, some of them still clapping, many of them still wiping tears from their cheeks.

"Isn't that the Fortuyns over there, the ones who adopted little Jan?" Egg said. "And there's the doctor who set Sem's broken arm last year."

"Where's Edda?" Lotta asked. "I wanted to ask her what she thought of it all."

Milou was searching the crowd too, still desperately hoping to spot a trio with hair as dark as midnight and eyes that were almost black. She saw no one who matched that description, though. The glee she'd felt when performing was gone, snuffed out by overwhelming despair. Milou looked for the cowled figure she'd seen earlier, but that person seemed long gone as well. There was no one lingering in the theater. No one making their way to the stage to find her.

Where was her family?

"Are you all right?" Sem asked quietly.

Milou couldn't speak. She couldn't even shake her head. She took a deep breath and closed her eyes for a moment. All was not lost. It was just a setback. If they weren't here, then they obviously hadn't seen her advertisement. Milou would just have to wait until they did the next show—she'd send advertisements out to France, Belgium, and Germany too.

"Milou?" Sem repeated.

"I'm okay," Milou said, trying to believe her own words. "They'll come, one day. I just need to wait a bit longer."

There was a tinkling behind her, and Milou turned to find Lotta now sitting on the stage, running her fingers through a basket full of coins.

"How did we do?" Egg asked.

The others all crowded around Lotta, but Milou couldn't make herself let go of the curtain. Perhaps, when she looked around again, she'd see her family waiting.

Lotta grabbed a handful of silver coins. "It will take a little while to count it all to be certain, but . . ." She let the money slip through her fingers and tinkle into the basket again. "This looks like more than double what we'd hoped for."

Milou smiled, thoughts of her family buried beneath a deep sense of achievement. "We did it," she said breathlessly. "We're fr—"

There was a sharp pinch at her ear and a screeching of curtain rails above her. The curtain was wrenched from Milou's fingers, and someone grabbed her hair. She was pushed forward, her neck pulled backward, and found herself looking up a large nose, a thick mustachio sprouting out from underneath it. Her blood turned cold.

Rotman.

Milou caught a glimmer of metal in her peripheral vision. A cold, sharp point pressed against her collarbone. Sem straightened to his full height, his gangly limbs poised to move. Lotta staggered to her feet, clasping Fenna and Egg tightly. Milou's scalp was burning where Rotman held her hair in his fist, and she felt certain her neck would snap if he pulled it any further back.

"Nice show," Rotman growled. "It seems I underestimated just how profitable you lot could be," he continued, eyeing their money basket. "I suppose that might cover *some* of the damage you did to my ship."

"Go!" Milou cried to the others, struggling to get herself free. If she could hold Rotman off for just a few moments, the others would have time to flee. "Run!"

The others remained unmoving.

"Leave!" Milou repeated.

Sem shook his head. "No."

Egg coughed, his face pale. He shook his head too. "We're not leaving you."

"How sweet," Rotman growled in Milou's ears. "I have some delightful plans for the five of you."

Sem took a step toward Milou, his fists clenched.

"Ah-ah!" Rotman said, bringing the tip of his knife closer to her neck. "I'll have no nonsense. Especially not when I have such a lovely surprise for you. There's someone I'm very eager for you to meet again."

Milou's first thought was Dolly. The image of those sharp fangs and Sem's still-healing wound flashed in her mind. Was he going to feed them to that beastly dog?

"She should be here any moment now," Rotman said. "As for the the rest of you, behave yourselves, or little Milou here will no longer have a head attached to her neck."

Click-clack.

Milou's heart seemed to stop.

Click-clack-click-clack.

"It can't be," Lotta said, her eyes turning to the curtains.

Rotman smiled gleefully. "She's been *ever* so keen to see you again."

Click-clack-click-clack.

Milou's mind conjured the image of blank, staring eyes.

"No," Egg choked.

Click-clack-click-clack.

Milou knew that sound as well as she knew the faces of the four terrified children in front of her, but her mind still refused to believe it.

Click.

Clack.

Click.

Milou was just contemplating whether Rotman was playing a cruel joke on them, when the curtains were wrenched open. A large, rotund silhouette stood on the edge of the stage, face hidden in shadows. The five of them stared up at it.

Clack.

Click.

Two steps in, and the small lantern behind the stage illuminated the figure's hawk-like face and furious beady eyes. Milou's legs went completely limp, and she sagged against Rotman.

Gassbeek was back from the dead.

✤ THIRTY-FIVE ✤

THE MATRON'S FACE LOOKED pale and sickly, but her expression was just as brutal as it had always been. Her chest heaved up and down as she glared at the orphans, fury radiating from every inch of her. Milou felt bile climb up her throat. What she was seeing couldn't be true; and yet . . . it was.

Gassbeek was *alive*, and Milou was certain she'd die herself, right there and then, from the horror of it.

"*Hallo, kindjes.*"

Sem shook his head. "You're dead."

The matron clucked her tongue. "You really should have checked more carefully. I was no deader than you are right now."

"How?" Lotta asked.

"An acute episode of terror-induced catatonia. That's what the doctors in the asylum called it. I spent twelve days in a lumpy bed, staring at a gray wall, unable to talk or move. I did, however, have a lot of time to think about how much I'd like to rip each one of your limbs off."

Her friends fell silent. Milou was starting to lose feeling in her legs.

"Pleasant reunions aside," Rotman said, addressing the matron, "is she here yet?"

She? Who else could there be?

Gassbeek nodded. "You keep a firm hold of that one." She reached out and grabbed Lotta by a pigtail. "I'll take this one. The other three can carry our money between them."

She twisted her fingers, and Lotta whimpered in pain. Fenna let out a deep growl, right from the chest. Gassbeek paused, cocked her head, and then laughed. Fenna launched at Gassbeek, grabbed her arm, and shoved her away from Lotta. From the stage roof, Mozart let out a shrill, angry shriek.

Gassbeek gaped up at the owl, then down at Fenna.

"These children aren't very bright, are they?" Rotman growled. He pressed the blade closer to Milou's throat, and she gasped as a sharp sting bit just below her chin. "If you do not do as we say, I will spill more than just a droplet of this one's blood. Four orphans would be enough for my ship. I'd just have to work you all a little harder to make up for losing the fifth, that's all."

Fenna lowered her gaze and stepped away from Gassbeek.

"Let's get this over with," Rotman said, dragging Milou to the steps beside the stage.

She staggered along with him, her feet barely touching the floor. What did he mean by "get this over with"? Was he going to kill them? How had they found them? And who else were they waiting for?

The air was bitingly cold as they made their way to the windmill. The crowds were gone, and Milou could see a trail of swaying lanterns making its way down the road, back to the city.

As they rounded the corner, Milou saw a horse and carriage pulled up outside the front door—with Rose Speelman stepping out of it. She was carrying the enormous Little Tulip record book in her arms and wearing an impatient frown. It was the second figure, however, that made Milou bite back a scream of fury.

Edda Finkelstein was standing there, arms crossed, and wearing her polder warden uniform.

She'd betrayed them.

"*Goedenavond*!" Rotman said cheerfully. Milou's hair was suddenly released, and the knife disappeared from her throat. Rotman put a heavy hand on her shoulder. "I was just retrieving the little darlings, so sorry to keep you waiting."

"I'm still not sure why you asked me here," Speelman said. "And I am entirely confuddled as to why this couldn't have waited until morning."

"Let's get inside so we can explain," Gassbeek crowed. "The children can get us each a nice mug of warm milk while we talk."

"My father is still not well," Milou said hastily. "He'll be upset if we disturb him."

Speelman shifted the record book onto her other hip.

"Yes," Edda said, to Milou's surprise. "Perhaps it is a little late in the day—"

"Nonsense!" Gassbeek squawked, elbowing her way to the door. "Meneer Poppenmaker doesn't mind at all."

Before Milou could think of anything else to stall the inevitable, Gassbeek shouldered the door open, and they were all marched inside.

"Matron Gassbeek," Speelman sputtered, staggering in behind them as Edda closed the door. "It is polite to knock first—"

Gassbeek whirled from her spot in the middle of the kitchen, a delighted smirk on her face.

"Mevrouw Speelman," she said. "I have already checked with Meneer Poppenmaker here"—she nodded toward the chair in the corner where Puppet Papa sat—"and he really doesn't mind us intruding. Isn't that so, Meneer?"

"Stop!" Milou shouted, but Gassbeek *click-clacked* across

the room and stood next to Puppet Papa. "Just stop, please."

"Stop what, Milou?" the matron said, feigning innocence.

Milou squeezed her lips together and scowled. This shouldn't be happening. They had been free just a few minutes ago. And now Gassbeek was going to take everything from them, like she always had done. Milou realized she had no fight left in her. Beside her, she saw her friends' shoulders droop in resignation.

Their escape, the ship, the show. It had all been for nothing.

Edda Finkelstein had lived up to Milou's suspicions.

And, on top of it all, her parents hadn't come home to her.

"Matron Gassbeek," Speelman said, looking between Milou and the matron with a look of confusion. "What is going on here?"

"Let me show you," Gassbeek cawed, patting Puppet Papa on the shoulder. "These little orphans have woven quite the deception for you, and it needs exposing."

Then with a smirk aimed straight at Milou, Gassbeek wrenched Puppet Papa's cotton head from his grass-filled body.

THIRTY-SIX

SPEELMAN'S SHRIEK RICOCHETED OFF the walls. She dropped the record book and held her hands over her mouth to hide her horror. Milou sank into a chair by the table, too distraught to cry. She barely listened as the matron began to explain to the Kinderbureau agent that the children had left her for dead, stolen from her, forged documents, and run away like petty criminals. Instead, Milou glanced at Edda, who was showing no signs of shock at seeing Puppet Papa for what he really was. In fact, her face was completely blank, except for the tiniest crease of her brow.

"Why would you do this to us?" Milou stared at Edda. "You've ruined everything."

Both of Edda's eyebrows rose. "I didn't—"

"You knew all along, didn't you? It was you at the window that first night, wasn't it?"

Edda nodded. "I knew, but—"

Gassbeek's voice reached a crescendo. "They are charlatans!"

"I don't believe it," Speelman said. She was holding Puppet Papa's head and frowning. "How can five little *orphans* manage all this?"

"These five are nothing but trouble," Gassbeek shrieked. "Trust me, I've had the unpleasant misfortune of knowing them all their pathetic little lives. You have no idea how pleased I was when I heard the doctors talking about the show. Bram Poppenmaker indeed. The very name on that stupid little doll of yours, Milou. It seems that was enough to pull me from my stupor."

Milou swallowed, casting a guilty glance at Edda, who was glowering at Gassbeek and clasping her locket.

"I just . . ." Speelman said. "I'm not sure what I should do about this. I'll have to consider the legalities—"

"There's nothing to consider." Gassbeek cut her off. "These children lied. They are still *my* property and need to be brought back to the Little Tulip immediately. Meneer Rotman here has already agreed to purchase them."

"We are not property!" Milou said. "And we are not coming back with you."

"Girl, be quiet and let the grown-ups talk," Gassbeek said with a wave of her gnarled hand. "Now, Meneer Rotman and I will take them back to Amsterdam. You need not bother yourself with these delinquents, Mevrouw Speelman. I will make sure to it that they are suitably punished."

"We have the money to buy our adoption," Milou said, nodding toward the basket of coins by Rotman's feet. "Take it and leave us be. We don't need Rotman to adopt us, we are fine as we are."

"That is my money," Gassbeek said. "They stole it from me."

"No," Fenna croaked.

Gassbeek shot Fenna a dangerous look; one that promised repercussions. Milou watched in amazement as Fenna—shy, timid Fenna—stared right back at the matron, unblinking and fierce.

"You can't do this!" Sem cried. "We earned this money."

"They are lying," Gassbeek snapped. "It's mine, and I shall be taking it back right this instant."

"She made a deal with Rotman," Lotta cut in. "She was going to sell us and keep the money for herself. And Rotman is nothing more than a charlatan. He plans to work us until we break. We had to rescue Egg from his ship, where he was *chained* belowdecks."

"Oh my." Rotman chuckled. "These five little darlings have such delightfully dramatic imaginations. Dolly and I cannot wait for them to join our seafaring family."

"You tried to kill us," Egg cried. "You nearly did, in fact."

Rotman's eyes glimmered with mirth. Gassbeek's smile was—as ever—all teeth, but no soul.

"And Gassbeek," said Lotta, "is not only a miserable witch. She takes money that should be spent on the orphans—"

Gassbeek grabbed Lotta's pigtail. "Liar!"

"Mevrouw Gassbeek," Speelman said. "The Kinderbureau does not abide the manhandling of children—"

"Nonsense," Gassbeek said. "I was manhandled plenty when I was an orph—" She cut herself off with a shake of her head and let go of Lotta's hair. "Fine," she spat out. "But you will be silent, Lotta, if you do not want to earn more of my wrath."

"It's true," Milou said. "What Lotta's saying. I heard them strike a deal. He even laughed when he said he could bury our bodies at sea. And this Dolly he claims will be our mother is a *dog*."

"Don't be so rude!" Speelman cried. "I will not abide any name calling."

"It's true!" Milou yelled back. "She's a real dog, not a woman."

Rose Speelman pinched the bridge of her nose in frustration. Milou glanced at Edda, whose expression had hardened.

"This is ridiculous," Gassbeek squawked. "These children

are proven liars. They are simply trying to weasel themselves out of the trouble they've gotten themselves into."

"That's not true!" Lotta cried.

"Enough!" Speelman slammed her fist on the table, making everyone jump. "You five have not only broken the law by forging official records, you have intruded on private property," she said. "I will not listen to more of your nonsense."

Gassbeek grinned triumphantly. Milou balled her fingers into tight fists. From Fenna's shoulder, Mozart let out a shrill *screeeeeeeeech*.

"This ends now," Speelman continued, picking up the record book and placing it with a *thunk* on the table. "These records *must* be put right. The five of you *must* have legal guardians, and the fees *must* be settled immediately or you *must* return to the orphanage."

"Perhaps you should leave the children in my care and investigate their claims further," Edda said.

Everyone turned to stare at the polder warden.

"Absolutely not," Speelman spluttered. "This is being settled this very instant."

"But—" Milou started.

"No!" Speelman cried, her cheeks flushed. "The rules are the rules, and I will not abide them being broken any further." She opened the record book. "From this day forward, you will be charges of Meneer Rotman. And that is my final decision."

❖ THIRTY-SEVEN ❖

THE TEARS MILOU HAD been holding back finally began to trickle down her cheeks. Sem slumped into the chair beside her and squeezed her hand. Edda pulled Lotta and Fenna into a hug, and Egg was staring at the record book as if he might make it disintegrate with nothing but his mind.

They had fought so hard for their freedom.

And they had lost.

"Hurry along and fetch your belongings then, little *liefjes*," sang Rotman. "Dolly will be keen to get you settled in for the night, and it's terribly late already."

Reluctantly, Milou got to her feet and looked at where Puppet Papa's limp body lay crumpled and broken.

"I need a quill," Speelman was saying, patting down her cloak. "And an ink pot."

"Wait," interrupted Egg. "I can prove they're lying."

He was still staring at the record book. Then his eyes flicked to Milou's.

"She never recorded the Fortuyns' adoption," Egg said. "Do you remember? There was nothing in the book when we wrote our own adoption record."

Milou frowned, the memory tickling at the edges of her mind.

"*That's* how she did it," Egg said, more loudly this time. "She removed all records of those orphans whose adoption fees she kept for herself."

The kitchen fell so silent, they could have heard an eyelash drop.

"My records are, and always have been, utterly flawless," Gassbeek crowed. "Each orphan in that book is accounted for. There is no evidence whatsoever to back such a ridiculous claim."

"There is *always* evidence," Edda said coldly. "You just need to—"

"Look closely enough," Lotta finished. "Mevrouw Speelman, may I please see that record book?"

"No, girl," screeched Gassbeek. "You may not."

A charge of invisible energy seemed to pass between Lotta and Gassbeek; Milou could almost feel it. They both stood, shoulders stiffened and backs straight, glaring between each other and then at the record book that lay open on the table.

Gassbeek sucked in a sharp breath. "Don't you dare—"

Lotta sprang toward the table, but Gassbeek was closer. The matron scooped up the book and clutched it tightly to her chest as Lotta clawed at it.

"Give it to me!" Lotta yelled.

With her free hand, Gassbeek struck Lotta hard across the face. Redness blooming on her cheek, Lotta dived again at the matron. They both fell to the floor. It had happened within mere seconds, before Milou could remember how to move her limbs. In the corner, by Mozart's wardrobe, she noticed Rotman grinning wildly at the display.

Sem staggered toward the fight but stopped when Edda let out a yell of anger. The clock maker had a broom handle in her hands, which she held over her head as she strode purposefully toward the fighting duo. A carefully aimed kick sent Gassbeek sprawling onto her back. This was followed by swift jab of the broom handle that dislodged the record book from the matron's grasp. Milou gawped with astonishment.

It was over within a few heartbeats. Edda held the matron in a headlock, and Gassbeek cawed and squawked incoherently, her face growing redder and redder. Still lying on the floor, Lotta clutched the record book to her heaving chest with her twelve fingers.

"I'll find the evidence!" Lotta yelled, her lip bloodied and her eyes ablaze. "And you can't stop me from revealing it, you spiteful old crow!"

"This is absurd!" Speelman cried. "Never in all my life have I seen such appalling behavior!"

"I told you they were brats!" Gassbeek choked out.

"I'm talking about *your* vile actions, Matron!" Speelman said. "You should know better than anyone that striking children is against the rules!"

"She struck me too!" Gassbeek squawked, six thin red lines dribbling blood down her cheeks where Lotta had clawed her.

"You struck her *first*!" Edda said, her tone so furious that Milou barely recognized it. "And it is perfectly within my power to arrest you for such an action. Now." She glared at Speelman. "Sit yourself down and let Lotta speak freely."

Speelman opened her mouth to protest again, but Edda cut her off.

"You will hear these children out, or so help me I will put in a complaint about your conduct. I have contacts in high enough places."

Speelman slumped into a chair with a groan and waved a hand at Lotta. "You have two minutes."

Rotman's mirthful smile had turned forced. Standing beside him, Fenna clutched a startled Mozart in her arms.

"Egg," Lotta said. "Show me what you noticed."

"The little boy that the Fortuyns adopted, Jan," said Egg,

kneeling beside her. "When Milou and I were forging our own document, we saw that the matron hadn't recorded the adoption at all."

"Nonsense!" Gassbeek crowed. "There was no boy called Jan. They are trying to cover up the fact they tried to kill me—"

"Continue, please," Speelman said, raising a hand to silence Gassbeek.

Lotta was staring at the matron, and Milou could almost hear the cogs of her mind clunking away, working out the puzzle.

"There *was* a little boy called Jan. He was even at our show tonight," Lotta said, narrowing her eyes. Then she smiled. "He arrived at the Little Tulip in October, didn't he? Which means he'll be listed in the abandonment records."

She rifled through the pages, paused, rifled some more, and frowned.

"He's not in there because he never existed," Gassbeek squawked, smiling cruelly. "Now unhand me."

"No," Lotta said. "This doesn't make sense." She ran her finger along the inside crease of the book and then pulled it quickly away. "Ow!"

Her fingertip was bleeding.

"She's cut a page out," Egg gasped.

Speelman leaned over the book, scanned the page, then shot Gassbeek a furious glare. "They're right. You've sliced a page out."

"And if you look closely," Lotta said, pressing her nose right to the page, "you can see the imprint of Jan's name . . . *here*."

Gassbeek paled, and she began squirming again, but Edda held her tight. Rotman, meanwhile, was leaning against the sink next to Fenna, tapping his chin.

"I bet there's more," Lotta said. Sucking her finger, she flicked through more pages. "Here's another page missing. And another one."

"I've been set up!" Gassbeek cried.

"I wonder how long she's been doing this," Egg said, taking the book from Lotta. "I bet she—"

He stopped, his eyes widening on the page he had just opened.

"What is it?" Milou asked.

Egg looked at the matron. "An abandonment record," he said quietly. "For an *Elinora*, abandoned in a shoebox on the bottom step, June twentieth, 1838. Never adopted."

The matron screamed, her pointed boots clacking furiously on the kitchen floor as she kicked and stomped.

"I was owed that money!" she cried. "I spent my *entire* life in that miserable place."

"Matron Gassbeek," Speelman said sternly, slamming the record book closed. "Fraud on this scale is punishable by imprisonment. That money was meant to go to the Kinderbureau, to be shared out amongst *all* our orphanages."

Gassbeek opened her mouth, but then snapped it closed again.

"I have to say," Rotman said. "I am very shocked that the matron has been so duplicitous. Mevrouw Speelman, I think I shall just take these orphans and go. I have a ship to repair!"

"Duplicitous?" Gassbeek squawked. "You're a fine one to talk!"

Rotman's smile widened, as his mustachio twitched in double time. "I have no idea what you're talking about—"

"Matron Gassbeek," Speelman interrupted, ignoring Rotman completely. "I will be reporting this to the police at once."

"You can't do that!" Gassbeek cried. "I can't go to prison! Please!"

"Come now, orphans," Rotman crooned. "Let's get you settled in your new home, shall we? My ship is much more impressive than this rickety old windmill. You will love it, I just know you will."

Milou glared at him. Fenna and Sem took a step away. Egg glowered, and Lotta snorted. Gassbeek began thrashing wildly in Edda's grip.

"I'll make a deal!" the matron squawked, her face as terrified as those of the orphans she had tormented. "I have information on a larger, much more sinister orphan trade—"

"Come now!" Rotman repeated, more loudly this time, reaching out and grabbing Fenna's arm.

"Rotman's entire trade is off the backs of helpless orphans!" Gassbeek cawed. "He threatened me. I had no choice—"

"The matron is clearly still insane," Rotman growled, pulling Fenna toward him, who immediately began to struggle in his grip. "Perhaps she needs to go back to the lunatic asylum."

"Let Fenna go," Milou cried.

"No," Rotman growled. "I don't think I will."

In a flash of metal, Rotman's blade came out again.

This time, it was pointed at Fenna's throat, pressed right against her thumping pulse.

Mozart let out a screech, claws and beak aimed at Rotman's face, but the merchant slapped the bird away. With a flutter of ruffled feathers, Mozart spiraled up to the cupboard top. Milou picked up a candlestick from the kitchen counter. The sight of Fenna helpless in Rotman's grip was enough to make Milou recklessly angry. She would not let him hurt her.

"Meneer Rotman," Speelman cried, eyeing his knife in horror. "What are you doing?"

"I am taking what belongs to me," Rotman said, his mustachio trembling. "Five orphans, just as Matron Gassbeek promised me." With his free hand he picked up the basket of coins. "And the money these little brats owe me after setting fire to my ship."

Sem, Egg, and Lotta came to stand next to Milou. Edda

wrestled to keep Gassbeek contained, as the matron wriggled and mumbled around the tea towel that now protruded from her mouth.

"Let Fenna go," Edda said. "These children are not going anywhere with you."

Rotman chuckled. "And who, exactly, is going to stop me?"

No one spoke. No one dared. The knifepoint was too close to Fenna's jugular. A single twist of his wrist would kill her.

"Well?" Rotman boomed. "Which one of you pathetic idiots is going to stop me?"

"I am," said a deep voice.

It had spoken from near the stairwell, on the opposite side of the room from every single person in the kitchen. Startled gasps sounded as everyone spun to peer into the shadows under the stairs, to where Puppet Papa's headless body was slumped over the side of the rocking chair, just as Gassbeek had left him. Slowly, his right arm raised up to grab the side of the chair. Then his left one. He pulled himself upright, his back to them, then slowly turned.

"Let the child go," Puppet Papa said, in a voice like grinding bones.

❊ THIRTY-EIGHT ❊

THERE WAS A *THUD* behind her and Milou spun, only to find Rose Speelman had fainted headfirst onto the table where she'd been sitting.

"*I* will stop you," Puppet Papa said in a ghoulish grumble, raspy and ominous. Milou could practically hear the hairs rising on everyone's arms. "Let her go now, and I'll let you live."

Milou caught a tiny glimpse of a white glove above the stairwell door. The same white gloves, she thought, that had handed her coins at the gate earlier that evening.

Who was it?

She peeked at the others.

Rotman was gawping at the rocking chair. "How—"

"Surely you must have heard the rumors?" Milou said, her voice dropping to a menacing whisper. "This windmill is haunted. Did you not read the sign at the gate?"

Rotman blinked in disbelief. Gassbeek was now clutching Edda in terror, and the clock maker's Eyebrow of Curiosity was halfway up her forehead. Speelman was still facedown on the table, muttering incoherently to herself as she slowly came to.

"Heed my warning," Puppet Papa growled. He raised his hands up in front of him, as if he were ready to throttle Rotman. "Or I will crush your skull and pull your brains out through your nose."

Milou watch Rotman's hand twitch. She would have laughed, if not for the fact that Fenna was still trapped beneath that cruel blade of his.

"I'll cut you open before you have a chance," Rotman said, but his voice trembled as much as his mustachio.

Milou kept her eyes fixed on the blade, noticing with silent glee that Rotman's hand was lowering. She shared a pointed look with the others. With the adults no longer looking her way, she used her eyes to indicate that they should move soon to free Fenna.

"Who . . . who are you?" Rotman yelled, squinting at Puppet Papa.

"Your greatest nightmare . . ."

The blade lowered a fraction more, and Milou felt a gentle tingling in her ears. It ran down the back of her shoulders and gave her a nudge of encouragement.

"Now," Milou mouthed to the others.

Sem swung his leg; it connected with the back of Rotman's knee, and the merchant tipped forward. At the same moment, Fenna twisted at an impossible angle, sliding out of his loosened grip as if she were made of water. She tucked and rolled out of reach. Lotta staggered over and threw the contents of a mug into Rotman's face, just as Milou brought the candlestick down on his knife-wielding hand, sending the blade clattering to the ground.

She kicked the knife under the table as Rotman swayed and rubbed at his eyes. When his gaze met hers, he roared in fury and strode toward Milou with deadly intent. He had made it only two steps before Egg appeared on the table behind the merchant and brought the record book down hard on his head.

Rotman crumpled, landing on his stomach.

It was over within a few hammering heartbeats.

"Did I kill him?" Egg squeaked.

Rotman let out a muffled groan in response.

Edda pushed Gassbeek into a chair. The matron squawked in indignation but remained seated as the clock maker grabbed some puppet string from the table and began tying the merchant's hands behind his back.

"You did not kill him," Edda said. "But he will wish he was dead when he wakes up. I intend to make sure he is locked in the darkest cell in all of Amsterdam, with nothing but rats and fleas to keep him company."

Speelman sat up, blinking furiously. "What's happening?" she asked. She looked down at Rotman and gasped. "How—"

Gassbeek gave a muffled squawk behind her tea-towel gag, her expression pained and defeated.

Milou, however, was staring at Puppet Papa, who was now slumped once more into his chair. Two white gloves appeared around the edge of the stairwell door, pushing it open. The cowled figure Milou had seen earlier stepped into the room, face still hidden in deep shadow.

The white gloves reached up and lowered the hood.

Milou's heart stopped dead.

It was a man she had never seen before, yet she knew him immediately.

He looked . . . like Liesel's portrait.

He had a potato-shaped face and one eye slightly larger than the other. Two plum-sized ears stuck out of the side of his head. And his hair . . .

His hair was the color of a sky-burnt sunset.

Milou couldn't speak. Her mouth was as dry as grave dirt, and her chest felt as if it were being crushed.

"Bram Poppenmaker?" Sem gasped.

The man was silent for what seemed like an age, his eyes boring down at Milou and his cheek twitching in annoyance. And then, with a low and disconcerting voice, he spoke.

"Indeed."

❧ THIRTY-NINE ❧

MILOU REALIZED SHE WAS biting the inside of her lip when the coppery taste of blood curled around her tongue. Her father was standing right there in front of her. He'd seen her message and come back.

She made a step toward him, wanting to wrap her arms around him, but stopping as she felt a sharp pinch on her left ear.

Why was he not overjoyed to see her?

Why was he . . . glowering?

"Excuse me," Speelman said, pushing through the five of them to get to Bram. "Meneer Poppenmaker. On behalf of the Kinderbureau, I apologize that these orphans have intruded on your property, stolen your identity, created a cotton copy of you, and caused general pandemonium. I shall see to it that they are suitably reprimanded, once I work out what to do with them—"

Bram Poppenmaker turned the full force of his glower onto the Kinderbureau agent, silencing her instantly.

"I want to hear from this pandemonium of Poppenmakers myself," he said. "I want to know why they saw fit to use my name, and my *daughter,* to drag me back here."

Milou noticed his voice cracked slightly. There was sadness leaking from beneath that angry glare; she could see it clearly, even though he was trying to keep it hidden.

"Bram," Edda said. "Perhaps we could all sit down and discuss this calmly."

"Is this your doing, Finkelstein?" Poppenmaker said, his words biting the air between them. "You seem to be in on it all. Why doesn't that surprise me?"

"It had nothing to do with Edda," Milou found herself saying. "It was all me."

Bram's gaze bore through her. "And who, exactly, are you?"

"My name is Milou Po—" She stopped, trying to swallow the lump in her throat, but it wouldn't budge. A gentle tingle tickled her neck. "I am Milou Poppenmaker," she said with a confidence she didn't truly feel. "*That* is who I am."

Bram cocked his head slightly. "Is that so?"

This was it. The moment she had been hoping for. The answers she craved, needed, were just a few moments away. And yet, Bram Poppenmaker barely even acknowledged her.

"Milou," she repeated slowly, waiting for him to show any indication of recognizing her. "It's me, *Milou*."

"And what are you doing in my windmill, Milou *Poppenmaker*?"

The bite to his words made Milou flinch. Why was he pretending not to know who she was?

"It's a long story—"

"It seems you're rather good at telling stories." He set Puppet Papa aside and sat down on the rocking chair, crossing his legs and then his arms. "So why don't you tell me exactly how you came to be in my windmill."

"I grew up in the Little Tulip Orphanage in Amsterdam," she began. "I was left on the roof . . ."

His gaze remained cold and fixed on her. If he now realized who she was, he was doing a very good job of not showing it. A tiny flutter of doubt settled in her. Still, her ears tingled softly, urging her to continue.

"That was twelve years ago . . ."

Still no response.

"In my basket was a cat puppet, made by you."

The tiniest frown creased his brow, but still he didn't

speak or acknowledge that it was he who had left her there.

Anger surged through Milou. Her ears prickled in warning, but she ignored it.

"I followed the coordinates you left for me. They led me right to that tree of yours."

He blinked. That was all.

"I found your name, and my mother's, carved up on the highest branch. I found the handkerchief with the rings ... Why are you pretending you don't know me? You know full well who I am, seeing as you abandoned me and never returned!"

Milou didn't realize she was shouting until she saw him flinch.

"I waited twelve years for you," she said, quieter this time but just as resentful. "I spent every single morning staring out the window, wondering if that would be the day you came back for me. And then, when you didn't, I thought perhaps you needed me to find you. I dreamed of you. I wrote down every little detail, every little clue, hoping to work out how I could find you. And here I am—"

Her voice caught. Tears burned a path down her cheeks.

"You had another daughter," she whispered. "Did you love Liesel more? Is that why you left me?"

She didn't know what else it could be. This was not how she had expected her reunion with her father to go. All these years of waiting, wondering, wishing—she had never considered she'd be met with this cold, hard look he wore, and his insistence on pretending he had no idea who she was.

"Do you even realize what it was *like* in that orphanage?" she continued when he still didn't respond. It infuriated her. "The matron was cruel. We were worked until our fingers cracked. We slept in cold rooms, in beds barely big enough for one, let alone two or three. She was going to *sell* us. Do you not care about any of that?"

Bram Poppenmaker blinked again. He opened his mouth to respond, but Milou cut him off.

"Please don't pretend you don't know who I am. All I want . . . all I've ever wanted . . . is answers."

"Milou . . ." Bram sighed, and now, finally he looked sorry. "I am not your father."

Milou blinked.

"You're lying. You're . . . you must be . . . My baby blanket," she mumbled. "It's velvet, just like your cloak. You stitched my name onto it, I know you did. And . . . and my puppet. You made it. I must be your daughter!"

She looked at him, searching his face for any hint of dishonesty, but she couldn't see any. His glower had softened, replaced with a new emotion that turned Milou's insides into a maelstrom of anguish.

He pitied her.

"But—"

Her words clogged her throat as she studied his features again. If she squinted, which she did just then, she thought that maybe, just maybe, their noses had the same rounded tip, but his was much longer. And his eyes were the brightest blue, not nearly black. And that red hair . . .

He looked *nothing* like her.

"I'm not your father, Milou," he repeated softly. "I'm sorry, but that is the simple truth of it. My wife, Annaliese, died many years before you were born. When Liesel was not much younger than you, in fact."

His words echoed around her head, and it felt as if she had fallen down a well. Even though her mind was insisting it was just a cruel lie—it *had* to be—her heart could see the truth of it in his eyes. He wasn't lying.

Bram Poppenmaker was not her father.

"I had only one child," Bram said quietly. "And I loved her very much. I would never have given her up. Liesel was everything to me."

Milou's trembling stopped, and her ear tips turned to ice. "Liesel *was*—?"

Bram's face crumpled. "Liesel is dead."

❧ FORTY ❧

MILOU'S HEART DIDN'T BREAK, it shattered. The tingling at her ears fell deathly still. An anguished cry filled the room. Milou turned to find Edda had slumped into the chair beside Gassbeek, her face completely pale and her eyes squeezed closed.

"Liesel . . . she's . . . ?" The polder warden's voice cracked at the edges. "She's *dead*?"

"Yes." Bram's expression hardened again. "No thanks to that cousin of yours."

Edda's eyes snapped open, filled with pain and fury all at once. "He loved her!"

"He killed her!"

The room fell silent. Eyebrows either furrowed or raised high, and it seemed like everyone had sucked in a startled, collective breath as Bram's words settled over them.

"No." The polder warden scowled. "He would never harm her. How did she die?"

"Consumption." Bram sighed. "The very same illness that took her mother."

Edda's scowl deepened. "How on earth can you blame that on—"

"She was supposed to be in bed, resting. I came back from Amsterdam late one night, only to see that unscrupulous cousin of yours hurrying away from the mill—even though I had forbidden his visits. I found Liesel slumped beneath the tree outside, paler than a ghost and shaking like a frightened mouse. A fever set in . . . It didn't get any better, no matter how much I tried—" He stared down at his gloved hands. "She died a week later, the day before her nineteenth birthday, in my arms."

Milou felt heartbroken. It didn't matter that Liesel wasn't actually her sister, as she'd believed. Not when she'd spent the last few weeks dreaming of what it would be like to meet her, to love her and be loved by her. They'd had so much in common, after all. Milou felt as if she had known Liesel, had already *loved* her.

"She's really gone?" Edda asked, her voice ragged. "She's been dead for twelve years—and you never thought to *tell* me? You let me think she'd just . . . left me." Edda was shaking, tears spilling down both cheeks. "Where is she?" she asked Bram. "Where did you bury her?"

Bram was silent for a moment, looking beyond the polder warden. He let out a long breath. "She's with her mother, of course."

Edda paled, her head snapping toward the window. Milou followed their gaze, to where the oak tree was framed perfectly in the center of the window.

"The flower garden," she whispered, understanding dawning on her. "You were tending to Mevrouw Poppenmaker's grave in Liesel's absence. That's why you were always under the tree."

Edda wiped a tear. "Liesel always said a flower garden was much more apt than a cold headstone. I just . . . I didn't want her to come back to find it overgrown or worse, barren. Little did I realize that I've spent the last twelve years tending to her grave too—"

Milou realized she'd been very, very wrong about the polder warden.

She hadn't hated Liesel. She'd *loved* Liesel.

It was written plainly over every inch of her anguished expression.

"You were friends with Liesel?" Milou asked Edda. "Was that why you've been loitering around here? Were you trying to find out what happened to her?"

Edda nodded. "She was the best friend I've ever had. The

only one, really. When my family first moved here from Strasbourg, she didn't stare at us like we didn't belong. She didn't care that we were different. But then she just *vanished*. I was hurt and angry, that she would leave without explanation, as if I meant nothing to her—not even a postcard. When months, then years passed, I bolted the mill's gates and refused to even look at it. And then the five of you turned up and brought it all back. And now I know—"

Silence fell heavily once more.

Milou's head was spinning.

"Liesel was stronger-willed than even you and I put together," Edda said finally, staring hard at Bram. "If she left her sickbed, she'd have done it by her own volition. I realize losing her must have broken your heart, but there's no use in blaming someone whose only crime was to love your daughter. And then punishing me for it, too."

"Theodora Tenderhart," Lotta said suddenly. "Was Liesel writing about herself? Did she know she was going to die?"

Bram nodded.

"She would have liked your ending," he said, smiling ruefully. "And she loved the puppet theater. Oh, how she loved it! Your show would have delighted her."

"Yes," Edda said, smiling slightly. "It really would have."

Fresh tears spilled from the polder warden's eyes. After another tense few heartbeats, she got to her feet. It looked like she was trying very hard not to cry. She faced the other children.

"Come on," she said, pulling Gassbeek up to her feet and nodding disdainfully at Rotman's still-prone figure. In all that had just happened, Milou had nearly forgotten about them. "Let's get these two reprobates into Speelman's carriage, shall we? I'll need to deliver them to the prison soon. Let's give Bram and Milou a few minutes to talk in peace."

Gassbeek made indignant protests, muffled by the tea towel, as Edda dragged her to her feet. Rotman was still unconscious. It took all four children to lift him, one limb each, and carry him out the door. Speelman tutted once, shot a sympathetic look in Milou's direction, then followed them outside.

The kitchen door was slammed shut by the wind, and Bram and Milou were alone.

Milou sat on the rocking chair opposite him, tucked her knees under her chin, and clutched them tightly. She didn't know what to say. Her ears tingled softly but constantly.

None of this felt right.

She couldn't have come all this way for nothing.

But if Bram wasn't her father, who was?

Who left her the watch, and the coordinates, and the puppet?

And why did they lead her here, of all places?

"Liesel—" Bram began, then took a deep breath and let out a sigh. "Do you know, I haven't said her name aloud since she—"

A hot tear rolled into the corner of Milou's mouth; partly for Bram's sad story, partly for the fact that everything she had ever believed in had just been torn from her. Even the sister she had spent the last few weeks pining for.

Bram lifted one of Puppet Papa's limp arms and smiled. "This is just the kind of madcap ruse Liesel would have come up with. You've got a fine imagination; I'll give you that. It was her last, dying wish that I fill that theater with her stories, so that she could live on through them."

"You promised her you wouldn't stop the puppet shows?" Milou asked, glowering at the puppet maker. "So why did you leave?"

"Because my heart cannot bear to be here," Bram said. "This place . . . there are too many memories of her—and her mother. Every item in this mill is a memory that hurts too much to hold on to. I left with nothing except the clothes on my back and a few boxes of boring work documents. Just sitting here, I feel like my heart is shattering all over again."

Milou's ears tingled again, more insistently this time.

There had to be something she'd missed.

Something to make sense of it all.

A thought was trying to push its way to the forefront of her mind, but she couldn't quite grasp at it.

She was so very, very tired.

And so very, very confused.

Bram Poppenmaker was now looking at Liesel's portrait of him. He seemed to have forgotten Milou was there entirely, lost to his memories.

She untucked the pocket watch from under her collar and held it out to him. "Do you really not recognize this?"

Bram shook his head. "Sorry, I don't."

Milou hurried to the back door and got her coffin basket. "This?"

Again, Bram shook his head.

Again, Milou's ears prodded her on.

She set the coffin on the floor and began to unpack it, setting her clothes and then the cat puppet aside. She unwrapped the handkerchief and held the rings out to him. "These?"

Bram jumped to his feet, his expression transforming instantly.

But it was not the rings he was looking at; it was her puppet.

Carefully, he picked it up. "This is Liesel's. How did you—"

The door opened and the Kinderbureau agent marched in, looking pleased with herself.

"Milou," Speelman said. "It's time to go."

Behind Speelman, her friends wandered back in, all looking resigned.

"Wait," Milou said.

Bram was turning the cat puppet over in his hands, looking grief-stricken once more.

"I've waited long enough, I really must get you back." Speelman turned around, only to walk into Edda, who had just appeared from outside.

The polder warden was staring at Milou's coffin in wide-eyed horror, looking as if she'd seen a ghost.

"That coffin . . ."

"It's all right," Lotta said. "It doesn't have a body in it. It's just—"

"No," Edda cried. "I *made* that coffin."

❋ FORTY-ONE ❋

MILOU'S EARS PRICKLED SHARPLY at the tips, and her heart shuddered almost to a stop. She looked at the basket, then back to Edda. A sliver of hope began to beat in her chest.

Edda shook her head. "I made it for my previous cat, Madame Meowkins. Those clasps . . . the weave . . . Look, it even has the claw marks from that pesky hound . . . I thought she'd chewed up the whole thing. How on earth did you—"

"My parents abandoned me inside it," Milou said, hardly able to breathe. "When I was about a week old, according to Gassbeek."

A heavy silence settled. Bram sat down heavily in the rocking chair again, frowning at Milou and Edda, clutching the cat puppet tightly. A chill crawled up the back of Milou's neck, and her ears prickled wildly, but when she tried to speak, no sound came out.

"It was December 1880," Egg said. "On an orphanage rooftop, under the full moon."

"It must have been the same night that Liesel died," Sem added. "Milou said you were seen leaving Poppenmill under the full moon that month."

Bram paled.

Edda made a small croak, her eyes wide as she turned back to Milou. "But—"

"There's more," Lotta said officially, reaching into Milou's sleeve and pulling out the Book of Theories. "A velvet blanket that looks like it could have come straight out of the Poppen-makers' workroom. The cat puppet, which certainly *did* come out of his workroom—it belonged to Liesel. A pocket watch with the coordinates of the oak tree just outside Poppenmill. Two wedding bands wrapped in a handkerchief embroidered with the name A. Poppenmaker—"

Lotta kept talking, but Milou's ears were now rushing so loudly her friend's voice sounded muffled and distant. She rubbed at her ears as she watched Edda's expression change from confusion to utter shock and Bram's face get impossibly paler.

"It can't be," Edda whispered, clutching that locket of hers with both hands.

The clock maker took Milou's pocket watch, her face paling too. "This is his." She looked up at Milou, eyes glistening with tears. "Oh, sweet cheese, do you think—"

She and the puppet maker shared a look.

"No. It can't be," Bram rasped. "I would have known."

Milou looked up at Lotta, who was frowning thoughtfully. Fenna and Egg were casting nervous glances between Milou and Edda. Sem inched closer toward her, his eyes never leaving Edda.

Neither Bram or Edda moved or spoke for several long moments.

They were both too busy staring at Milou.

Then, letting go of the pocket watch, Edda reached up and gently tilted Milou's face this way and that, examining every detail. The tingling on Milou's ears intensified, running down the sides of her neck and back up again.

"How did I not notice?"

Sem squeezed in closer. "Notice what?"

Edda shook her head again, staring deeply into Milou's eyes.

Milou's breath seemed to be stuck in her chest. Finally, Edda's shaking fingers let go of her chin, and the clock maker took a step back.

"You look just like him."

The world seemed to tilt around Milou. Sem's hand clasped around her elbow and held her tight.

"But you have *her* nose," Edda continued.

Milou felt rivulets of thick, hot tears sliding down both her cheeks. Yet still, her lips seemed unable to form words.

"Whose nose?" Egg asked.

"Liesel," Lotta whispered. "She was named Anna*liese*, after her mother. That's why her handkerchief had the initial A on it. Is that right?"

"Yes," Bram said softly, getting slowly to his feet. He took Milou's chin in one gloved hand and studied her. "Dear God, Finkelstein, you're right. She's Liesel's—but . . . but, how could she have hidden this from me?"

"The dresses," Sem said. "The aprons around the middle. Perhaps Liesel made them to hide her growing stomach?"

Bram seemed not to hear him, but Milou's ears were ringing with his words.

"But Bram would have noticed her having the baby!" Edda said, sending a questioning glare at the puppet maker. "You must have known."

Bram let go of Milou's chin and closed his eyes. "I did not."

"Maybe Milou was born elsewhere," Lotta said. "Somewhere close—"

"The theater!" Egg said. "That *might* explain the blankets we found on the stage. It *would* explain why she left the mill that night, even though she was so ill."

Her friends' voices were getting louder, but the tightness

in her chest and throat was getting worse. Milou tried to answer but couldn't. She couldn't even nod. Edda and Bram seemed just as much at a loss for words.

"And the wedding rings," Lotta said. "Perhaps they were planning to marry, as soon as you were born. But Liesel was already too sick. Oh! He must have been heartbroken when he learned Liesel had—"

"Who is he?"

Milou's voice was barely audible, but it silenced the room, nonetheless.

Edda wiped a tear from her cheek and shook herself. When she spoke again, her voice cracked on almost every word. "Thirteen years ago, my cousin came to live with me. He and Liesel, they were . . . well, they were very close, although—oh, Milou, I never suspected they had—and then he left so suddenly, just after Liesel did, without any explanation. I simply assumed he . . . your *father* . . . had gone to find her, wherever she had gone."

Father.

The word shot through Milou's heart like an arrow. It broke her apart and then pieced her together again; slightly more whole than before, but still achingly hollow in places.

"The people around here—" Edda wiped at a tear. "Let's just say they didn't think much of a scruffy boy with a wild look about him and a large dog that ate everything she could get her jaws around. They didn't know the kind-hearted, slightly awkward boy I knew. Only Liesel saw it because, as with me, she was the only one willing to *look*."

Milou's throat clogged again. The tears seemed to thicken, curling over her chin and down her neck. The ear tingling became a gentle, soothing caress.

"Here," Edda said, clasping her locket again. "I have him here."

With shaking fingers, Edda reached up and pulled it up over her head. Milou took the locket from Edda and looked down at it, her hands shaking so much she thought she might drop it. A six-fingered hand appeared and helped her unclip the small clasp. But as her friends gathered more closely around her, Milou's fingers closed around the locket. She looked up helplessly at them, then took a shaky breath and opened the locket.

Inside was a photograph of a young man with a wolfish grin. His unruly hair was as dark as midnight, and his eyes were almost black. At his feet lay a large gray hound—its paws the size of breakfast plates. And on the corner of the photogram, etched in neat handwriting, was a name:

Thibault.

❊ FORTY-TWO ❊

MILOU STARED AT THE picture of Thibault.

    The claw marks.

    The pocket watch.

    The wildness of her very own features.

    It had all come from him.

    Milou clasped a hand around the pocket watch.

> Beneath the stars I found you.
> Under the moon I lost you.

    Her parents had fallen in love, sitting in the oak tree, watching the stars.

    Then her mother had died, on the night of a full moon.

The inscription hadn't been for Milou at all.

It had been for Liesel.

"I don't know why he left you the way he did," Edda said. "How he could have borne it. But I do know he always did what he felt was right."

Milou snapped the locket closed and handed it back to Edda. She had wanted answers, and now she had them.

Her mother was dead.

Her father was gone.

Her heart felt hollow.

"Sorry to interrupt," Speelman said, without sounding sorry in the slightest. "But I need to get the orphans back to the Little Tulip tonight." She gave Bram a big, toothy smile, then nodded her head at Milou. "I suppose you'd like to keep this one, yes?"

Bram blinked.

"Excellent." Speelman dropped the record book on his lap and handed him a quill. "Please sign here, that's it, thank you. Now, the rest of you, let's go."

"No," Milou said. "You can't take them back there."

"Rules are rules, dear child," Speelman said, hefting the record book up.

Milou looked to Bram pleadingly. "Can you—"

Her grandfather sighed. "Milou, until a few moments ago I was a childless widower. Now I have a surprise granddaughter to take care of. I can't take on five . . ."

"Well then," Speelman said brightly. "That's that. *Kindjes,* gather your things, say goodbye, do it quickly."

Milou blocked the doorway, her mind whirling. "Please don't—"

"Wait," Edda said.

They all turned to her expectantly. She was holding Lotta protectively.

Speelman frowned at her.

"These children are perfectly adept at caring for themselves," Edda said. "They've certainly proven that. Their tenacity is quite astonishing. Surely, there must be some way around all this?"

The Kinderbureau agent sighed. "Firstly, I would require a legal guardian be named for any minor without a biological parent or relative. Secondly, tenacity does not impress the Kinderbureau nearly as much as accurate records do. And thirdly, the children have nowhere to live."

"They can live here, of course," Bram said matter-of-factly. "Edda, would you still be interested in buying this place?"

Edda looked stunned for a moment, then nodded. "Yes, but—"

"Excellent," Bram said. "I'll take the fox-shaped clock as first payment, if you still have it?"

The Eyebrow rose. "I do. But—"

"Liesel loved that clock," Bram said with a small smile.

"And this place will only crumble into the canal if it's left uninhabited. These children, no doubt, will make good use of it. Liesel would have liked that."

"The *children* need a *guardian*," Speelman cried in exasperation. "The records—"

"If it is merely a question of silly paperwork," Edda said, "I will sign as their guardian."

Milou heard her friends each suck in a surprised breath.

Lotta clung to Edda.

The others stared at her.

"It would be my honor to be their guardian," Edda said. "If they'll have *me*, that is."

Four sets of arms tangled themselves around the polder warden's middle.

Milou wrapped her own arms around herself.

Speelman clucked her tongue.

"Oh, very well," Speelman said, lifting the record book. "That's the matter settled then. I honestly can't take any more surprises, so I think I shall just take the fees and leave you to it. I still have two criminals to deliver to the jailhouse before I can go to bed."

Lotta counted out fifty guilders, put them in a burlap onion bag, and handed it to the Kinderbureau agent while Edda signed her name. Rose Speelman took one last look at Puppet Papa, then at the children, and shook her head in disbelief, disappearing once more into the cold night.

Bram stood, running a hand through his hair. "Come on then, Milou," he said. "Let's go home."

"But . . . is this not home?" she asked, realization kicking in. "Why would we leave? Where would we go?"

"I have a houseboat in Antwerp. That's where I've been the past twelve years. I can't live here. The memories are too painful. I'm sorry, but we're leaving. Tonight."

The resulting silence was louder than a winter storm.

She watched as several emotions played out on her friends' faces. Fenna looked confused, Lotta seemed shocked, and Egg shook his head, as if he hadn't heard Bram properly. It was Sem's expression, however, that twisted her insides.

He looked nothing short of heartbroken.

"Say your goodbyes," Bram said. "I'll gather our stuff."

Milou shuffled, uncomfortable beneath their bewildered stares. She realized she had no idea how to say goodbye to them. Neither, it seemed, did they.

A moment later, Bram appeared beside her again.

"Ready?"

He nodded courteously to Edda, then took Milou's hand and guided her to the door, her coffin basket under his arm. Milou's feet moved with him, but her gaze remained fixed on the four gawking faces behind her. Sem tried to muster an encouraging smile for her, but it wobbled too much to be even slightly convincing.

This is what happened with orphans.

They found a family, and then they left.

There was no reason why it should be any different for her.

And just like that, she was out of Poppenmill.

The four faces she'd come to know better than even her own were gone.

The door closed.

❧ FORTY-THREE ❧

MILOU WALKED MECHANICALLY TOWARD a carriage parked up beyond the front gate. Bram heaved her coffin basket onto its back and, hands shaking, Milou unfastened the clasps and opened the coffin lid to put her cat puppet inside.

On top of her clothes, in the same spot as always, were her treasures: a lock of red curly hair, tied with an emerald-green ribbon; a charcoal portrait of her; the poster for Cirque du Lumière; and, of course, her Book of Theories. The journey to Antwerp would take several days. Plenty of time for her to begin filling the blank pages with new theories about where her father might be. Milou opened it. The book had been a comforting presence throughout her time at the Little Tulip, but now, for some reason, that comforting feeling seemed gone.

She opened to the first page, her eyes falling onto one particular line:

My family would never leave me—

Sem had refused to leave them, even if that meant giving up his dream.

They'd all followed her from the Little Tulip to Poppenmill.

They'd all stayed, despite the risks, to raise the adoption fees.

They'd pulled her from that frozen canal and carried her home.

And when Rotman had her by the hair on stage, all four of them had refused to leave her behind.

And yet here she was, leaving *them*.

"Hop up then," Bram said, patting the front bench. "It's a long journey—"

"Wait," she said.

Milou rubbed at her ears, hoping for a tingle or a prickle to guide her.

But her Sense was silent.

Milou rubbed at them again.

Bram looked down at her in befuddlement. "What's wrong with your ears?"

Milou gave up the rubbing and sighed.

Emiliana's words came back to her.

A shadow follows you . . . the dead kind.

Could it have been her mother all this time?

If so, why wasn't Liesel helping her now, when she needed guidance the most?

Milou knew the answer already.

This was a decision she, and she alone, could make.

She looked up at Bram, who was waiting for her to speak.

"We could stay here," Milou said. "Together, we could make the theater everything Liesel dreamed it would be."

"Milou—"

"You've been hiding from this place for twelve years. You've all but forgotten her."

Bram's gaze flickered toward the oak tree and the flower garden graves below it. Then he closed his eyes for a moment. "Forgetting is easier than remembering. It's far less painful."

"I belong here," Milou said. "I never knew her, but I want to honor her memory, nonetheless. And I belong with *them*." She turned and pointed to the four faces pressed nose-first against the kitchen window. "I always have."

Bram nodded grimly, and sighed. "Then you should stay here."

"And you?"

She saw his answer in the pained frown that creased his brow. Milou could tell that looking at her reminded him of the daughter he'd lost, and the young man he felt had stolen her from him; that it wasn't just being back at the windmill that threatened to break his heart all over again each day—and that he couldn't survive doing anything less than forgetting it all.

Bram Poppenmaker wasn't ready to remember.

Perhaps he never would be.

Milou reached up and took her coffin basket into her arms. "Goodbye, *Opa*."

Bram ran the back of a gloved hand down her cheek.

"Goodbye, Miloutje. For now."

She gave him a small nod, then turned toward the mill.

Her friends were already outside, their faces agog with disbelief.

Egg shook his head. "Are you—"

Lotta blinked. "Aren't you—"

Sem opened his mouth to speak, then hiccuped once.

Milou placed her coffin on the ground. "I couldn't leave. This is my home. And you're my—"

Her words were cut off as the four of them leapt forward and smothered her in a crushing embrace.

"Family," Fenna said, somewhere beyond the tufts of hair in Milou's face.

Milou extracted herself from the huddle and smiled at them, pleased to find her stomach was no longer twisting and churning. She'd made the right choice, she knew.

"Yes, family."

Peering behind her, she saw Bram staring at the five of

them. He gave her a small smile and an even smaller nod, then clucked his tongue at his horse. In a rattle of wheels and clatter of hoofbeats, the carriage pulled slowly away from the gates of Poppenmill.

Bram Poppenmaker was gone.

Again.

❧ FORTY-FOUR ❧

MILOU SAT ON THE lowest branch of the oak tree and watched as Bram Poppenmaker's carriage rattled down the canal road. Her friends sat beside her, the tips of their noses glowing in the lantern light that still dotted each branch. As the carriage finally merged into the nighttime gloom and disappeared from sight entirely, Milou let out a long, shaky breath. She pushed her cat puppet to her chest, right over the pocket watch, until she could just about feel its heartbeat *tick-tocking* in tandem with hers.

"What now?" she whispered, looking up to the constellations for an answer.

Instead, it was Sem who responded. "Sleep."

Fenna yawned loudly.

"I'm going to get the mill working again this spring," Lotta announced. "I haven't asked Edda yet, but I wonder if we could get it to generate more electricity for the theater."

Sem perked slightly. "I've had some more thoughts about puppet making. Bram's designs are lovely, but I have ideas of my own."

"We should make more of Fenna's whistling too," Lotta said. "Imagine it: stories, puppets, light shows, and our very own bird songstress."

Fenna let out a little giggle, her eyes twinkling in the lantern light.

"As wondrous as that sounds," Milou said seriously, "Egg and I have important shawl-identifying business to attend to first. It'll take us a while to knock on every door in Amsterdam."

"It's a good thing I have a map of the area already," Egg said from near the tree's trunk. "We can cross each house off as we go."

Milou couldn't see his face, but she could hear the smile in the stretchy sound of his words.

"This place is a dream," Lotta said, kicking her trouser-clad legs happily. "I never want to leave. There are so many possibilities, so much to do."

"Right now, I really do just want to dream," Sem said sleepily. "For a week at minimum."

A door creaked open behind them, and Edda emerged from her farmhouse. She walked down the stone path toward them.

"I suppose you want the five of us tucked up in bed," Lotta said with a sigh, leaping down from the branch. "It's very late. Way past our bedtime."

"Um." The clock maker blinked. "Yes . . . I'm sure that's very sensible, but actually, I'd like to talk to Milou first, if I may?"

Edda directed her question to Milou, her expression a little cautious.

Milou nodded.

Egg and Fenna hopped down. Sem toppled over, landing on one leg. Lotta caught him before he wobbled over completely. Fingers to her lips, Fenna whistled sharply, and Mozart swooped down onto her shoulder from one of the upper branches. The five of them disappeared over the bridge and into Poppenmill, becoming hazy silhouettes behind the gauze curtains: a puppet show of stumbling tiredness.

Edda stood silently for a moment beside the flower garden, her expression hidden in the shadows. Her shoulders heaved once, heavily, then she scrambled up to sit next to Milou. "I never was very good at climbing this thing," she huffed as she settled herself on the branch, looking down as if it were on a cliff edge. "Liesel and Thibault never teased me about it, and they'd even sit down here with me for a while, but as soon as

I went in to bed, they'd clamber to the very top to watch the stars."

"I know," Milou said with a small smile. "I found their names up there."

An awkward moment passed. The wind howled.

"You saw us through the window that night, didn't you?" Milou asked.

Edda smiled. "I did. I don't know what I was expecting to see, but I can assure you, the sight of five children building a fake father was certainly not it." She let out a big sigh. "I'm sorry if my nosing around worried you." She went quiet, her expression unreadable. "You really don't like me, do you?"

"I didn't," Milou admitted. She grimaced. "But mainly because I thought you might be a werewolf."

The Eyebrow of Curiosity arched like a pulled bowstring, then Edda burst out laughing.

Milou groaned. "I know it's absurd."

"Oh, Milou," she said. Her chuckles subsided, and she sighed heavily, turning serious. "I think you're absurdly *magnificent*. All five of you. The past few weeks, watching what you children have achieved. The tenacity of it. The utter brilliance of it." She smiled warmly. "This world needs more absurdity like yours. Please don't ever change."

Milou began to smile, then bit her lip.

Perhaps Edda was right. They had achieved a lot together, but that didn't stop her from worrying that perhaps her friends wouldn't have been put in quite so much danger if it hadn't been for her wild imagination and silly theories.

"You being a werewolf is not even the most absurd thing I've ever convinced myself of."

She took her Book of Theories out of her sleeve and handed it to the clock maker. Edda smiled as she read the first few entries, then she closed the notebook, gave it back, and reached into her own jacket pocket.

"That's why I wanted to talk to you, actually." She pulled a piece of card from the pocket and held it over her chest. "As I said, I haven't spoken directly to Thibault in twelve years. I've certainly not heard of any werewolf-hunting or secret spying, I'm afraid, but he does have a sense of wild adventure in him. Just like you."

She handed the card over.

"What is it?"

"A photograph he sent me a couple of years ago. No return address, of course, but I suppose it was his way of letting me know he's not forgotten me. You can have it, if you like."

Milou lifted a lantern from above her head and held it closer to see better.

Her breath hitched as she realized what she was seeing. She blinked a few times, peering closer. The image remained the same.

It was an air balloon.

It hadn't taken to the air yet but seemed like it was about

to launch. Hanging beneath the round black balloon wasn't a gondola, however, but a simple woven basket. She squinted at the photo, realizing it was set against a snowy landscape. Two figures could just about be seen inside the basket. One had a mass of midnight-dark hair and thick goggles over his eyes. The other was a large wolfhound.

She turned the photograph over. There was only a single line scribbled on the back:

You should see the night sky up here.

Edda leaned in, flipped the photograph over again, then tapped the corner of the picture. There, in scratchy handwriting, were three words and four numbers:

Svalbard, Arctic Circle, 1890

Milou's scalp tingled and a smile tugged at the corners of her mouth. "I wonder if he befriended any polar bears."

"It wouldn't surprise me if that silly wolfhound of his managed to eat one whole."

Milou jolted. "Do you think he's ever been to Java?"

Edda shrugged. "I don't know. You'll have to ask Thibault about it all one day. I'm sure you have many questions for him."

"Yes, I do," Milou admitted wearily, tucking the photograph into her Book of Theories. "At least seven very *big* questions. But for now, I just want to do gloriously normal, family things. Like asking Sem to teach me how to ride that bicycle, watching Fenna train Mozart, helping Lotta make electricity, and Egg . . . well, he needs my help the most, and I intend to do everything I can for him."

"And Bram?"

"My grandfather knows where I am, if he wants to see me. And my father, well, perhaps he should be the one to find me. It's up to them if they want to remember the past or not, but I'll remember my mother with all my heart until the day I die. And you can help me."

"I certainly can," Edda said, smiling. "I have many stories about her."

Milou jumped to the ground and held up a hand to help Edda down. The clock maker stumbled only slightly less than Sem had, grabbing the tree for support as she slid down.

"Ow," Edda said, sucking her fingers. "Splinter." She looked at the offending part of the tree. "Oh."

Milou followed her gaze. Carved elegantly into the trunk, next to where Egg had been sitting mere minutes ago, were five new names:

Fenna

Sem

Lotta

Egg

Milou

Her heart fluttered. All thoughts of air balloons, polar

bears, and wild adventures disappeared, replaced with a warm bubble of contentedness that spread right through her.

Milou really was *home*.

It might not be perfect, or conventional, but it was *hers*.

They were hers, and she was theirs.

"Come on." Edda gave her hand a gentle squeeze. "I hear it's way past your bedtime."

They started back toward the mill, but the clock maker stopped after just a few steps and frowned. For the first time since Milou had met her, Edda looked completely puzzled.

"What... I mean... how..." Edda shook herself. "Should I make you all some warm milk first? And read you a bedtime story? Is that... is that what I'm supposed to do?"

"Yes," replied Milou, grinning wolfishly. "That's *exactly* what you're supposed to do."

❊ EPILOGUE ❊

ON A CRISP, AMBROSIA-SCENTED night, an owl patrolled its kingdom with sharp-eyed diligence. Its mismatched wings sliced through the star-strewn sky as it swooped and soared over fields and canals. Spring had been slowly but steadily tiptoeing its way across the land, breathing color into the bleakest corners, teasing tentative tulip shoots out from the soil, and whistling soft lullabies to the three fluffy, newly hatched owlets snuggled in their oak-top nest.

The polder was emerging from a long, cold, dark slumber, yawning out new life, new wonder, new beginnings.

Even the crescent moon that night seemed warmer and

brighter than ever before. And its shimmering yellow glow illuminated two very dissimilar, unfamiliar sets of footprints in the softening dirt, which the owl's keen eyes tracked with ease.

The longer and thinner set led, determinedly, in a ruler-straight line down the road. The other, rounder set wove drunkenly in and out of the first, drifting now and again toward the canal edge, then toward a gate post, then back again, then off again, and so on.

The footprint trail ended at the base of the owl's own leafy oak tree. With a squawk of territorial fury, the owl spiraled toward its nest and peered down, round-eyed and sharp-beaked, to see just who was intruding so brazenly. It let out a shrill screech of warning at the man lurking ominously on the ground below, drenched from head to toe in the tree's deep shadows.

The lurker in question, however, paid the owl no notice. He stood, stiff-backed and unmoving, watching the windmill in deathly silence, his face lost to the darkness.

If the owl had been in any way knowledgeable about human fashion, it would have noticed that the man wore a long Parisian-style jacket and a top hat unquestionably designed in London. His gloves were made of Peruvian wool and his boots of Bavarian leather. Around his neck was a silk neckerchief, decorated with a delicate batik pattern, and, in one gloved hand, he gripped a crumpled poster.

If the owl had been able to read, it would have noticed that upon this poster, the man had circled, in bright red ink, four words:

Your

Daughter

Is

Back

Unaware of the eyes bearing down on him from above, the man reached up to take his hat off, revealing hair that was as dark as midnight and eyes that were almost black. In all the years that he had been traveling the world, not once had he considered ever coming back to this place. It was nothing but pain to him, or so he had thought.

His shoulders heaved up and then down as he watched the six hazy silhouettes behind the kitchen's gauze curtains: a puppet show of familial bliss, steaming mugs, and cuddling bodies, so at odds with what he had been expecting.

There was a scraping noise from behind the tree, and a huge gray wolfhound emerged from the gloom to stand beside him. Its jaws were wrapped around the head of the stone gargoyle it had torn from a front gate, gnawing contentedly at it. The man remained silent and still, brooding and yet, also, bewitched by what he was seeing.

As if sensing her human's despair, the wolfhound dropped the gargoyle and howled, long and soulful, up toward the yellow slice of moon. It pierced through the quiet, startled the family of owls in the branches above them, and sent a single wet tear sliding down the man's left cheek, which curved under his chin and then dripped down onto his boot.

The howl ran on, and a face appeared at the windmill's kitchen window. A small, heartbreakingly familiar nose pressed right up against the glass, and eyes just like his own scanned the darkness. As the girl rubbed frantically at her ears, the man stepped tentatively out of the shadows toward her, beckoning the howling wolfhound to follow.

"Come, Andromeda," he said, in a voice as rough as an arctic storm. "It's time we remembered."

ACKNOWLEDGMENTS

It really did take a village to raise this book-child of mine, and I therefore have a tremendously long list of people to whom I owe gratitude (get ready for the Dunglish).

First of all, my infinitely *wonderbaar* agent, Jenny Savill, who took these five little orphans on in their infancy and provided me with endless wisdom and encouragement to raise them properly. I'd also like the thank everyone else at Andrew Nurnberg Associates for championing this book and working so hard to find it a home with all my wonderful international publishers.

My editors on both sides of the pond: Naomi Colthurst, Kendra Levin, and Maggie Rosenthal. *Hartelijk bedankt* for helping me shape this story, solve its never-ending plot holes, and for generally being a joy to work with. *Dank u* to the entire Puffin & Viking teams, who have welcomed me into the PRH family and made this whole experience truly *magisch*. In particular, huge *dankje wel* to Stephanie Barrett, Janet Pascal,

Jane Tait, Roz Hutchinson, Lottie Halstead, Lucy Upton, Kat Baker, Zosia Knopp, and Andrea Kearney. And to Ayesha Rubio, for bringing my characters and setting to life in her *prachtige* illustrations and cover art.

I also owe enormous *dankbaarheid* to the entire MA Writing for Young People Community. The tutors: Elen Caldecott, Julia Green, David Almond, Steve Voake, Janine Amos, Jo Nadin, and Luce Christopher. Thank you for providing unrivalled wisdom, inspiration and support. And *a hele grote* thank you to C.J. Skuse, for being the first one to see potential in this story and encouraging me to drop all else and crack on with writing it.

My writing *kameraden*: Lucy Cuthew, who not only has the most beautiful hair, but also the sharpest eyes, kindest words, and endless plot-fixing cleverness. Wibke Brueggeman, for the bleary-eyed, caffeine-and-twix-fuelled writing sessions that got us both through our first drafts. Yasmin Rahman, who hates everything about the genres I write but reads my work (somewhat) enthusiastically, nonetheless. I'd never say this to her face, but she's pretty wonderful. Nizrana Farook, for reading an early draft and pointing out all the (owl-related) tangents I had gone off on. Sophie Kirtley, Alex English, Sue Bailey, Rachel Huxley, Kate Mulligan, all my workshop pals, Team SWAG (you know who you are)—I feel so lucky to have you all.

Rachel Betts, my all-time favourite Dutchie, who has been

pulling my hair and cheering me on/up since we were in kindergarten. Vera Tooke: book research assistant, fact-fudging coconspirator, and *de echte beste moeder in de hele wereld*. My much taller siblings, for only ever looking down on me in the physical sense—you made writing about sibling bonds much easier, so *dankie dankie*! And my father, who provided me with endless weird-spiration growing up, which I can now channel into all my stories.

Dylan: love of my life and chef of my dinners (the two being only "coincidently" connected). I'm not sure there are words adequate enough. I wouldn't have gotten to where I am now without you. And Felix: my bluntest critic, fiercest supporter, and the funniest creature in this universe. Thank you for making me laugh every single day.

And finally, Maisy Moop, for warming my lap and keeping me glued to my chair so that I had no other choice but to keep writing.